Our Lady of the Potatoes

Our Lady
of the Potatoes

DUNCAN SPROTT

faber and faber

LONDON · BOSTON

First published in 1995
by Faber and Faber Limited
3 Queen Square London WC1N 3AU

Photoset by Intype Ltd, London
Printed and bound in Great Britain by
Mackays of Chatham PLC, Chatham, Kent

A CIP record for this book is
available from the British Library

ISBN 0–571–17458–2

2 4 6 8 10 9 7 5 3 1

Our Lady of the Potatoes

The Murphys began their history not at the beginning but in the middle, on a boat in the English Channel, low in the water, in chaos. It was an Irish boat, stuffed full of Irish nuns and Irish soldiers, all of them swearing and praying and vomiting in the dark, the sacred and the profane all mixed up together.

The nuns shouted Hail Marys loud enough to be heard in Heaven above the howling of the elements, but the wind and waves carried on smacking their faces nonetheless. Their black and white habits flapped like giant gulls trying to take flight.

The soldiers swore and sang to keep their spirits up, to keep their minds off death and judgement, but the sea and the sky soaked their scarlet uniforms all the same, like bedraggled birds, the colour of flames and the colour of blood.

The nuns and soldiers prayed and swore their best, but the wind whipped the words out of their mouths and left them speechless, waiting for the end of the world, or the beginning of a new one; Heaven or Hell or the coast of France.

The Irish boat was a fresh start. Before that everything was so awful that the Murphys did not care to remember a thing about it. The voyage was bad enough, but on the boat, hanging over the side, spewing out his guts, was a pale Irish youth with hair like straw and his face a shade of emerald green, grandfather of the most famous Murphy of them all.

The green sea came up higher than his head, and his vomit came up to keep it company. His stomach turned itself inside out like an umbrella, threw up vile yellow juices, took his breath away, and squeezed him dry.

At dawn he became aware of vague grey shapes in the mist. He heard the crash of waves on a beach and angry voices cursing in a language that was not his own. It sounded as if everything that could go wrong had gone wrong; as if nothing would ever go right again.

He sicked up the remains of his Irish vocabulary over the side, thinking he would not be needing it any more.

The captain of the Irish packet pushed mild wild Denis Ogue O'Murphy – his initials spelling *doom*, which was what he felt – overboard, and the Wild Goose briefly flew.

As he took wing, all his old life flew with him – the thatched cabin without the luxury of windows, the beasts stamping and stinking inside the house, his mother's round face the colour of smoked bacon, the steady drizzle, the mud and shite. All Ireland, green and damp and dreadful, went with him, sewn into his skin, and he would never be rid of it. Ireland would not be left behind.

He landed flat on his pale potato-face on French soil. He bit his tongue. He bloodied his hands and knees. He muddied his trunzers. In the left-hand trunzer pocket was one shrivelled potato, sprouting in the dark with a life of its own, a charm against the rheumatism. The fact of the blood made him swear himself, and his first French word, learned from the soldiers, came into his bloody mouth.

'*Merde*,' he said, '*merde*.'

And so the sixteen-year-old Paddy, man before his time, was turned upside down, inside out and became a Frenchman. He vowed a vow then and there on the beach, covered in French mud and French shite, ready to begin the new life that seemed little different from the old one: 'I will never go back,' he said.

Years later he would tell his son, 'Leave the past behind. Forget as quick as you can. Yesterday is no use to you. Leave history alone . . .'

Denis Ogue O'Murphy did not want to remember. It was here and now that mattered. *Aujourd'hui*, as he learned to say. He remembered only Le Havre: the place where you took the boat back to Ireland. Le Havre might be the end as well as the beginning after all.

From the beach, Denis O'Murphy wandered he did not know quite where in a language he never did quite know. He was conspicuous in a red uniform with yellow facings that grew more and more mud-spattered and bloodstained, that he wore patched and repatched for ten years without putting his arms and legs inside a new one. He grew into his uniform and he grew

4

out of it – by turns towel, bandage, handkerchief and blanket –
as a soldier in the Irish Regiment in the service of the French
king, Louis XIV.

But though he was a Wild Goose and a French frog and a
Paddy all at once ('Three in one,' he laughed, 'like the Trinity'),
he was proud to be a Paddy first, and prouder still to be a
Murphy of Ballymollymore before that.

The Irish fought wild, fought fierce, fought blind, fearing
nothing, killing anything that stood in their way. The army
taught Denis O'Murphy how to stand up, how to handle a gun,
how to handle himself, how to handle death – for death was
always standing in front of him. He gave death a run for his
money. War made Denis O'Murphy a man.

He saw ten years of blood and butchery, ten years of sliced
flesh and licensed murder. He spent ten years shivering in the
arms of a different woman for every night of the week, till he
discovered Margaret O'Connor, who pursued the Dillon Regiment out of Dublin and all over Europe, picking up the pieces,
picking up who and what she could.

'No girl wilder this side of Connemara,' laughed Denis O'Murphy, 'Peggy O'Connor, wilder than the wild.'

They were married, two wild things wanting to be tame. In
the winter of 1699, with frostbitten toes and chilblains on his
fingers, but with Peggy O'Murphy clinging on to them, and a
great grin on his face, they fetched up at Rouen and the Irish
wife became a mother. The Wild Goose clipped his wings and
the years of wandering came to a stop.

Denis O'Murphy tried to cut the memory of war from his mind
like the bad bits of a rotten potato, but there were days when
death came and sat down beside him and did not want to go
away. He tried to wipe out the horror of his past but still woke
screaming in the night, and no amount of prayers or whiskey
would make the nightmares leave him alone. And then death
ran off with his wife.

Denis O'Murphy found a new Irishwoman to keep him warm
at night, but death hung about, shivering. Death climbed into
bed beside him, held Denis O'Murphy's cold hands, whispered
in his ears, and danced away with him.

He was buried in his red uniform, dead before his time, the grandfather she never knew.

It was 1713.

'Unlucky thirteen,' wailed the Widow O'Murphy.

II

Daniel Murphy, the son, repeated his father's story. White as a lily, he joined the Irish Regiment, soldiered, shivered, starved. He drifted away from Rouen, north and south, speaking half English, half French, a half-language full of broken pieces that would never fit together.

When the cold edged deeper inside him he gave up the art of death and made shoes for a living.

'So that the Murphys will never go barefoot,' he said.

And he found an Irish wife, so that the Murphys would stay Irish to the bone.

'Peggy O'Hickey,' he laughed, 'the wildest of wild girls, and the most beautiful.'

On her marriage, Peggy Murphy gave up her profession, stopped following the army into battle in a capacity that everyone knew about but no one liked to mention, and peddled old clothes instead.

They settled down at Rouen, thought French, drank French, spoke French after a fashion, and dragged with them everything that was Irish and would travel.

Nothing ever parted Daniel Murphy from the locket with a piece of shrivelled shamrock inside it, for good luck.

Nothing ever made him take the shrivelled potato out of his pocket.

Nothing would ever make the exiles forget the banshee, or the leprechaun, or the day they had watched the little people walking up a wall *in Montpellier*.

There were parts of France where nothing was heard out of anyone's mouth but the soft lilting music of Cork and Waterford. There were places where the Irish ate nothing but snails and frog's legs, but the Murphys themselves kept body and soul together with potatoes baked in their skins, as they always had and always would; *pommes de terre dans leur robe de chambre*, as they began to call them.

'Nothing on the menu,' laughed Peggy Murphy, 'but whiskey and potatoes.'

During the day honest, smiling Daniel Murphy, dressed in black coat and black *pantalons*, hammered nails and cut up leather, intent on constructing the finest pair of brogues in the city of Rouen.

At night Daniel Murphy's bloody past would descend upon him in a black cloud. He twitched and roared in his sleep. He dived out of bed in his dreams and cracked his head on the armoire, squealing like a pig having its throat slit. He bayoneted Peggy Murphy and beat her black and blue, sure that he was sleeping with the enemy.

Mrs Murphy regularly screamed blue murder, prayed her husband would not throw himself right out of the window, and clung to his flailing arms and kicking feet, smacking his face and wailing like the banshee till she woke him up.

Then, quite calm, Daniel Murphy would wonder where he was, cross himself, say his prayers and go quietly back to sleep.

In the end Mrs Murphy tied him to the bed with stout ropes. She knew well enough what battle was like. She had the red and black nightmares of her own.

Peggy Murphy had acquired her expertise in the world of second-hand clothes on half the battlefields of Europe. She had spent her youth stripping stiff corpses of bright and bloody uniforms, helping herself to gold lockets with miniature wives and smiling children. She fingered fat purses full of cash. She rifled the breeches pockets of the bleeding dead.

She still felt sick in her stomach at the thought of it fifty years afterwards. She screamed her nightmare till the day she died, and nothing would make it go away.

She dreamed herself a magpie, stealing everything that shone; a bird of prey and a bird of carrion, making her living from the dead. She dreamed cold corpses lying in the snow, stark skeletons dressed in faded red; she was a crow pecking the lips off handsome faces; she dreamed grass growing through cracked boots; she dreamed herself a snail oozing through staring eyes.

Bloody rain trickled down her cheeks, bloody tears, like a miracle-working Madonna. She could not decide whether her dream was a dream of the past or the future.

Mrs Murphy soldiered on. She bore child after child and gave them all French names. Daniel Murphy, after the traditional Irish custom, spat on each one.

'For good luck!' he said, and his spit went pit-pat on the baby's cheek, making it lucky for ever.

The Murphys smiled and sang and tried to forget their past. They were good times, or they were supposed to be, but with the good times came the bad.

Brigitte Murphy, the first child, died in 1716 aged one year and five months, of smallpox.

Denis-Michel-Dominique Murphy died in 1717 aged one year and eleven months, of smallpox.

Marie-Marguerite Murphy died in 1720 aged three years and two months, of smallpox.

Jeanne-Marguerite Murphy died in 1721 aged three years and two months, of smallpox.

Jean-François Murphy died in 1722 aged three years and six months, of smallpox.

Marguerite-Modeste Murphy died in 1723 just nine months old, of smallpox.

And Michel-Augustin Murphy died on the day he was born, before he had a chance to smile.

The Murphys had thought to make a new beginning, to forget death and escape death, but each time there came the new hope of a new life, death came sidling back, knocked on the door, broke it down. Death climbed the creaking stairs and snatched all Mrs Murphy's babies away from her.

Smallpox was everywhere and the Murphys could do nothing about it but pray for miracles. They tried not to love their children, tried not to mourn, but they went about with hearts like stones all the same. They tried not to feel that their troubles were a punishment for the life they had led before, but they could not help wondering.

Peggy Murphy became used to her children dying. She some-times looked at them hard, wondering if it was worth her while to feed them, wondering whether they would last the winter.

It was not until 1724 that she bore a child who survived beyond the age of five, but with the birth of Marguerite-Louise-Geneviève Murphy there was a change for the better and the seventh child became the eldest.

'Lucky seven,' said Daniel Murphy, laughing as he spat.

Mrs Murphy put it down to the power of prayer and the power of magic. Having begged Our Lady for a child who – just the once – lived, she promised to call all her subsequent children Marie: in gratitude, and as a precaution.

As if to prove that her intercessions had been heard, the next three children survived as well: Marie-Brigitte, Marie-Madeleine and Marie-Victoire, all of them golden-haired, with pale skins and perfect smiles.

The Murphys hurried them, like the good Catholics they were, to the *curé* of Saint-Éloi within the hour, to be baptized; lest they too should die, lest they too went with the unbaptized babies to Purgatory instead of straight to Paradise as instant angels.

At grace before every meal Daniel Murphy would recite the dead children's names with tears in his eyes.

'Brigitte . . . Denis-Michel-Dominique . . . Marie-Marguerite . . . Jeanne-Marguerite . . . Jean-François . . . Marguerite-Modeste . . . Michel-Augustin . . .' he said. 'They've gone to a better world . . .'

'And please God,' prayed Mrs Murphy, 'the list won't grow no longer. Please God, no more death.'

And they would cross themselves and fall on their food like savages.

After each baptism the delighted parents blew and dribbled red wine into each girl's mouth in order to prevent epilepsy and drunkenness for the rest of her life.

Daniel Murphy rubbed each pair of tiny lips with a gold *louis* so they would stay red for ever.

He pressed *petits pois* into the chubby cheeks to encourage dimples – then the height of fashion.

Where the fancy took her, Mrs Murphy administered correctives to Nature, thinking how she might improve on God's work, always mindful of how much money a perfected daughter might fetch on the open market.

She pummelled Madeleine's head three times a day before meals with her plump fingers in her quest for a more aesthetic shape.

She bound Geneviève's head with strips of linen to make it long and narrow in the current Paris style.

Victoire's nose, not quite *comme il faut*, she bandaged up, and pinched and prodded until it conformed with more acceptable models.

Meanwhile she was careful to conserve the ample bosom that was her own principal attraction.

'The wet-nurse is the fashionable thing, to be sure,' she told her husband, and she farmed her daughters out to strangers, with the strictest instructions.

'Remember the sow rolling on her piglets . . .' she warned.

Mrs Murphy did her exercises twice a day, maintained her breasts in perfect shape, and drank her mother's milk herself.

As if the deaths of seven infants were not enough trouble, the authorities arrested Mrs Murphy in 1729 on a charge of notorious misconduct.

She flew into a passion, fought and scratched, and screamed that she had done nothing wrong. She shed tears and shrieked with the injustice of the accusation. She denied all knowledge of the charge. She swore she had not been soliciting for an improper purpose.

The magistrates of Rouen let her off with a caution, but reminded her that in former times common prostitutes had been rounded up and had their ears and noses slit.

Afterwards, when the authorities were out of earshot, the Murphys, husband and wife, screamed with laughter till the tears poured down their cheeks, and Mrs Murphy carried on earning her living as before.

Worse was to come. On the night of 4 February 1735 Daniel Murphy's door was broken down by gentlemen of an exquisite politeness, gentlemen dressed in black who took him away without giving any explanation.

Peggy Murphy was left confused and distraught, surrounded by grizzling infants, not knowing what her husband had done wrong or where he had been taken.

Daniel Murphy also led a double life and had other sources of income. He was agent to Daniel O'Brien, later Earl of Lismore, who was himself charged with the affairs in France of the Chevalier de Saint-George – the Young Pretender, who would be the Catholic King of England as James III – who waited his chance and bided his time in exile at the court of Rome.

Callers visited Murphy's workshop not only to have their

feet measured but also to leave messages and instructions. The Murphy residence had become the headquarters for communications between Versailles and the Stuart court in exile.

Now the Lieutenant-Général de Police had received a complaint from the Comte de Lismore: that Daniel Murphy had taken a false key and stolen papers from Lismore's desk – papers relating to the Pretender's movements, papers that could be sold to the enemies of the Chevalier de Saint-George.

Daniel Murphy was guilty of burglary.

The gentlemen in black took Murphy away to Paris and locked him up in the Bastille, leaving his wife in indifferent health and without the means to support herself.

The Benedictine nuns of the Abbaye d'Arcis at Nogent-le-Rotrou took her in, looked after her four daughters, nursed Peggy Murphy back to health, prayed with and for her at all hours of the day and night, and attempted to reform her immoral habits of life.

Peggy Murphy recovered and began to put on weight. Her damp washing criss-crossed the cloisters, flapping in the wind, as if trying to escape.

In the summer months she tucked up her skirts and worked in the convent gardens with the black-and-white clad nuns, all of them wearing straw hats against the sun. And she introduced them to the cultivation of the *pomme de terre*.

She chanted the daily offices with the sisters while her daughters ran wild and barefoot. They acquired the habit of the rosary and devotion to the saints of France, and perfected their French at the knee of *la Mère Supérieure*.

After eight months of living on bread and water, manacled to the wall of his cell and sleeping on straw among rats and mice, Daniel Murphy was released. His hair had turned white, his back was bowed and his eyesight was impaired, but he was free.

He was free on condition that he stayed away from Paris, where – according to the Comte de Lismore – he was dangerous to leave at large because people would offer him money on behalf of the English government to reveal his secrets.

Daniel Murphy limped back to Rouen and kept his mouth shut. His wife and daughters travelled home in the carrier's cart, singing, and life returned to normal.

It was at Rouen two years later, on 21 or 22 October 1737, that Peggy Murphy was delivered of her twelfth and last child, her fifth surviving daughter.

She was born laughing. Mrs Murphy carried her up the stairs at once, to make sure she would rise in the world. To make doubly sure she climbed with her on to a rickety chair, jigging and jiggling her up and down, singing fragments of Irish lullabies.

Within the hour they carried the new baby to the *curé* of Saint-Éloi to be baptized. Afterwards they blew and bubbled the finest red wine into her red lips and Daniel Murphy spat carefully on her smiling face.

'For good luck,' he said, 'all the luck of the Murphys!'

They called her Marie-Louise.

III

Mrs Murphy was determined that her youngest daughter would not have a hump-back, twisted legs or an elongated head. She decided Marie-Louise did not need all the trouble and effort of a cosmetic assault. She could not risk her experiments going wrong.

'Marie-Louise is already perfect,' she said.

Her elder sisters had been fed on a mixture of cow's milk and flour that stopped some babies screaming so effectively that they came home from the wet-nurse nailed up in a box.

Marie-Louise was spared all that and stayed alive.

'To Hell with my bosom,' declared her mother, and fed Marie-Louise herself.

In her spare time Mrs Murphy revived her second-hand clothes business. She made money when and where she could.

When lying and stealing were the only means of keeping her family alive through a severe winter, Mrs Murphy would lie and steal accordingly.

She kept up a steady supply of dead men's teeth for sale to the medical profession. She would seize on the opportunity of a passing corpse and haggle with the surgeons about a reasonable price.

When she was desperate she sold herself.

It was not enough to be poor but honest. Even the blessed saints themselves, some of them, had sold their bodies in order to eat, in the absence of any other source of income. It was a precedent.

She consoled herself with the thought of Sainte-Marie l'Égyptienne sailing to Egypt, selling herself to the sailors one after another in order to pay her passage. Sainte-Marie had sold her body and yet she had been received among the saints in Heaven.

'God will provide,' Mrs Murphy told her husband. It was what Père la Chose had taught: 'God will teach us what talents we have.'

'A family must survive . . .' murmured Daniel Murphy.

14

'There's more than one way to Paradise,' said his wife.

Mrs Murphy made sure her girls were never left alone in a room unless *La Sainte Bible* lay open on a table beside them.

They slept in the same direction as the floorboards so the Devil did not take control of their dreams.

She bathed their inflamed eyes with Holy Water provided by the *curé* of Saint-Sauveur.

When the comforts of religion were exhausted, the Murphys turned to the traditional beliefs of old Ireland that they had exported with them, passed down from mother to daughter, father to son.

Mrs Murphy kept a wine-bottle full of the blood of a black cat, efficacious in the treatment of all diseases, except smallpox.

When Marie-Louise contracted thrush her mother stuck a live frog in her mouth for her to suck. Marie-Louise rolled her eyes, whimpering, terrified the frog would jump right down her throat.

When frogs were out of season Mrs Murphy held the goose's bill open in Marie-Louise's mouth so that she inhaled the cold breath. The sick-room rang with honking and stank of goose-shit but Marie-Louise recovered. Her mother's miracles always worked.

On the *fête* of Saint-Michel Daniel Murphy slaughtered the goose and sprinkled its blood all over the house – although he had forgotten *why*.

Marie-Louise grew up protected by all the charms her parents could remember.

A necklace of blue beads prevented her from catching colds, quinsies and bronchitis. A dried rabbit's foot on a string round her neck brought her all the luck of Ireland.

She carried the back tooth of a horse wherever she went, to bring her more luck. She kept a coin with a hole in it in her purse to bring still more luck, endless luck, and she spat on it at every new moon to make the luck work. The purse was made of weasel skin, which guaranteed further luck and ensured that she would always have money.

She wore her stockings inside out to frighten away the witches. She crushed her empty eggshells with the heel of a shoe so that the fairies could not turn them into boats. She kept the loaf of black bread the right way up on the table lest a ship full of Irish cousins sank on its way to France.

Until she believed that nothing could go wrong and that she was proof against all disaster. She believed that her purse would always be full of money, even though it was nearly always empty. She began to believe that she led a charmed life, that somehow to be a Murphy meant that she had all the magic in the world working for *her*, and that she would live for ever.

The invisible powers that controlled the world of the Murphys had to be appeased, though.

Marie-Louise always crossed herself when she saw a magpie, for the magpie was the Devil.

She always squashed black beetles with her right-hand thumb so that she would be forgiven the Seven Deadly Sins. The black beetle had his uses.

'Now I can do just what I like!' she laughed, and gave in to gluttony and sloth.

'But she's a good girl really,' said Daniel Murphy, 'for she never whistles after dark.'

Nor would she comb her hair after sunset. She would never look into a mirror by candlelight in case she saw the Devil peeping over her shoulder.

When she yawned she made the sign of the Cross over her mouth so the Devil did not rush down her throat and take up his residence inside her.

She always spat into her right-hand shoe before she put it on, for luck. She spat for luck before she did almost anything, so there were times in the Murphy household when there was nothing to be heard but little Marie-Louise gobbing on the floor and shooing the chickens off the chairs.

Her mother was careful to keep on the right side of religion. A Holy Water stoup stagnated in every room of the battered apartment. A *Sacré–Coeur de Jésus* dripped blood perpetually over Mr and Mrs Murphy's bed.

Mrs Murphy kept praying, and considered that eternal life was no more than her due after the trial and torment of this world here below.

She would genuflect constantly before the plaster statue of the

Virgin Mary that clung to the wall of her *salle à manger* high above the street, as near to Heaven as anyone in Rouen could get without climbing the spire of the cathedral.

She lit candles beneath the statue for her relations in exile in France. She lit candles for her family over the water in Ireland. She lit candles for her husband and daughters, till the apartment flickered like the church where they went regularly to Mass, a forest of flames, and there was candle wax spattered all over the floor.

She prayed for relief from toothache, and for the growth of her potatoes free from blight. She prayed for the health of Daniel Murphy. She prayed on the hour every hour for the blooming of her five daughters, for their preservation from accidents and disfiguring diseases.

Mrs Murphy did a great deal of praying. She sprinkled Holy Water over her furniture and over her family whenever contagion threatened.

'It can do no harm,' she insisted. 'It might do us all a power of good.'

When Brigitte and Marie-Louise fell ill with smallpox Mrs Murphy's heart sank but her faith was unshaken and the Holy Water flew.

She sent the other girls away to Nogent-le-Rotrou and sat by the bed fanning the invalids' faces with the pages of *La Sainte Bible*, keeping up a ceaseless chant of Hail Marys.

Brigitte's face disappeared under a thousand spots. Her long blonde hair had to be cut off, though it fetched a good price from the wigmaker. Then Brigitte lost her eyebrows.

Marie-Louise's nose vanished and her head increased in size by a third. On the ninth day the *curé* came to administer absolution and extreme unction, and left the sisters 'in the hands of the good God'.

Brigitte's pustules turned black and gave off a foul stench. Marie-Louise lay beside her, quite still, her face the colour of coal, and the weeping Mrs Murphy prepared herself for the loss of two more children.

But on the thirteenth day there was a victory for prayer. The fever subsided and the girls began to itch and thrash about on their straw.

'Please God you'll both get better,' said Mrs Murphy, 'but if you dare and scratch yourselves you'll be so ugly that no man will ever want to love you.'

Marie-Louise, terrified of not being loved, clenched her fists and lay moaning, chewing her blanket.

'If I don't scratch,' Brigitte whispered, 'I shall *die*.'

Marie-Louise lay awake at night listening to the scrape scrape scrape of Brigitte's fingernails.

At last both girls opened their eyes, were restored to life, and after a year the red spots disappeared. Brigitte's face was left scarred and ravaged. She emerged ugly, thinking she would have to trudge to Nogent-le-Rotrou and become one of the holy sisters herself.

The miracle was that Marie-Louise's complexion was unmarked, save for one pock on her right cheek, which her mother covered up at once with a black taffeta patch in the shape of a star.

Having kept the tail-end of her family breathing, Mrs Murphy's next concern was to preserve the girls' chastity.

They wore the oldest, filthiest dresses. They plastered their hands with mud and smeared coal-dust on their faces. They kept their charms hidden to protect themselves from men.

When the disguise was washed off once or twice a year, the girls rose from the tin bath looking more impossibly beautiful, Mrs Murphy thought, more ravishingly pretty than any other girls in the whole of Rouen. Always excepting Brigitte, who now wore false eyebrows made of strips of mouse-skin.

'But even Brigitte,' Daniel Murphy insisted, 'even Brigitte has her attractions. A pretty face is not everything.'

Most of the time the girls ran wild on the streets of Rouen. They watched the tide and the ships come and go. They smiled at the sailors, ran errands for them, and made themselves useful in whatever way they could. They roamed the quays crowded with workmen and hauled their youngest sister with them.

Marie-Louise, aged five or six, would gaze up at the great black cathedral of Notre-Dame and listen to the clamour of the bells.

In the Place du Vieux Marché she remembered poor burning

Jeanne d'Arc and crossed herself. She thought of Jeanne's ashes floating on the Seine and said her prayers. In particularly hard winters Mrs Murphy sold bits of the genuine cross held by the Maid of Orléans and charred fragments of the genuine stake she was burned at. The Murphys watched open-mouthed as their mother's relics worked the miracles she promised they would and turned into instant cash.

'Believe!' she told them, laughing. 'Miracles happen!' Rouen swarmed with people and bustled with business, but it was not big enough for the Murphys. Daniel Murphy's customers were the Irish poor, who only wore shoes on Sundays. He no longer made fine boots for foreign couriers. There were no more orders for a dozen pairs of shoes at a time for the Comte de Lismore. The months in the Bastille had ruined Daniel Murphy's health.

Peggy Murphy's sideline in bright girls had a certain notoriety. She decided she might benefit from a change of scenery. She thought it was time her daughters' careers began in earnest.

'My girls are wasted in Rouen,' she told her husband. 'We should be living in Paris.'

The authorities knew too well who and what Mrs Murphy was for her to be left alone for long. They had cautioned her about loitering on street corners after the hours of darkness. It was only a matter of time before they arrested her again.

'I have my good reputation to consider,' she told her husband.

She thought of her former business, more lucrative in a place like Paris, where clients were better-off and more discriminating.

Daniel Murphy wondered now whether he might be able to creep back into Paris unobserved.

Paris was, in any case, cheaper than Rouen.

News reached the Murphys of the great Irish frost: of the dead eaten in the fields by dogs; of whole parishes desolate; of roads littered with the dead; of Irishmen dying of actual starvation, with hardly the skin of a potato left to live on.

Daniel Murphy heard tell of cousins over the water opening the veins in the necks of their cattle and, in the absence of any other beverage, drinking the blood.

He considered returning to the old country, going back to the old life, but he had never crossed the water at all.

'There's no wine to speak of in Ireland,' said Daniel Murphy.

'No croissants,' said his wife, 'no chocolate . . . no pâtisserie . . . *no food!*'

The Murphys had become more French than Irish. They thanked their lucky stars and decided to stay in France. They began to call themselves *Monsieur et Madame* Murphy.

In the middle of the winter of 1743 the Murphys disappeared, leaving a deserted apartment and a deserted workshop, with the rent unpaid, the door hanging open and a débris of half-finished shoes, smashed crockery, broken bottles and filthy straw.

A horse-drawn barge bore them southward on the Seine with their decrepit furniture: tables with their legs in the air, battered chairs piled high, boxes of old clothes, wicker cages full of thin chickens, and a vociferons black pig.

On top of it all rode the five daughters, muffled up in moth-eaten furs, singing the old Irish songs their father had taught them:

Geneviève, nineteen, her smiling face painted white, with rouge on her cheeks, lamp-black round her eyes, ready to spread her wings and fly into the arms of any man who would take her, regardless of for how short a time.

Brigitte, sixteen, her smiling face cratered like the moon, inclined to be solemn, by trade a maker of false pearls, with her nimble fingers practised and ready to be led wherever fate might lead them.

Madeleine, eleven, her smiling face patched up with powder and cream, fresh from her first acting experience as an angel in the Rouen nativity play, and still wearing her wings.

Victoire, nine, with a doll in her arms and her smiling face covered in red spots, her heart pounding with excitement, on the watch for a man who might be interested in giving her a kiss.

And Marie-Louise, six, still a little girl, hugging the pig and looking about her, wide-eyed. Her skin remained miraculously unmarked, her one dwindling pock-mark still covered with a star-shaped patch. Her face remained under its mask of mud and coal dust, hidden away to preserve her virtue.

Daniel Murphy tied Marie-Louise and the pig to the side of the barge, unwilling to lose overboard his two most prized possessions.

The Murphys came to Paris, seeking their fortune. They made their way towards the Palais-Royal, headquarters of the second-hand clothes trade, haunt of the better class of prostitutes – a place that was the private property of the Duc d'Orléans, where the police of the capital had no authority to make arrests.

Marie-Louise amused herself in her new surroundings by collecting the white snails that silvered the paving stones in the Palais-Royal gardens. She liked to put a snail on a plate of flour and cover it up overnight. In the morning she would reveal the initial of her true lover's name in the flour.

Her snails always traced an elaborate Letter L.

'Liam . . .' she mused, 'Laurent, Luc, Lazare . . .'

'*Louis,*' smiled Madame Murphy, hugging her, 'King Louis . . .'

Then she would tip her snails into boiling water and the Murphy family, *Monsieur*, *Madame* and *Mesdemoiselles*, true Frenchmen, would sit round the creaking table in their dilapidated apartment high above the Palais-Royal, and eat them.

Marie-Louise always left the black snails alone.

'The black snail means death!' her sisters told her.

Madame Murphy was reluctant to eat snails at all, thinking of her dreams, but she ate them nevertheless.

When her parents' new acquaintances asked Marie-Louise what she wanted to be when she grew up, expecting her to answer 'Old-clothes woman, like *Maman*', she would amuse them by replying, 'I want to be like my *sisters*.'

IV

Monsieur Murphy sat at a café table near the Palais-Royal think-ing about shoes. The Dublin newspaper was within reach. Irish snuff and Irish tobacco filled his waistcoat pockets. The skirl of Irish bagpipes filled his ears. Paris was not a foreign city at all; Paris was home.

Madame Murphy stood in the Place du Palais-Royal in all weathers, shivering beside a stall piled high with second-hand clothes. She spent the day dancing on the spot to keep warm, shouting her wares, doing a brisk business, holding ragged dresses up in the air, smiling at passers-by. Her patter was loud and gruff and incorrect, but French all the same.

Her daughters stood up on the stall, holding out their skirts for the public to admire, smiling and turning round and round: their mother's models. They had strict orders to smile constantly, to attract the attention of the public in any way they could.

First and foremost they caught the attention of Monsieur Bou-cher, the artist, his face spotted with cobalt blue, his eye-glasses speckled with viridian. He sidled up to a frozen Madame Murphy on her first morning in business, his eyes sparkling, and asked whether he could hire her daughter to sit for him.

'Which one?' demanded Madame Murphy. 'There are five.'

Boucher pointed. 'The one with the hands,' he said.

'Ugly Brigitte!' she said, astonished.

Boucher drooled over Brigitte's hands, kissed them, held them, and told her how beautiful they were.

'I did not know,' laughed Brigitte, 'that hands could be beautiful . . .' And she went off to have her hands made instantly famous. At sixteen Brigitte was suddenly the richest member of the family, and required to lend her parents money.

'I knew there was luck in Paris,' declared her mother, and she kept shouting her stock till she was hoarse, in the hope and expectation that there was everlasting luck just round the corner.

Madame Murphy sold only women's clothes: a mountain of

ancient silk taffeta dresses, frayed at the hems and rotten under the arms from years of sweat. She sold the torn, muddy clothes of suicides fished out of the Seine: dead women's clothes, stained with blood and caked with filth. She sold sumptuous Versailles dresses embroidered with gold and silver braid, thrown away because a Marquise had grown fat and split the seams; last week's fashions, this week too outrageous to be worn in polite society.

The dresses crackled with frost in winter, hummed with flies in summer, and stank all year round of old perspiration, decayed food, and occasionally the last hint of a scent that had once been à la mode. Picking over the festering heap on Madame Murphy's stall were the hundreds of women with too many mouths to feed, women too poor to buy anything new; women who had never worn new clothes in their lives.

Marie-Louise sat at home with her mother every evening with the candles lit and the windows tightly shuttered, watching as she tipped her day's takings out of her leather bag on to the table and counted coins into tottering piles: money for old clothes, money for hiring out her daughters, money for services rendered and favours granted.

'Money for lying on our backs,' she laughed.

Marie-Louise remembered all her life how one night she had stood, aged six, on a table in the wine shop, by candlelight, in the middle of a crowd of stinking men, men roaring with laughter, smoking foul thick tobacco: drunk men, breathing whiskey over her. She remembered the clink of glasses, their quarrelling voices.

She danced on the table wearing her pink taffeta dress, because there was no room to dance on the floor. She remembered the drone of the hurdy-gurdy, and her mother yelling, 'How much am I bid? Who will put a price on my lovely lovely girl?'

No one had told Marie-Louise she was for sale. No one had mentioned her going away. She remembered her panic, her heart beating twice as fast as usual, her eyes looking wildly round the room as she wondered what would happen and who would want to buy her.

She remembered the bidding, and how she had carried on dancing, clicking her heels, with her hands straight down by her sides, holding the pink dress with the hole in the back that revealed a bare patch of white skin, and her feet going up and down as the price went higher and higher – until the wine shop was in uproar and she was being sold for more money than she had heard of in her life.

She kept dancing, with the smoke up her nose making her sneeze, the shouts ringing in her ears, and the red eyes of the men staring at her, laughing, and their glasses rising and falling regularly from belly to chin and back again. Men with bristly faces, Irish men, rough men, men wearing second-hand clothes.

She remembered them all holding their breath, and in the sudden silence her mother's deep, rough voice: 'Marie-Louise – she's not for sale, Messieurs, she's mine – my darling girl's not for sale at all at all.'

Her mother roared with laughter, pulled her down from the table and jiggled her up and down, clutching her to her enormous bosom.

'No one shall have my darling,' she shouted. 'Not yet . . . she's not ready . . . We will fatten her up, Messieurs . . . So start saving up.'

Although her mother hugged and kissed her and pinched her cheeks to make her laugh, she had briefly, momentarily, hated her for doing it.

On another occasion her mother had shouted, 'A girl is a millstone round a mother's neck. A girl is a leech.'

She would never let her daughters forget her first feeling of shame at having brought yet another girl into the world.

'A boy might support his poor parents in their old age,' she moaned, 'but a girl brings nothing.'

Then she had cheered up. 'A girl can earn a living just as well as a boy,' she said. 'There are ways enough for a girl to be a breadwinner.' She paused for breath, then yelled at them, 'So stay alive, and don't be doing anything stupid.'

The girls grew up into perfect examples of their sex, five minor miracles (except perhaps Brigitte), and the day came when Madame Murphy was moved to kneel in the gloom before the altar of Saint-Germain l'Auxerrois and give thanks to Our Lady for enabling her to transform her daughters into profit-making ventures.

24

As she prayed she kept her fingers crossed. 'Just in case,' she murmured.

The Murphy girls fell, one after another, on their feet, sold into the more genteel reaches of prostitution.

'The Murphys is lucky,' Daniel Murphy told his wife. 'Every one of them a lucky girl.'

Except Brigitte. At an early age Brigitte had been told to watch a pan of water, and had allowed it to boil over.

Her sisters screamed at her, '*Oo la la*! You have boiled away all your sweethearts.' Brigitte's hopes of marriage faded on the spot. She gave up all hope of being anything put plain Mademoiselle Murphy. She resigned herself at the age of nine to being an old maid for ever.

Daniel Murphy loved Brigitte none the less. He would go round the table every evening, hugging and squeezing the five girls, kissing them four times each, twice on each cheek, in the French manner.

'*Un pour moi, un pour toi, un pour le bon Dieu,*' he said. 'And one more for good luck.' Twenty kisses.

'You must get used to being kissed,' he said. 'All the men in the world will want to kiss my beautiful daughters.'

He went round the table again, kissing them all four more times, forty kisses, and four more for his wife.

'Lucky I didn't have the twelve daughters,' he laughed, 'I should be worn out with the kissing . . .'

Marie-Louise herself took a long time to get used to being kissed. One New Year's Day they had all gone to walk in the Tuileries, and found the gardens thronged with people. Marie-Louise had shut her eyes, playing a game, and spun round and round and lost herself in a sea of ladies' dresses, a forest of gentlemen's legs.

She felt like a girl who did not belong to anyone, who did not belong anywhere. She squeezed through the gaps between people, scraped by swords, bruised by parasols. Smooth hands that were not lost strayed on purpose to stroke her skin. Hairy hands plunged deep inside her dress. Hot fingers clutched her, poked at her private places. She told herself she was only lost for a short time, that she would soon be found, and held back her tears.

Then someone picked her up, held her high above the crowd, squealing and kicking, and she was being passed from hand to hand, kissed by everyone, handed from man to man and kissed and kissed and felt all over.

She squealed and screamed till she found herself on the ground with her family, and her sisters gripped her shaking hands firmly and would not let go. And she promised them, no, she would not let herself be lost again, she would never let them out of her sight.

'I did not like to be touched,' she told them, 'just there. I did not like it.'

Her mother said, 'You'll like it well enough one day.' And the sisters smiled darkly at each other, as if they knew much more about touching than their mother did.

But it was as if something had woken up inside Marie-Louise and would not go to sleep: as if everything had changed, as if nothing would ever be the same again. She saw all Paris with fresh eyes; and men, who before she had liked and believed, she was now reluctant to trust.

Her innocence vanished. Men would take from her whatever they could. Men were just *jeanchouarts* on legs. For a long time she did not want to have anything to do with men, or think about men at all.

Shortly afterwards Daniel Murphy, the kind Papa, came home with a wooden box which he placed on the table among the candles. She heard his soft voice, Irish-French, calling '*Une surprise!*'

The girls peered over his shoulders, exclaiming, as he had taught them, '*Parbleu! Nom d'une pipe!*'

Inside the box, lying still, was a bright green spotted creature, eight *pouces* long, with a diamond patterned skin, a blue face, a long tail and bright beady eyes.

The girls smiled, asking '*Qu'est-ce que c'est?*'

'*Lézard*,' said Daniel Murphy. 'You have to lick him all over.'

The girls drew back, making faces.

'If you lick him your tongue will have the power of taking the sting out of a burn. For ever!' he said.

The girls frowned, wearing their most serious looks.

'Come on now,' said Daniel Murphy, hands in the pockets of his frog-green *pantalons*, 'Who goes first?'

He looked hard at Geneviève, aged twenty, sparkling in a dress stolen from the wardrobe of the Opéra-Comique.

'The eldest!' he said, smiling.

Geneviève raised a delicately-drawn eyebrow, smiled her best sarcastic smile, and said, 'I would rather drink my own piss than lick a lizard.'

Brigitte, seventeen, rolled her eyes, kept her mouth shut and her fists clenched, ready to hammer her father.

Madeleine, twelve, fingered her rosary and her lucky beads, crossed herself and said, 'I would rather die than lick that creature.'

Victoire, ten, in a dress too big for her, ran from the room with her mouth full of vomit.

'*C'est obligatoire!*' smiled Daniel Murphy. 'You must! For Papa!'

He looked at Marie-Louise, aged seven, and smiled again. The lizard flicked his tail and ran across the table. Marie-Louise stuck out her hands to stop him running over the edge and he was suddenly sitting in her palm, tickling her.

She poked her tongue out, ran it round her lips, gathering her spit, then thought better of it and put her tongue away.

Daniel Murphy showed the black gaps between his teeth and twinkled his eyes at her. Then, without any fuss, she put her hands up to her mouth and licked the lizard's tail and spotted sides. The lizard's tongue flickered in and out. She licked his pale belly.

'He doesn't taste nasty,' she said, 'he tastes of nothing at all.' She went on licking.

'*Voilà!*' she said, 'he tastes nice!' She looked at Victoire, still wiping sick from her mouth, and said, 'Go on, I dare you.'

Monsieur Murphy pressed his bristles to Marie-Louise's cheeks and the elder sisters settled down to licking the lizard as well.

'There's nothing a Murphy can't do!' said Daniel Murphy. 'There's no such word as *can't.*'

Marie-Louise grew, and she grew more beautiful, until she caught the eye of Monsieur Boucher as she ran along the Rue de Richelieu behind the Palais-Royal, and she too was scooped up to be his model and made her mother howl with delight.

Marie-Louise would undress behind a screen and emerge in her pearly white skin. Boucher was interested in more than her hands. She sprawled on her stomach with her legs in the air. She became familiar with the plaster busts and seashells and urns and lyres that littered his studio and was paid for doing nothing but being herself.

After three hours of sitting like a statue she was unable to move, and a young man was detailed to rub her limbs, to bring her circulation back to life, until the agony of pins and needles went away.

She came to like being rubbed. It was quite different from the way she had been touched that day in the Tuileries. The young man looked into her eyes as he pummelled her, and his eyes glowed, were on fire, looking deep into hers.

A different part of her was roused from sleep. The warmth inside her was alive, as if the sparks in the young man's eyes had set her on fire too. She began to feel that she was part of the world of touchers and holders herself, that she was just like everyone else, that she belonged after all.

At the same time Madame Murphy took charge of Marie-Louise's education. She took her to the morgue at the Châtelet and made her look at the dead bodies. She saw the depressed, the homeless, the loveless, who had thrown themselves into the Seine, who had thrown their lives away. She took the dead chins between her thumb and forefinger to make sure she was not haunted by their ghosts.

She stood in the Place de Grève to watch the branding of felons with the *fleur-de-lis*. She watched the women thieves being burnt on the face and shoulders with *V* for *Voleuse*. She heard the sizzle of flesh, the women's dreadful screams and gasps. She saw the disfigurement. She was not allowed to grow up in ignorance.

'Stay alive,' Daniel Murphy told her, 'live a long time.'

Madame Murphy did her best. She dispensed wise advise and sharp remarks.

'*Parlez Anglais!*' she screamed at her daughters. 'You never know when we might have to go back over the water . . .'

'If you bite your nails your fingers will fall off . . .'

'Stand up straight . . .'

'If you tell a lie your face will split open . . .'

Madame Murphy supervised the rubbing-in of lotions guaranteed to keep her daughters' skin soft and smooth and prevent them from growing old.

'Use the magic cream,' she told them, 'and you will be young for ever.'

As for Brigitte, she hid the worst of her pock-marks under black taffeta patches and made up for the loss of her face by smiling.

She plastered her hands with scented lotions to preserve them in all their glory. In her spare time her fingers magicked false pearls out of wax.

She would let no one forget that her hands had been immortalized by the most famous painters. As a result, she refused to put her hands in water. While she indulged her delusions of grandeur, lying in the bath before the fire, soaped ånd massaged by her sisters, with her hands held up in the air, Marie-Louise would be covered in mud, filthy from carrying coal and stoking fires, her hands black with boot-polish.

Some imagined the Murphys, always wearing false pearls, to be nobles who had fallen on hard times. The Murphys encouraged the illusion, more attractive than the reality of their cramped existence on the seventh storey above the street, with the pig sitting on all the chairs.

They were good at pretending. In Paris Madeleine Murphy quickly became a familiar figure under the colonnaded portico of the Comédie-Française and on the stage, where as 'Madame Corbin' she played the role of the statue in *Pygmalion* and was praised for her singing voice.

And when it did not suit them, the Murphys were good at keeping quiet and not being seen. It was in the blood. They were never quite comfortable being themselves, but happier being something else as well. They melted into shadows, never quite what they seemed: rogues, tinkers, thieves, gypsies and gentry rolled into one.

'The Murphys can do what they like,' said Daniel Murphy. When it suited him he could be the lowest of the low, stick out his hand and be one of the beggars beside the road. He could also be one of the oldest of the Murphys of old Ireland, hanging

on to the coat-tails and coat of arms of the O'Murphys of Ballymollymore. They looked upwards, always on the watch for ways
in which they could climb.

Victoire Murphy had already gone up in the world. Under the
name of 'Madame Saint-Gratien' she sang at the Opéra-Comique
and attracted a crowd of admirers. She hid the pock-marks in
her face under the thickest layer of powder and became part of
the scenery painted by a friend of the family – Monsieur Boucher.
She existed to be looked at.

Victoire had her protectors, men who owned a share in her,
much as they might own a share in a racehorse: men who paid
for her stabling and fodder, and in return enjoyed the privilege
of visiting her two or three times a week to stroke her flanks
and take a ride on her back.

But Victoire had engaged too many protectors and ended up
with an unwanted daughter and no father to pay for her upkeep.

The child was taken in by her elder sister, Geneviève, then
living with a Monsieur Melon, whose only occupation was gambling. And Geneviève brought up Victoire's baby as her own,
leaving Victoire free to sing in the evenings, to lie in bed all day
– with or without a long string of benefactors, one of whom,
Monsieur Patu, a lawyer to the Parlement, was to be the link
between Marie-Louise and the start of her own glorious career.

Towards 1750, when she was twelve, the sisters took Marie-
Louise to the most notorious quarters of Paris and showed her
the ropes of her profession. She saw the pregnant women without
means of support. She saw the lowest women plying for trade
in the street. She saw women with hordes of starving children,
women who had sold their teeth for something to eat.

She was to learn from Victoire's mistake.

Madeleine took her to see the smart end of the business: the
gilded rooms, the priceless jewellery, the golden knives and forks,
silver plates, silk sheets; a world of liveried and powdered footmen and glittering diamonds.

'The choice is yours,' said Madeleine.

They began to give Marie-Louise kissing lessons. She learned
what would please men. Kissing alone was allowed. Under no

circumstances would she lose her virginity. She prepared to begin the rehearsals.

Madeleine warned her, 'If you fall in love your heart will break.' And Marie-Louise solemnly promised that she would not fall in love.

At first she was revolted by men's hairy noses tickling her face, the noses of men old enough to be her grandfather, puffing and blowing all over her, sniffing her like dogs' noses, as if her smell alone was what mattered.

She kept her eyes tight shut. She did not want to see the slobbering mouths that strayed all over her body, poking into every flap and fold of her skin, as if she were nothing but a plate of meat.

She disliked the smooth-talking tongues that tried to force their way behind her lips, tasting her, rolling her around their mouths as if she were some fine wine. She clenched her teeth. No garlic-flavoured tongue was going down her throat. She wanted no man's spit on her tongue.

She thought, I'd rather have the frog in my mouth. I'd rather kiss the lizard.

But the men seemed to think that her resistance was part of what they had paid for. They thought that, having paid, they could do as they liked. She fought them. They held her down. She cried out and shed tears. They held their hands over her mouth and carried on regardless.

Her nails flew out and scratched their faces. She bit like an animal and beat with her fists. She made the fullest use of her delicate knees. She had been taught how to defend herself.

The men seemed to enjoy her violence, and came back to be punched and scratched and bitten and kneed in the groin some more. For a while she fought on, tearing at men who had been carefully chosen to accomplish her training, to inure her to disgust, to help her to sublimate her feelings and be indifferent to the most repulsive clients as long as they handed over their money.

She brushed up against the parameters beyond which no decent girl would go. And in the end she bore almost everything without a murmur.

Victoire told her, 'You can get used to anything . . .'

31

Then her diet changed and Marie-Louise was fed on men like the gods in Monsieur Boucher's paintings: young men with smooth skins, who made her smile with their compliments; men whose breath did not repel her; men whose tongues found their way behind the portcullis of her teeth; men with whom – had she not been strictly warned – she might have fallen in love. They pressed gold *louis* into her palms and kissed her until she was exhausted.

She moaned to Brigitte, 'I shall be kissed to death . . .'

But it was not long before she came almost to enjoy the snuffing of warm breath. She began to find the varying texture of men's skin quite interesting. She began to find a strange fascination in her new employment.

She went sometimes to Madame Fleuret, a *lingère*, who taught girls about lace and fine linen, and shifts, shirts, caps, coifs, and peignoirs; and who trained girls in the finer arts of the bedchamber, and fixed girls up with permanent and often startlingly lucrative positions.

Marie-Louise continued to sit for Monsieur Boucher, and sat waiting for something to happen, waiting for the right man to turn up, waiting for the beginning.

'Everything has a use,' said Madame Murphy, smearing mud on her youngest daughter's cheeks. 'Even dirt might save your life one day. It will protect you till the time is right . . .'

'Even *merde* might save your life,' her mother said.

Marie-Louise turned up her nose.

'Poor man's gold,' said her mother, 'mark my words.'

Marie-Louise made a face.

'Don't!' snapped her mother. 'The wind might change . . .'

Marie-Louise laughed.

'And don't sit in the sun,' said her mother, 'we don't want you turning into a baked potato.'

V

At Versailles prowled the very high, very mighty and very excellent prince Louis XV, by the grace of God King of France and Navarre, in search of a new mistress.

He had been married at fifteen – too young, said all Versailles – to the daughter of Stanislas Leszczinski, the deposed King of Poland, then living in exile in France. Marie Leszczinska was twenty-one and the match was seen as a mismatch. They were married without having set eyes on each other.

At first, though, all went well, and the legend was repeated that Louis had made love to his Queen seven times on their wedding night.

The Queen, charming, plain and devout, liked to consume two hundred oysters at a sitting. After ten confinements she was heard to complain that she was nothing but a machine for bearing children.

Her doctors advised that ten children was enough, and that it would be dangerous to have any more. Marie Leszczinska failed to pass the information on to the King. Instead she made a fuss about letting him into her bedroom, and gave religious reasons instead of medical reasons.

She could not sleep with him, she said, because it was the *fête* of Sainte-Geneviève, or Sainte-Béatrice, or Saint-Jérôme . . . There were so many saints in the ecclesiastical calendar that she need never look for another excuse; she need never sleep with Louis again.

The day came when Louis stormed out of the marital chamber shouting for his valet to bring him a woman, any woman. The valet obeyed orders. There was a succession of temporary mistresses, followed by Jeanne-Antoinette Lenormand d'Etioles, Madame de Pompadour, a permanent fixture.

The Pompadour was the perfect mistress. She was lively where the Queen was dull. She was amusing where the Queen was boring. She was the heart and lungs of civilized Versailles. She organized operas, music and amateur dramatics; she cultivated her salon and made the King forget his melancholy. She made him forget about the horror of death.

But the former Mademoiselle Poisson made herself ill by subsisting on a diet of nothing but celery soup, truffles and hot chocolate: nothing but aphrodisiacs, in an attempt to turn herself into something other than a cold fish.

'Poisson by name, Poisson by nature,' laughed all Versailles.

The diet made the Pompadour fat. She lost her health. Her breasts sagged. Her figure shrivelled up. Her face turned yellow. She acquired a double chin and a haunted look.

By the middle of the century Louis had lost all interest in the physical Pompadour. They remained on the best of terms, were the best of friends, and the Pompadour retained her barnacle grip on affairs of state, but eventually she sent out crisp white cards to her acquaintances to announce the termination of sexual relations between her and the King. She advertised to her intimate circle the vacancy for a new royal mistress.

Louis did not want and could not afford the colossal expense of a second Pompadour. One mistress running six châteaux of her own was enough. He wanted a cheap girl to make him forget the horror of being King.

The Pompadour was behind the plan, as she liked to be behind every plan. She wanted to hang on to power. She hired and fired generals and ministers, dabbled in politics, extended her patronage to any man whose face she liked. She thought she was doing a wonderful job. The whole world of civilized France revolved round Madame de Pompadour.

In spite of all this, Louis said later that he had never loved her. When she died he was asked, 'If you did not love her, why did you not send her away?'

Louis replied, 'If I had sent her away it would have killed her.'

Thus, at Versailles, they were searching for a girl. Louis had had other mistresses since the Pompadour, but the perfect girl had not yet been discovered.

The Pompadour herself kept her eyes and ears open.

Her brother, the Marquis de Marigny, scanned crowds and interviewed strangers.

Dominique-Guillaume Lebel, Premier Valet de Chambre du Roi and go-between-in-chief, walked the streets of Paris at night

34

in search of the girl of Louis' dreams, the girl to end all girls, the girl of a lifetime. She had to be young, the younger the better, because he wanted to be warmed up, and because he was afraid of venereal diseases. He wanted a girl who was alive, a different girl, a special girl. Sometimes Lebel wondered if he would ever find her.

In 1751 the wildest thing on two legs this side of Killarney was fourteen and still sitting for François Boucher in Paris. She lay on her stomach, propped up on her elbows, with her feet in the air. The lucky blue ribbon was entwined in her hair, the ends held in her fingers. Her feet were filthy from the bare boards of the studio floor. The sofa she lay on was stuffed with horsehair, prickly, yellow, covered with mouldy silk sheets.

Boucher was using his imagination. He did not quite paint what he saw.

'The Bouchers,' he said absently, touching the front of his *pantalons*, 'always interested in flesh . . .'

The sofa was not what she was used to. She preferred the warmth of straw, but the opulence went only as far as the edge of Boucher's canvas; beyond it was a screen supporting the rich drapery, then empty wine bottles, paint-stained china, dirty washing, a bare window with jagged glass.

'Meat, that is,' he said, putting a paintbrush behind his ear.

The damp silk was alive with bugs. The sofa was full of fleas that made her itch. She needed to smack at what was biting her, but could not. She must keep still.

'Raw meat,' he said, with a paintbrush between his teeth.

He thought he had caught her beatific smile, her contented look, her honey side. Then he wondered if he had not allowed himself to invent it, to make it all up. The usual temptation.

'It's all to do with eating,' he muttered, 'with appetites.'

Marie-Louise wondered if she was as perfect as he seemed to be making her. If she was not too good to be true.

Boucher saw her as a collection of disparate pieces, fragments of a dozen different girls, like a jigsaw puzzle.

'All about food,' he said, 'all to do with hunger.'

All to do with desire, he thought. He shrugged his shoulders and sketched in the pages of an open book in the bottom left-hand corner; the outline of two pink roses, intertwined, down

35

on the bottom right-hand side. It was common knowledge that he preferred to dispense with models, to do without them; that he liked to make things up. He enjoyed playing at God. A model triggered pictures in his brain. Models were never exactly what he wanted; real life was never quite perfect enough.

'Nature itself,' he murmured, 'is too green, too badly-lit.'

Sometimes he felt the whole picture was off the top of his head, a complete fabrication, right down to the yellow sofa. She could be any one of a hundred girls, any girl, every girl.

'The word made flesh, flesh made paint . . .' he said, 'a kind of incarnation . . .'

Her mind did not run on luxury, or love, or men. She dreamed about food. She worried where her next meal was coming from. She was afraid of what Boucher might do to her. She was cold.

Boucher ignored the goose pimples, put flesh on her bones and fattened her up.

'About the realization of an idea,' he said, 'an ideal . . . an ideal beauty.'

He took no notice of the blue rings under her eyes or her chewed nails. He had not tried to capture the reality of her situation. He was painting a dream. He was performing a miracle.

'Flesh turned into paint,' he murmured, 'more real than the real thing.'

The real Marie-Louise smelled bad. She did not often see soap. A rat had died beneath the studio floor. Boucher himself stank of sweat. His teeth were rotting. She inhaled the smell of paint, the not unpleasant smell of turpentine. She was on the point of vomiting up her last meal. She wished she was somewhere else, away from the eagle glare of the artist's eye. Sometimes she wished she was dead.

'Immortal,' he declared, 'you will last for ever.'

The real Marie-Louise had mosquito bites all over her face, marks in her flesh where her clothes were too tight, spots on her bottom like any other girl.

'Do you like?' he asked, stepping back from the canvas.

She stood up to take a look, holding the white sheet over her nakedness.

'*Fantastique*!' she said. It did not look like her, she thought. Her hair was the wrong colour. Her eyes were too blue. He had spirited away her moles and freckles.

'We never see ourselves as we really are,' he said. 'The nearest you can get is in the looking-glass – and there you are back to front!'

Boucher laughed and squeezed her arm. She stood beside him, looking. She shrugged her shoulders, did not know what to say.

'It does not feel like you?' he said. 'You are afraid I do not like you the way you are?'

She saw herself through his eyes, saw herself as she really was. She did not recognize herself at all.

'I have made something new out of you,' he said. 'A portrait is full of lies. I have imagined you. I have made you up!'

She laughed.

'You are afraid Monsieur Boucher has butchered you?'

She looked doubtful. The girl in the picture pouted, she thought.

'Look,' he said. He picked up the canvas, took it to a mirror and held it up to the glass. 'There,' he said, 'what do you see now?'

'That's me now,' she said, smiling. '*C'est moi*!'

Boucher grinned, kissed her, a smack on the lips.

She thought, All mouth.

'Rose,' he said, pointing. 'Symbol of love.'

All *bouche*, she thought, all *pantalons*.

Boucher's pupils saw to it that there was no shortage of reproductions. Marie-Louise Murphy was much in demand. Within days half the gentlemen of Paris carried her in their pockets. She rubbed up against a thousand hearts. Paris lusted after her, an instant idol, the most famous image of her day.

Madame Murphy thought differently. 'The painting does not look anything like my daughter,' she said. 'And what in the name of God is the *book* for?'

Boucher smiled. 'She will look like this one day,' he said. 'The book is to pass the time . . .'

Rumour decided that Louis XV had commissioned the painting. Or the Pompadour's brother, who owned the picture, or a copy of it at one point. Or that it was painted expressly to whet the King's appetite.

'Where else,' asked Rumour, 'could such a girl have ended up but in the ogre's palace?'

Marie-Louise Murphy became the Girl in the Boucher. People recognized her features in all his other canvases, including those painted years before Boucher knew her, years before she was born. She became the girl in all the Bouchers.

In old age she insisted that she had sat for the Premier Peintre du Roi. Everyone said so. It was common knowledge.

In later life Boucher gave up using models altogether and painted from inside his head, where the lighting was perfect, where the girls were perfect and sat perfectly still.

He had just the one type, just the one woman, repeated over and over again. Marie-Louise was the mirror for his obsession. His divine beauty. His Venus. His darling girl. His inspiration.

Dominique-Guillaume Lebel strode fast through the Parc at Versailles on long legs. His pockets were full of blue silk condoms embroidered with the *fleur-de-lis* in gold thread. He pointed to left and right as he went. His assistants moved fast to scoop up his candidates for interview. Timid girls they led by the hand. Reluctant girls they bribed with gold. Wild girls they carried kicking and squealing towards the golden château.

Lebel's eyes wore their habitual wicked glint, their lizard alertness, but for Lebel there was nothing new. He had seen everything, he was tiring of the charade of kidnapping girls, tired of the legend of Louis; as if it might be true that he slit their throats, drank their blood, bathed in it . . .

Lebel knew exactly what he wanted, though the King's taste was not always Lebel's taste. He was at the summit of his career. He had at his manicured fingertips all the secrets of Versailles. There was nothing Lebel did not know about what went on between the sheets at the château. His eyes bulged, as if he had spent his whole life seeing too much, as if he knew more than was good for him. Wigless, his bald head shone in the sun. His eyes flashed diamonds. Without Monsieur Lebel all life might grind to a halt.

He sprang up the Orangerie steps on absurd red high-heeled shoes, peering from side to side, on the lookout for something new, something bizarre to wake up the King's jaded fancy, so exhausted with doing nothing. Somewhere in the Parc, he was sure, lurked the right girl, the dream girl, the girl who would make Louis go weak at the knees not just the first time he saw her but every time, all the time. A girl to make the King faint with desire.

Later Lebel slouched in a gilded chair in the Trébuchet, the Bird Trap, a room where chickens, geese, ducks and guinea-fowl waited to be killed for the royal table: a living larder with wicker cages from floor to ceiling, loud with the frenzied flapping of clipped wings.

Here Lebel lined up his handful of smiling girls. He had taken young girls away from their parents, had them educated in a convent and trained up in everything that might please the King. One more mouthful for him to chew up and spit out when he was tired of her boring conversation. The man could get away with anything.

Lebel looked and pondered. He might order a change of dress, a change of hairstyle. A bath often worked wonders. There was no telling what might be hidden under a layer of dirt.

He had to be careful. It was no good dressing a girl up to look like 100,000 *livres* only to find she had webbed feet or supernumerary breasts, or – horror of horrors – was no longer a virgin. Or worse still, to find the *fleur-de-lis* branded on her shoulder, a thief, a girl already labelled as Louis' own property. Such things had happened.

The King did not know what he wanted. Nothing was denied him. So many beauties he could not make up his mind which to have next. He wanted them all. He was a divinity, to whom different rules applied.

He would often turn up his nose at Lebel's selection of girls, turn on his heel and leave the room. As if the girls looked too like the Queen, too like the Pompadour, too like last night's girl. Always he must have something new.

Lebel dismissed them all, knowing it was hopeless, that none of these girls would come up to the monarch's exacting standards. He shooed them out of the Trébuchet like chickens, set them free.

*

Victoire Murphy's protector, Claude Patu, had acquired an Italian friend, a Monsieur Giacomo Casanova, Chevalier de Seingalt, who attached himself at once to Patu's ménage.

Casanova walked with them in the Jardin des Tuileries.

He went with Patu to hear Victoire sing at the Opéra. He trailed home with them afterwards to the Rue des Deux-Portes Saint-Sauveur. He hung about and would not go away. He had nowhere to go. He asked if he might make himself comfortable on a chair for the night.

Victoire's younger sister, a pretty, ragged, dirty little creature, appeared in the doorway and offered her bed to the Chevalier if he would like it.

She wanted to charge him three *livres* for the privilege.

Marie-Louise took Casanova to her room, where there was a rotting mattress stuffed with straw supported on two or three boards.

Casanova laughed. 'Do you call that a bed?' he said.

'It's where I sleep,' she said.

Casanova refused to sleep on it. He would sleep on the floor.

Marie-Louise pouted and put her tongue out at him. His eyes lit up. Then she asked, 'Were you going to undress for bed?'

Casanova said, 'Of course I am.'

'There aren't any blankets,' she said.

'Do you sleep in your clothes then?' he asked.

'I do not,' she said, indignant. They slept naked, like real Frenchmen.

'*You* sleep in the bed,' said Casanova, 'but I want to watch, and you can have three *livres* for that.'

'All right,' she said, 'but you mustn't *do* anything.'

The prized possession must be preserved intact.

'Not a thing,' said Casanova, grinning, 'I promise.'

He ogled as she took her clothes off. She lay down, covered herself up with an old curtain, shut her eyes and giggled.

Casanova stretched out his hands to tickle her ribs. She squealed, laughed, refused to let him, and opened an eye.

'You promised you wouldn't do anything,' she said. She put her tongue out at him and giggled again.

Casanova complained about the mud. She explained that the dirt was her protection. Casanova called for hot water, washed her with his hands, and found she would let him do anything except take away her virginity, which was worth 600 *livres*.

Casanova did not possess 600 *livres*.

'I'll think about it,' he said.

He paid 12 *livres* each time he visited her. In twenty-five visits he parted with 300 *livres* for nothing.

Victoire opened the door to Casanova twice a week, her smile broader every time, thinking that the Italian was the greatest money-spinner she had ever come across.

It was Casanova who described Marie-Louise as 'white as a lily', 'a perfect beauty'. It was Casanova who took the credit for introducing her to Versailles. It was Casanova who claimed to have commissioned the miniature of her lying on her stomach on a sofa, resting on her arms, with her bosom on a pillow.

'Casanova?' laughed Marie-Louise Murphy. 'You can't believe a word out of his mouth.'

Whether she was sent by Casanova or by Boucher, she found herself on her way to Versailles, hardly able to believe what was happening to her, in a public coach that rumbled through woods that were full of painted whores and lurking thieves. Her sister had cleaned her up, pulled her into a dress borrowed from the Opéra-Comique, fastened a string of Brigitte's false pearls round her neck, and set off with her for the rendezvous.

At her first sight of the City of the Sun, Marie-Louise Murphy rubbed her eyes, as if Versailles might be made of honey, or golden pâtisserie; as if it might melt in the heat.

'This is a dream!' she said. 'It is not real!'

'It's not a dream,' said Victoire, 'it's not a fairy tale, it's a nightmare come true.' She pointed to the grey-blue cobbles.

'Look!' she said, '*merde* everywhere. Nothing is more real. It's all made of shite, and the people inside are all full of shite too.'

Marie-Louise wrinkled her nose and laughed.

Monsieur de Saint-Quentin, or Monsieur Quentin de Champplost, or Monsieur Quentin de Champcenetz – or whoever it was whose name Casanova had scrambled or forgotten – locked the Murphy sisters inside a garden house with a mosaic floor and cherubs flying on the ceiling. They were prisoners among spades and forks, stifling in the enclosed space, with flies buzzing against the dusty windows.

Here, after they spent half an hour thinking they had been tricked or forgotten, came Louis XV, by the grace of God King of France and Navarre, King of Shadows, King of Secrets; alone, incognito, with a key to unlock the door.

'*Bonjour, Mesdemoiselles*,' he said, grinning. He gave no name. He was just The Gentleman Who Wanted To Talk To You. He smiled. He took the miniature from the pocket of his cinammon velvet coat. His eyes sparkled like coals. A smirk flickered over his face. He looked hard at Marie-Louise, wondering whether she would do, whether she would be safe to take into his bed, wondering what she might steal. He could not stop smiling.

'I have never seen a better likeness,' he said.

He sat down on a garden chair. Dust and cobwebs adhered to the cinammon velvet breeches. He took Marie-Louise's hand, pulled her on to his knee, caressed her arms, stroked her bosom, squeezed her bottom.

Victoire looked out of the windows, wanting to watch, trying not to watch, not knowing where to put herself. The royal hand worked its way under Marie-Louise Murphy's skirts and assured itself of her virginity.

He kissed her cheek. He kissed her on the lips. He sniffed her skin, inhaled the fragrance of her adolescence. He could not stop kissing her.

Marie-Louise Murphy grinned. She could not stop grinning.

'What are you laughing at, Mademoiselle?' asked the King.

'You, Monsieur,' she said, 'because I know you. You can stop pretending. Your face is on all the coins!'

She pulled out the weasel-skin purse and showed him.

'You're just like the face on the six-*livre* piece,' she said.

Louis laughed. He asked her if she would like to live at Versailles, with all the diamonds, rubies, emeralds, sapphires she wanted, three meals a day, as much pâtisserie as she could eat, and all expenses paid.

'Well,' she said, 'I'll have to ask my sister.'

Marie-Louise, in the pay and employ of Victoire, had been drummed into thinking before she agreed to anything.

Victoire laughed. 'Of course!' she said. 'Nothing would give us greater pleasure.' And she burst into tears.

Louis XV disappeared fast, leaving Monsieur de Saint-Quentin to see the girls off the premises.

'We'll let you know,' he said vaguely, leaving them to find their way back to Paris with the weasel-skin purse heavier by the sum of a thousand *louis*.

Madame Murphy screamed, incredulous, and had to be given liquid refreshment to restore her composure.

'24,000 *livres* for half an hour in a garden shed,' she sighed. The Murphy family fanned her, gave her more whiskey, and spent the night dancing on the roof.

Marie-Louise would not wash her face because Louis had kissed it. She would not wash her hands because Louis had held them. She would not change her dress because it had been fingered by Louis himself.

'*Lui-même,*' she said, 'Himself!' And the name stuck. Himself, she called him, just as Madame Murphy referred to her husband.

Victoire spent a week banging doors and smashing plates, alternately kissing and pinching her sister. She cried herself to sleep every night, dissatisfied with every man she met.

Marie-Louise wondered if she was dreaming. Her feet did not seem to touch the ground.

VI

The Pompadour, swathed in green silk printed with pink roses, asked, 'Did you ever bathe ... in milk, Mademoiselle?'

'I did not,' said Marie-Louise, who had only rarely bathed in anything. 'I never did at all.'

'Not ass's milk?' asked the Pompadour, fanning herself calmly, unable to believe the whiteness of the girl's skin, or that she had ever bathed in anything so ordinary as water.

'Never, Madame,' said Marie-Louise. 'Most days I would be covered in mud ...'

The Pompadour nodded, smiled her icy smile, fanned herself vigorously, looked Marie-Louise Murphy up and down. She liked the look of her. She thought she was in no danger of being toppled by such a girl. She thought she looked none too clever.

The Pompadour rang her bell and Madame du Hausset, her *femme de chambre*, appeared, bustled around Marie-Louise, unlaced her at the back and whipped the borrowed dress of camellia pink watered silk right over her head, leaving her naked but for her shoes.

Marie-Louise shivered on the hearth-rug in the Pompadour's golden salon, and did not know where to put her hands.

The Pompadour rang again and a gentleman in black and gold came to peer down Marie-Louise's throat and gaze deep into her eyes. He poked her stomach, hunted for bugs in her hair, and felt behind her ears.

He bowed to the Pompadour, smiled, and left the room without a word.

The Pompadour smiled curiously, fanned herself frantically, then rose up out of her golden *fauteuil* and swept from the salon in a whisper of silk, leaving Madame du Hausset shaking her head, tut-tutting, wrestling with the task of pulling the protégée back into the pink silk and lacing her up again.

The Pompadour decided that Marie-Louise was not ready for Versailles.

'She is not old enough . . .' she said.

Louis frowned.

'Her breasts must be given time to grow . . .' she said.

Louis thrust his hands into his pockets, searching for something that was not there.

'She must be kept away from men . . .' said the Pompadour.

Louis smacked his left fist into the palm of his right hand.

'Her virginity must be preserved . . . She must not be a fallen angel . . . Some education would not go amiss . . .' she said.

Louis did as he was told.

If Marie-Louise was to survive the contemptuous smiles and sarcastic comments of the Court she would have to be trained in all the complex etiquette of the château. Accordingly, the sisters of the Couvent de la Présentation in the Rue des Postes, Paris, received an extra pupil for a lightning course in culture and civilization.

Marie-Louise was at once surrounded by pale nuns with thin lips, nuns who never stopped smiling, nuns who had never seen the sun.

They veiled her as a novice, and made her walk about with the *Exercices Spirituel* of St. Ignatius balanced on her head to improve her deportment.

'A waste of time,' whispered Soeur Véronique to her neighbour in chapel, 'for a girl who will spend her whole life lying down . . .'

Mademoiselle Murphy woke at five-thirty each morning to a dawn chorus of chanted psalms, and spent the day under a régime of unrelieved austerity. Every action was framed by prayers, punctuated by bells and the ceaseless singing of the sisters in the distance, slightly out of tune.

The nuns taught her to read and supplied her with a kind of instant fashionable knowledge: they trained her to memorize facts without requiring her to demonstrate that she understood them. As a treat she was allowed one hour's instruction in elementary arithmetic on holy days.

Everything took second place to religious and moral instruction, so that her grammar remained imperfect and she was at times at a loss for the right word. She was filled instead with a love of virtue and a hatred of vice, a complete contempt for worldly goods, and a deep distrust of the wicked ways of the opposite sex.

She learned the fashionable way to smile, to show her teeth but not too much. She learned never to roar with laughter. She went about smiling fashionably till her jaws ached.

The girls smiled whether they felt happy or not. They danced girl with girl to an invisible band, with Soeur Angélique shouting the steps and the tune, because the nuns could not afford musical instruments.

The smiling practice went on, until the girls' jaws seemed permanently fixed and their eyes sparkled of their own accord.

Marie-Louise learned to curtsy fashionably and performed a perpetual curtsy wherever she went. She bobbed up and down in her sleep to imaginary monarchs.

She learned the genteel way to take snuff, the polite way to sneeze, and the least disagreeable way of blowing her nose.

She was drilled never to stamp her feet, never to shout, never to swear or show emotion of any kind, and never to display anything so vulgar as an appetite.

She learned that news of the death of a relative must be received with complete equanimity; that the death of a child must be accepted with the same composure as a letter from a distant cousin.

She learned that at Versailles death must never be mentioned, that the idea of death was unthinkable. It was necessary to pretend that everyone would live for ever, that she was among the Immortals. Death did not exist.

Versailles, the nuns told her, was the next best thing to Paradise. The King and Court must be worshipped, if not sacrificed to as well. No one suggested to Marie-Louise Murphy the idea that she might be the sacrifice herself.

At bath-time the girls would drape themselves in an all-enveloping sheet, gathered in at the neck, so that only the bather's head stuck out. The sides of the sheet had to be draped over the edge of the bath so that the girls never saw themselves or each other naked, and so that modesty and decorum were preserved.

From the sacred environment of the convent most of the girls went straight to the altar, devoid of all instruction in the mysteries of contraception, abortion and child-bearing. Some were shocked by the onset of menstruation into thinking that they were bleeding to death.

All mention of the arts of the bedroom was forbidden. For the sisters of the Couvent de la Présentation sex did not exist any more than death.

It was a rare girl who reached her wedding night armed with the most rudimentary facts of life, of what would be expected of her as Madame Telle-ou-Telle. But for Mademoiselle Murphy alone, special lessons were arranged, with the octogenarian Soeur Jacqueline, who was deemed to have had the most experience of the profane sciences no one was ever meant to mention.

Mademoiselle Murphy learned exactly how to avert an unwanted pregnancy, how to deliver a baby in an emergency, and how to avoid becoming pregnant in the first place.

Soeur Jacqueline drew elaborate diagrams and taught all the obstetric practices of the seventeenth century, advising that a newborn child should be wrapped up in the bloody skin of a freshly flayed sheep, and that the best way to procure an abortion was to chew parsley.

Marie-Louise absorbed all the *recherché* rules of Versailles etiquette. She learned the difference between the forms of salutation expected by a Duchesse and a Vicomtesse. She learned to distinguish between a Prince of the Blood Royal and a Prince not of the Blood Royal, and so on.

She was taught the proper way to wield a knife and fork, how to be dressed and undressed by her *femme de chambre*, how to be totally dependent on other people. She mastered all the gentle art of doing nothing.

Most importantly, she learned how to move.

When the girls of the Couvent de la Présentation appeared in public it was for no other reason than to practise walking, for of itself exercise was well known to be hazardous. The new generation of Court ladies emerged only to rehearse the short sharp steps, moving very fast but without ever lifting their feet and without ever breaking into a run, that were *de rigueur* at Versailles.

'Running,' Soeur Jacqueline warned, 'is highly dangerous.'

A girl running full tilt in a voluminous dress would work up an unladylike sweat and perhaps fall over. To be overheated inside multiple layers of petticoats and laced up under the wicker basketwork that held the vast lengths of silk in place was asking for a chill and asking for trouble.

'And a pregnant lady who runs,' warned Soeur Jacqueline, 'runs the risk of losing her child.'

Thus the short steps that carried ladies from one end of the vast château to the other; fast enough for a journey not to take all afternoon, slow enough for them to maintain their dignity. Thus the convent girls appeared to glide, as if they were mounted on silent wheels and not possessed of anything so common as feet.

There were more pressing reasons why Mademoiselle Murphy must wait before making the transition to Versailles. She was not French. It was no matter that Monsieur Murphy had served his time in the Bourbon army; he had also served his time in the Bastille.

There was every chance of his daughter being in the pay of one of France's enemies. She could easily take advantage of her position to poison the King, to stab him in the dark. A foreigner had to be properly investigated.

Monsieur Meusnier, Inspector of Police, settled down on the seventh floor of the building opposite the Murphys' apartment. He stared into the Murphys' windows. He was close enough to overhear their quarrels and conversations. He kept a watch on visitors and noted the lights burning at all hours of the night.

The Inspector scribbled everything down, pretending to practise the trade or profession of a man of letters. He observed with some interest the removal of the Murphy girls' clothes – three, four, eight, fifteen, twenty times a day.

For six months the Murphys were the most spied-on family in the capital, and in due course the Inspector submitted his report to the Pompadour. The document was full of the minutest details of the private lives and private habits of all the Murphys. When the Inspector could discover no more he had resorted to making things up.

Monsieur Lebel was not prepared for what he found in Paris. The squalor of the Murphys' lives was something of a shock. In the rabbit-warren of ramshackle apartments behind the Palais-Royal he sat with Madame Murphy discussing her daughter.

No, he smiled, he would not take a glass of Irish whiskey.

Chickens scratched about the floor. A black pig snuffled and snapped around his ankles. An Irish wolfhound nudged his nose into Lebel's groin, sniffing. A white cockerel perched on a window ledge, crowing every ten seconds.

No, he smiled, he would not accept a glass of Irish beer.

Lebel looked down at his green velvet Court suit, the spotless *pantalons*, the diamond buckles on his red shoes. He forced himself to think of business.

No, he smiled, he would not drink a glass of home-made wine.

The stench of animals was stifling. He stood by the window, held a lace handkerchief to his nose. He felt a desperate need to scratch his scalp. His hands felt as if they had been dipped in glue.

No, he smiled, nor a dish of Irish tea.

He stopped his mind wandering, focused on Madame Murphy, huge, vast-bosomed, showing her black teeth; mother of the beautiful girl. He wondered how such a grotesque parentage was possible.

No, he smiled, nor a glass of water.

Her face was purple, like smoked ham. Her voice deep, like a man's, foreign. She shooed rabbits, made the chickens squawk upwards, set the pig off grunting.

'How much had you in mind, Monsieur?' she asked, offhand, her accent French but not French.

Lebel picked a figure, the lowest possible.

She did not reply.

He raised it. Doubled it. Doubled it again.

The Divine One's mother stayed silent.

Lebel launched into his explanation, the justification of his presence. How indebted his client was to Madame Murphy and her husband, without ever mentioning his client's name. He spoke of the need for discretion. He flattered her. He was bidding for the price of keeping her mouth shut.

Madame Murphy knew perfectly well who Lebel was talking about, who Lebel was, and what he was: the royal pander.

'She's a fine decent girl,' said Madame Murphy slowly.

Lebel doubled his *livres*.

'Nothing but the best for my very best girl,' she said.

Lebel doubled again.

She knew very well he had come hotfoot from Versailles on purpose to see her, on purpose *to purchase her daughter's virginity as cheap as he could.*

'We will not let our Marie-Louise go for nothing,' she said.

Lebel raised the sum again.

'Did your client have any thoughts of my daughter bearing him any children at all?' she asked casually.

She thought, I cannot have her sent back home again. I cannot have her turned out on the street in the family way.

Lebel added 10,000 *livres.*

Monsieur Murphy was, unfortunately, not at home. Hardly aware of what was going on, he would smile, nod his head to anything his wife said, and carry on sipping his whiskey. A gentle man, an easy man, a quiet man.

Then Madame Murphy suddenly said yes, she would allow her daughter to live at Versailles – all found, all expenses paid. She agreed to the diamonds, the conditions, and to Lebel's final offer.

Monsieur Lebel made his most solemn promise that they would look after her daughter for the rest of her life, however long she lived, whoever was on the throne of France, and whatever happened.

Madame Murphy smiled her best smile. Gold clinked in her hands, glinted on the shit-encrusted table. She poured him whiskey to clinch the deal.

Lebel was laughing inside, still within the King's limit. They chinked glasses. A half-price mistress, sold to the only bidder.

He drank, choked, and could not stop coughing.

'The whiskey,' he said and made for the door, with Madame Murphy talking away as if she had kissed the Blarney Stone, talking about Lebel did not know what, for his mind was elsewhere, unable to understand this mountain of a woman.

He backed through the door, gasping, trying to escape, trying to breathe through the stench of animal excrement, the stench of the communal latrine pouring urine down the dark staircase. He slid his way, coughing, down through the chicken bones, dog bones, dead cats, rotting fruit, fish-heads, mussel shells, broken bottles and out into the Palais-Royal.

He clasped his hands behind his back, walking through the gardens. He looked for girls automatically. He touched the seat of his *pantalons* and found something damp.

'*Merde*,' he said. 'Chicken shit.' Then he laughed a long laugh. 'Murphy!' he murmured. '*Irlandaise*!'

Up on the seventh floor Madame Murphy drank all the whiskey, unable to believe her own miracle.

The contract stipulated that the Murphys must stay away from Versailles, must give written notice of any occasion requiring their daughter's presence in Paris, must undertake not to divulge, reveal or disclose any fact, detail or particular of their daughter's residence in the town and château of Versailles whatever.

She had consented to the vow of silence and had sworn herself to secrecy.

'None of that matters, though,' she told Monsieur Murphy later. 'It's the money that matters.'

Madame Murphy sold her second-hand clothes stall the day after Lebel's visit, at his suggestion, and set about the acquisition of a carriage, a pair of horses, and a man to drive them.

She spent a week of afternoons buying dresses in the Rue du Faubourg Saint-Honoré, and appeared early in the day wearing her diamonds, having slept in them, unable to bring herself to take them off. After inspecting apartments in a more salubrious quarter of Paris, she disappeared in the direction of the spa of Bagnères with the intention of restoring her health, her physique, her complexion and her self-esteem.

Daniel Murphy gave up making shoes and spent his time drifting from café to café in a dream. The Murphys began to spend, confident that the source of their new wealth would never dry up.

With Madame Murphy's birthday approaching, Daniel Murphy had in mind what he could give her, now that he had all the money in the world. Something fine, he thought, something she would treasure for a lifetime.

Before Marie-Louise left for Versailles, he beckoned to her and said, 'Come with us and we'll buy your *Maman*'s present.'

They set off for the Rue du Faubourg Saint-Honoré and the

most expensive jeweller in Paris: Daniel Murphy in sea-blue velvet with silver buttons, his face properly scraped, his wig properly dressed, his new shoes squeaking in spite of having been steeped in urine for a week, and wearing the most expensive beaver hat he could find; Marie-Louise wore scarlet silk borrowed from the Opéra-Comique and her most fashionable smile.

Monsieur Murphy raised his hat and said 'Top o' the morning' fifty times before they were out of the Palais-Royal. They passed several hours fingering trays of diamonds and gold rings, and precious stones they had never heard of, bowed and scraped to by obsequious shop assistants. They could not decide what to buy.

'She said once,' said Marie-Louise, 'she would like to see some proper pearls, instead of all those false pearls of Brigitte's . . .'

'Pearls will it be then,' said Monsieur Murphy.

'The real thing, mind,' she said.

They walked home with a fine necklace of six strands of pearls that made Brigitte's work look shabby, and with Daniel Murphy's purse lighter by a considerable sum of money.

In the Rue du Faubourg Saint-Honoré he smiled and raised his hat to Madame Doolan, Madame Flannan, Madame O'Rooney, and to a hundred Irishmen, all of whom smiled back as if they expected all the luck of the Murphys to rub off on to themselves.

As they turned into the Jardin du Palais-Royal, Marie-Louise clutched her father's sleeve. 'Pearls are unlucky, though!' she said.

'Nonsense!' Daniel Murphy said. 'Not for the Murphys. Not now we have all the luck in the world.'

But that did not stop her thinking it. Nor did it stop her wondering why she had suggested they bought pearls in the first place.

She thought, In fact, pearls are the unluckiest thing you can possibly buy.

In 1752 François Boucher repeated the composition of the young girl lying on a yellow-green sofa. He painted the blue ribbon round her neck, twined it in her hands, made her feet sprawl out behind her. The blue eyes of Marie-Louise Murphy smiled in her face. The drapery was pink, her favourite colour. The open book on the left-hand side he replaced with a perfume burner, against the smells that made her feel ill, and a pink velvet cushion. The pink roses he moved to the left, and the two roses became one rose. The picture was less yellow. Her flesh was not quite so white. She seemed more alive. Her eyes sparkled. She was not pouting. She was plumper, had put on weight.

She preferred the new picture. She liked it better without the book in the corner. She asked who the painting was for, but Boucher would not tell her.

'Secret,' he said, 'but there is time for one more canvas before *sa Majesté* returns from his travels.'

She began to unlace her dress, ready to sprawl in her usual pose.

'Wait,' Boucher said, 'today you will be Our Lady, with your clothes on!' She fastened her dress and was at once a picture of unworldly purity. Yesterday profane, today sacred.

Her eyes fixed themselves on the middle distance, dreaming of Versailles. She sat still. A smile played over her face.

Boucher could see the halo hovering above the golden hair, and brushed it in before it disappeared for ever.

He treated her differently, she thought, with a kind of awe. He demanded no kisses, had set aside his smirks, his lecher's leer, his stolen gropings. She was the King's property, not Boucher's any more. She was no longer his model. She had become a potential patron.

She cradled a doll in her arms, radiated an aura of sanctity, was pure, holy, unspotted, the picture of innocence.

Before the paint was dry, the instant holy relic was packed in straw and thick cloths and rushed to Versailles on its way to work wonders.

Boucher's *Holy Family* was destined for the Queen's oratory, by some whim, some joke of Madame de Pompadour, who suggested that Marie-Louise Murphy would make quite a good Virgin.

Marie Leszczinska prayed hourly before the sacred Murphy and genuflected each time she passed the painting, a hundred times a day.

The King worshipped the profane Murphy in another part of

the château: his Venus, his Juno, his goddess of goddesses, his girl of girls.

The sacred image caused the Queen to shiver with a religious ecstasy that made her think of Paradise and flights of angels.

The profane image performed the daily miracle of making the royal *jeanchouart* grow in the dark inside his clothes like a potato plant.

Magic, he thought, *Abracadabrantesque* . . .

When the summons to Versailles finally came, it took Marie-Louise Murphy by surprise. She had wondered, sometimes, if Himself had really meant what he said, whether he was not playing some game with her.

She thought, we are not his sort of people, he will surely want grander girls than us.

She would not quite believe it until it happened. Then, one morning, the courier from the château was at the door, wearing a red velvet coat embroidered with gold braid, holding out a letter sealed with the King's seal, saying 'Be at So-and-So at Such-and-Such,' and his arms full of lilies.

She could not see a lily for the rest of her life without thinking of Himself. Lilies everywhere, until she fell in love with their perfect whiteness. Until she was sick of the sight of lilies and wished she would never see another lily ever again.

But on 25 March 1752 the sight of lilies could still make her heart leap.

'*Bonjour,*' the courier said, smirking, showing teeth that were themselves as white as lilies. The sort of young man she might have liked to marry, she thought, if she was free to marry a young man like an angel.

'*Bonjour, Mademoiselle,*' he said, 'it's your lucky day . . .'

VII

A plain carriage waited at the end of the Rue de Richelieu, unmarked by any *fleur-de-lis*, with nothing to show that it was a carriage from Versailles.

Marie-Louise Murphy climbed inside with her few possessions: a rosary, an ivory crucifix, a necklace of blue beads, a piece of blue ribbon round her neck with a rabbit's foot on the end of it, her weasel-skin purse – things the child in her clung to.

'You'll be after needing all the luck you can get,' her father said, kissing her.

She wore pink silk that showed off her newly-acquired bosom, a necklace of Brigitte's false pearls, all the best of the second-hand.

'Well, you won't be after needing any clothes for your new job,' said her mother, kissing her, and they all laughed.

She wore new shoes, one last pair made by her father, for a shoemaker's daughter could not go away on her great adventure in anything else, and they squeaked in spite of having been steeped in urine for a fortnight.

She felt as if she was returning to her convent, only they all knew she would not be coming home again. If she did come back, *when* she came back, she would be changed. She would be refined. She would be for ever dissatisfied with everything that was cheap, dismayed by everything that was not of the very best. None of the old things, none of the old ways would please her any more. She was going away to be spoilt, to be magicked into something she was not: to be turned into a princess but not a princess. Marie-Louise Murphy would never be the same again.

The Murphys bade her farewell, shed tears, kissed her, hugged her and gave her their parting advice.

'Look him in the eye . . .'

'Keep your shoes on . . .'

'Don't fall in love . . .'

'And don't get *pregnant* . . .'

The carriage door slammed, the iron-rimmed wheels ground

across the cobblestones, the horses snorted, stamped, disappeared into the mist at the end of the Rue de Richelieu, and there was a hole in Madame Murphy's heart.

Marie-Louise Murphy was on her way to Versailles, bundled into a carriage like a parcel, like a girl being kidnapped with the full consent and approval of her parents, carried off to the ogre's palace against her will, as if there was something dreadful about the appropriation of a girl of fourteen for the monarch's private pleasure.

'This is your great chance,' her mother had told her, 'the chance of your lifetime, your one and only chance, and you must take it now or regret it for ever.'

Marie-Louise Murphy was not being taken to live happy ever after in the castle of the Prince of her dreams. Louis XV, King of France and Navarre, might have been handsome once, but he could no longer be described as young. He was forty-two years old, much flattered about his looks and his figure. He was almost old enough to be her grandfather, and he planned to keep her in the attics.

On that particular morning the new mistress did not specially want to go anywhere. She felt as if she was still dreaming. Her feet did not reach the carriage floor but dangled in mid-air.

She worried all the way about what would become of her. For all her knowledge of the world she was still a child, with a child's fears: fear of the dark, fear of the unknown, fear of not pleasing him, fear of rejection.

She clutched her rosary, said all the prayers she could think of, thought of the money and tried to cheer herself up. She thought of the feather-bed instead of straw. She tried not to think of anything.

Then Versailles loomed, honey-coloured in the sun, and she tingled with excitement, amazed again by its vastness.

The coachman dumped her with a nod and she stood about, waiting.

Half a dozen gentlemen touched her elbow, slipped their arms through hers in the space of ten minutes, leering, trying to pull her along with them, hailing her as a long-lost cousin, as someone they knew in Nantes or Périgueux.

'Surely you are Mademoiselle Truc . . .'
'So, Mademoiselle . . . we meet again . . .'
'How strange to see *you* here . . .'
'Mademoiselle, let me show you my . . .'

But she did not know any of them. She would not be picked up by strange men, however rich, however handsome, however charming, not here, not today, not now. She had been picked up by the King himself. She was not anybody's relation, she was nobody's friend except His friend, and she was not going to speak to anyone but him.

Shortly afterwards she was gliding correctly behind Monsieur Lebel. He moved fast, bony, bird-like, with creaking shoes, and was way ahead of her before she had begun to move.

Everyone turned to look at her, as if all Versailles had been advised that today the new mistress would be delivered; as if they had made a special effort to come and stare and make instant judgements on her suitability.

Ladies came running to look and made loud remarks about her old-fashioned dress. She stood out at once. She was like nothing they had seen before. With lorgnettes raised, curiosity and desire aroused, gentlemen craned their necks and murmured admiringly as she floated past.

She caught glimpses of glittering salons, golden chambers, a jam of sedan-chairs inside endless corridors, the confusion of too many people jostling in a confined space. She passed princesses as young as herself playing carpet bowls. She noticed a *comtesse* having her portrait painted, watched by a crowd of idle courtiers with nothing better to do – who turned their heads to gape at the new girl, moving so fast that she attracted everyone's attention: a new girl gliding in quite the correct manner, whom nobody had seen before, whom nobody knew.

She passed gilded dog-kennels, and the dogs raised their noses from golden bowls to sniff as she went by. She caught sight of golden galleries full of gold-embroidered courtiers, full of the stinking public. The château seemed to be a vast market where everything was for sale: girls, women, kisses, fruit, flowers, birds. She saw chickens perched on the heads of gilded statues, chickens for sale, producing eggs for aristocratic tables, as if all Versailles were a vast farmyard devoted to just one thing.

And Versailles saw her as the King's new chicken herself, bound for the royal plate, by private and special appointment, a girl bought for the satisfaction of the monarch's private lusts.

The château was in total chaos, as usual, crammed with people. Versailles hummed with noise, the powerhouse of France, ridiculous and glorious at the same time. She liked Versailles at once. She *loved* it.

She saw Lebel bow his knee to the King's bed as he hurried through the Chambre du Roi, just as a priest might genuflect before his altar: as if here at Versailles the bed, and everything that went on in it, was an object of worship. Thinking it was the thing to do, she copied him.

On the top floor of the château, hidden among the roofs, Lebel showed her to a tiny apartment with walls of pale green silk covered with hand-embroidered flowers and golden leaves; there were pale green silk curtains embroidered with gold *fleurs-de-lis*; there were pale green damask chairs with gilt frames. A window looked out between two giant statues on the parapet over a vista of the pale green misty Parc. She looked down on to the perfectly-clipped green parterres and on to the Tapis Vert, impossibly green, and the impossibly blue blue of the Grand Canal stretching into the distance.

She peered down at the ever-present crowd. A muffled hubbub drifted up to her, with the strident music of the King's band that seemed to play without ever stopping and seemed always to play the same tune.

She heard the quiet, regular tramp of military boots on the gravel. At dusk she listened to the squawk of water birds, the plash of oars, distant voices, distant laughter, the screaming hilarity of girls like her out there in the dim shrubbery.

In the early evening her door was thrown open. A gentleman strode into the room carrying a worn leather bag, as if he might have come to wind the clocks.

He was stout and looked at her hard through his spectacles, as if he knew who she was and why she was here. He wore a scarlet coat with gold buttons and panted slightly, as if he had run up all the stairs.

'Come here, Mademoiselle,' he said. He spoke as if he was used to being obeyed. She walked to the window.

'Open, *s'il vous plaît*,' he said, looking at her mouth.

'Say AAH, Mademoiselle,' he said. Marie-Louise did as she was told, and realized who he was.

'Hmmm,' he said, sounding concerned. He put his cold fingers behind her ears and felt the sides of her neck. She felt his steady breath in her face.

'Hmmm,' he said, sounding alarmed. He gazed into her eyes and took her pulse. He inspected her fingernails, as if he was looking for evidence that she had sharpened them. He rubbed her teeth with his fingers, as if he was seeking for signs that she had filed them down for better biting.

'Remove your dress, Mademoiselle, *s'il vous plaît*,' he said. She climbed out of her silk taffeta, let it fall, whispering, to the floor and stood naked before him in her shoes.

The doctor ogled and said 'Hmmm,' sounding interested.

'Lie down, Mademoiselle,' he said. She lay down.

'Open, *s'il vous plaît*,' he said. She opened her legs for the doctor to peer inside with a lighted candle, dripping hot wax over her so that she squealed. He slid his fingers inside her and felt about, as if he were hunting for something she had hidden.

She felt his hot breath on her stomach.

'Hmmm,' he said, sounding perplexed, and poked her some more.

The doctor pronounced her free of a long list of diseases:

> *La gonorrhée* . . .
> *La syphilis* . . .
> *La diphtérie* . . .
> *Le choléra* . . .

He pronounced her fit to face Versailles, fit to face the future, fit to face the most strenuous exercise, fit to have the royal *zizi* placed inside her person.

The doctor smiled broadly. '*Enchanté*, Mademoiselle,' he said, '*enchanté* . . .' He patted her bottom, told her to put her dress back on, and was gone, slamming the door behind him.

Later in the evening her door burst open a second time, making the candles flicker and a second visitor interrupted her thoughts and made her jump. Before she had time to turn round from the window, he was in the room. He leaned on the door with his hands in his pockets, looking at her. Himself, breathing hard, as if it had been a major exertion to tear himself away from the business of being King of France and Navarre.

'*Bonjour*, Mademoiselle,' he said, and threw his wig on the bed. And then he said nothing.

She thought, He is shy, he is quite ordinary.

Her mind's eye had painted him in grander clothes. He looked no different from the men she saw in the Palais-Royal. He looked like any other man. He wore peacock-blue velvet. His shoes gleamed like mirrors.

She performed her perfect curtsy and kissed his hands, as she had been taught.

'*Bonjour*,' she said, and realized she did not know what to call him. She had forgotten what he looked like. She had forgotten the sound of his voice. She was surprised to find that it was husky, that it excited her.

His eyes, large, black, shining, were like blackcurrants, she thought.

He said nothing and she thought, then, that he was very shy, that he hardly knew who she was, that he did not know what to say to her.

She snapped out of her dream, thought she must have been staring at him. She smiled her perfect convent smile, asked a hundred questions, and his hand was on her shoulder, caressing her translucent skin, and then his hand was inside her dress, and her tongue was inside his mouth, and there were clothes in heaps on the floor.

As she slept her brain raced. In the early part of the night she felt as if she was immersed in a pool of water, with bubbles rising to the surface and everything in Versailles floating upwards: conical shrubs, silver *fauteuils*, golden tassels, golden knives and forks, all spinning slowly.

In the early hours her brain raced her through the Parc, naked, with antlers fixed to her head, flitting through golden trees, chased by a Louis on light feet that did not touch the ground, and all the time she glided more slowly, as if she wanted to be caught, and all the time the distance between them remained the same. It seemed that he would chase her for ever and never catch her up.

At dawn, when sleep finally overtook her, a cockerel crowed on her window-ledge every ten seconds, white, red-crested, magnificent, making her think she was waking up at home in Paris.

Louis. His blue-grey chin at daybreak, his bristled head, his stubble rasping against the sheets, like emery-paper against her soft cheeks. His incipient double chin, his *embonpoint*, product of half a lifetime of too much pâtisserie; his black eyebrows, questioning, raised in perpetual surprise although he was no longer surprised by anything. His red lips, soft; the blackened teeth, result of half a lifetime of too many bonbons; his periodic nightmare toothaches, his acute dyspepsia. She began to know him, became used to him. She looked into his glistening eyes, lost herself in kissing him, came up gasping for air. She breathed the smell of his cologne, stroked the hands that had never known what it was to be covered in mud or to tear the guts out of a chicken; hands that had never known bruises, hands that never did anything but explore the dark places beneath women's skirts. Ten fingers moving all at once, ten fingers that did nothing but drum his desk with boredom, at last with something to do.

'I live an idle useless life, Mademoiselle,' he told her. 'My life is a waste of time.'

He revealed the secret staircase that joined his private apartments to hers. He showed her how to send him messages that would not be intercepted by anyone else. He told her where she could and could not go; what she could and could not do.

Servants brought her delicacies she had never dreamed existed from the royal table. She was waited on hand and foot, treated like the lady she had been trained up to be. She grew accustomed to all the strangeness of the château and settled into a routine.

The shoemaker's daughter who had thought herself lucky to change her clothes once a month and bath twice a year was put under a bold régime of two baths a day, with strict instructions to get out of the water at the second shiver, and spent much of her time wearing nothing at all.

*

While Marie-Louise Murphy sat in luxury at Versailles the Irish in Paris called on her father, now passing himself off to the world as Monsieur Murphy de Boisfailly, in order to offer him their congratulations.

Long-lost cousins from Cork and Killarney pounded on his door asking, 'Is there any chance of a drink itself?'

Gentlemen who had kissed the Blarney Stone kissed Daniel Murphy on both cheeks in the Continental manner as if he were a close relative. Irishmen he had never seen before told him stories of his father's and grandfather's exploits and drank all his whiskey for him.

Monsieur Murphy dispensed the golden liquid all afternoon and carried on tipping up the bottle for the better part of the evening until his visitors, reluctant to leave, fell asleep in their chairs.

Madame Murphy's salon was crowded all day, thick with the smell of the not-often-washed, thick with the pipe smoke of her female relations. After a few glasses of her Irish cordial they fell to singing old Irish songs and telling old Irish stories, and expressed themselves over the moon at the good news they heard about her youngest daughter.

Monsieur Murphy would shake his head sadly, though the sparkle never went out of his eyes, and murmur, '*Hélas*, not one of them an honest woman.'

Later he forgot he had ever complained and spent his days in a state of quiet intoxication.

'Drink always,' he said, raising his glass to the room, 'you will never die.'

At Versailles Marie-Louise began to find her way about the labyrinth of the château, and to learn who was who.

'Beware of Madame d'Estrées,' her *femme de chambre* told her, 'she is dangerous.'

But when she met Madame d'Estrées she thought she seemed quite harmless and made friends with her at once.

Madame d'Estrées told her, 'Beware of Madame d'Estrades.'

Try as she did, Marie-Louise muddled the d'Estrades with the d'Estrées, and the Bourbon-Condés with the Bourbon-Contys. She confused the Duc de Choiseul with the Baron de Choiseul and mixed up the latter with the Baronne his wife.

But she saw few courtiers, did not mingle in society, and lived a retired life among the roofs, waiting for Himself to appear.

In time the servants, who addressed the King as *Sire*, began to refer to the new mistress as *Sirette*. Writers of journals and diaries who had hardly set eyes on Marie-Louise Murphy turned her into *La Petite Morphise*, or *Morfil*, or *Morfi*, or 'the new sultana', and faithfully recorded the slightest whiff of rumour.

The First Gentlemen of the Chamber greeted her civilly and inclined their heads when they met her in public. The First Valets of the Chamber – one of whom was Lebel, who slept on a fold-up bed in the King's bedroom, tied to his wrist by a silken rope lest he should require anything during the night – would carry Morfi's messages and do battle with the moths and mosquitoes that invaded her apartment.

The Premier Maître d'Hôtel, in charge of the royal food and drink, with a regiment of food-tasters, butlers, aides, yeomen of the pantry, yeomen of the laundry, yeomen of the scullery, porters and under-porters, running footmen and bearers of wine, equerries and head cooks, under-cooks, pastrycooks, errand boys, spit boys, uncorkers of bottles, basters of meat – all kept Morfi's meals ascending the stairs to her under a silver cover.

The polishers of parquet made her floor into a mirror she could see her face in. The head gardeners presented tributes of lilies and pink roses. She smiled with the same radiance on removers of cobwebs, repairers of chandeliers, lighters and snuffers of candles, killers of bats, ratmen, mousemen and cleaners of windows – who all attended to her daily requirements.

The Grand Maître of the Royal Wardrobe cared for her clothes with the same attention reserved for the clothes of the King.

The Premier Médecin du Roi and his seventeen consultants supplied Morfi with sleeping draughts, lip-salves, eye-drops, indigestion lozenges, reassurance and wise advice.

In the corridors the table-clearers, boot-boys, bell-boys and lower servants made her elaborate and formal bows. In the Parc the boatmen, coachmen, mole-catchers and clippers of hedges simpered and made obeisances when she passed.

The Garde du Corps of 1300 men kept watch over the King and never let him out of their sight (though he sometimes escaped) and saluted and presented arms when Morfi appeared in public.

In the Grande Ecurie, the royal stables, the Master of the Horse, forty-eight grinning pages and forty-two smirking valets laboured to supply carriages and horses for Morfi's daily outing. Ostlers, farriers, saddlers, spur-makers, sweepers of manure and forkers of straw vied with each other for her favours as she stepped down, smiling, from her carriage.

There were so many servants that no one knew exactly how many there were in total. Some were forgotten, still living in their quarters but performing no function, retired or infirm. There were so many servants that often there was nowhere for them to sleep. So many and so expensive were they that the royal household eventually stopped paying their wages and the *valets de chambre* were forced to beg charity of the *curé* of Saint-Louis because they had not been paid for two years and had no money to buy food.

Vagrants infiltrated the château precincts, begging Morfi for coins, but she received everything in kind. She had become like royalty: she had no occasion to spend money and never handled it.

The servants waited on some 10,000 courtiers, the Princes of the Blood and not of the Blood, the Ducs and Duchesses, Vicomtes and Vicomtesses, the Comtes, Marquis, Barons, Chevaliers and Messieurs and their wives, all of them sweating into velvet coats or silk dresses, all of them unwashed, all of them trying to stifle the smell with scent, or by piling on more and more clothes – to hide it by holding handkerchiefs soaked in scent to their noses; all of them trying to pretend that the *odour* of Versailles did not exist.

During the summer of 1753 Monsieur Murphy turned to toasting the saints in the ecclesiastical calendar in fine wine.

On 2 June he raised his glass to the immortal memory of Saint-Pothin.

On 3 June he drank the health of Sainte-Clothilde.

On 4 June he celebrated the canonization of Saint-Quirinius.

On 8 June he remembered Saint-Médard, invoked for toothache and thus of paramount importance.

In the middle of June he took to his bed and took the bottle with him.

The *curé* of Les Saints-Innocents asked Madame Murphy, 'Why do you not stop him?'

'He is a free man,' she said. 'He may do as he pleases.'

During the night of 16 June Daniel Murphy woke his wife to tell her he could hear the wailing of the *banshee*.

'Will you go back to sleep, man!' she said. 'Do you suppose the banshee would cross the Irish Sea in all this hot weather just to haunt you?'

Daniel Murphy said, 'I do, to be sure I do.'

On 17 June the *curé* of Les Saints-Innocents carried the viaticum through the Jardin du Palais-Royal under a scarlet ombrellino with a shivering golden fringe, preceded by acolytes in red and white robes, and Daniel Murphy's neighbours sank to their knees among the orange-peel and rotten apples and stinking black mud and crossed themselves devoutly as the *saint sacrement* passed by.

During the night of 17 June Madame Murphy and her elder daughters sat up with the sick man, fanning the pages of *La Sainte Bible* in his sweating face in order to bring down his temperature, but without success.

On 18 June Daniel Murphy de Boisfailly was dead.

'His poor hands cold like potatoes,' wailed the widow.

In the silence of the dawn the sound of the Irish women of Paris keening was heard, unearthly, like the yowling of cats, from high above the Palais-Royal gardens.

The daughters took turns to sit up with the body. They covered the mirrors with white sheets. They turned the engravings of Cork and Dublin to face the walls. They unlocked the locks in the apartment so the soul of Daniel Murphy could pass to its eternal rest.

The long sustained ul-lu-lu of the keening women went on and on, a noise no one could hear without great emotion, although few of the French people in the quarter knew what it was or what it meant.

Marie-Louise Murphy arrived in her Versailles dress of black silk taffeta, looking like 100,000 *livres*, perfectly turned-out. She made the rest of her family look shabby. She found her home small, dirty and cheaply furnished. She had become a stranger. She blamed herself for her father's death.

'It was them pearls,' she said.

She walked with her family behind the coffin to the cemetery of Les Saints-Innocents. She watched as her father's body was tipped into the ground with the skulls and knees and elbows of other dead men sticking out into his grave. Nobody said a word about the stench, but they held scent balls to their faces and breathed in as little as they could.

'All the luck of the Murphys . . .' sobbed Marie-Louise as she clung to Brigitte.

Madame Murphy denied that drink had anything to do with the demise of her husband.

'He was the sweetest and saintliest of men,' she said, 'and hardly touched a drop to drink in all his lifetime.'

Her daughters nodded, sniffed, and dabbed their eyes.

'A decent, respectable man,' wept Madame Murphy, 'who died in the arms of Holy Church amid the bosoms of his family, and anything else is a vile rumour put about by the enemies of Ireland.'

Marie-Louise blamed the pearls. 'Them pearls,' she said. 'If we had not bought the pearls he would still be alive today.'

Madame Murphy sat in a gilded chair and wailed and bit her knuckles.

'I cannot wear pearls given me by a dead man,' she said. 'I will not have them pearls in the house another night!' she cried.

She screamed at Marie-Louise, '*Malheureuse*! Why did you have to buy them?'

Marie-Louise walked slowly through the Palais-Royal, smiled on sympathetically by Madame Sheehy de Dunlaoghaire, by Madame Ryan de Kinsale and Monsieur O'Rourke de Fermanagh and a host of other Irish neighbours. She took the pearls back to the shop in the Rue du Faubourg Saint-Honoré.

Tears welled up in her eyes as she poured out her story to the jeweller: her father was dead, her mother refused to have the pearls in the house; she, Marie-Louise, could not wear them herself.

The jeweller smiled and said he understood perfectly. He examined the necklace with his eye-glass to make sure she had not substituted false pearls for the real thing and refunded the money.

He watched her walk along the Rue du Faubourg Saint-Honoré, shaking his head in disbelief.

'*Irlandaise!*' he said, laughing.

Back at Versailles Morfi's waiting was rewarded and she was showered with diamonds, sapphires, emeralds, gold trinkets and priceless treasures.

Himself would come and sit with her, to kiss her and to talk to her. He questioned her about her father's death. He had to know what were his last words; whether she had kissed the corpse; about keening; about her father's ghost; about the *pompes funèbres*; about the viaticum; about how the Irish did these things; about what the dead man wore in his coffin, how deep the grave was dug, about the smell of death. He had to know everything.

Louis XV was fascinated by death.

She had rarely seen him more animated. Death made him seem more alive. His black eyes glittered like jet and he kissed her more eagerly, pressed more jewels into her hands, and slipped away up his secret staircase to see her three, four, five times a day.

He would tell her to stand in the *Oeil de Boeuf* at such-and-such a time, so that he could see her as he went by: on his way to and from Mass, or as he went hunting. He would wink at her, or raise an eyebrow, or lift a forefinger in recognition that she was there. If he was close enough he might slip into her hand a note containing a further rendezvous.

She was summoned one morning to watch the spectacle of the Grand Couvert: Himself on display at his dining-table, to perform the miracle of the boiled eggs.

He sat pretending not to see her, quite different from the man she knew on the top floor. He acted a part, stiff, hieratic: he existed solely to be looked at. He tucked a white napkin into his lace collar to keep egg off his black velvet coat. He smiled an oily smile, used to the hundreds of strangers who kept coming, he could not understand why, to watch him eat his eggs.

She could tell he was bored with the drama before it began. She knew that he did not really want to eat eggs at all.

Liveried footmen, wigged and powdered automatons, paraded before him half a dozen of the largest eggs in France. He had to have the biggest, the best, the most beautiful, the most expensive of everything, like a big child.

He wished the spectators would disappear and leave him alone. Alone with Morfi, his secret, about whom no one was supposed to know anything. Morfi, kept caged just as he was caged.

For now, he contented himself with the performance. He picked up the golden fork, raised his hand, swiped at the first egg, and took the top off in one go. The perfect decapitation.

The crowd held its breath for a moment, then breathed out and applauded eagerly, as if he had done something quite out of the ordinary.

Egg ran down his chin in a golden, snot-like stream.

He performed five more beheadings. The crowd applauded more vehemently each time, gaped until they were bored with wonders, and wandered off in search of something new.

Up on the roofs Louis kept the royal chickens and the royal rooster that woke Morfi each morning and was, like her, his pride and joy. Louis was fond of his birds, reluctant to see them slaughtered for the table. In due course the rooster fell into a decline and neared the end of his natural life.

The red crest turned black. Towards the end Louis XV, in his royal-blue velvet coat with gold buttons, with the Order of the Holy Ghost across his chest, sat with the cockerel standing on his knees. Tears trickled down the royal cheeks. He sat up all night with Morfi by candlelight, helping the rooster to die. He talked to him, crooned, stroked the stiff feathers, fed him worms and bugs with his own hand.

The Premier Médecin du Roi gave his best advice. The fourteen doctors took the rooster's pulse, listened to his fading heart, inspected the scrawny tongue.

The rooster lay on a yellow-green velvet sofa, beyond all salvation, breathing more and more feebly. His eyes glazed over. The crest grew blacker. The mouth hung open, croaking, still trying to crow every ten seconds, and breathed its last.

The Premier Médecin listened one last time for the heart that had stopped beating. 'The chickens have worn him out, Sire,' he said, shaking his head.

*

Louis made further rendezvous, sent Morfi to Number 26 Rue de l'Orangerie, to the Hôtel d'Humières, to knock on the street door. Inside she was thrilled by the frantic beating of wings, the screech of exotic fowl, the demonic cries of his hunting birds, his birds of prey – falcons, kites, eagles, buzzards – birds with black staring eyes just like the King's eyes.

He lingered there with Morfi behind locked doors, tapping the cages, taking out the hawks. He threw scraps of meat, and live mice, to demonstrate their skill.

She was delighted by the jingling bells fixed to the birds' feet, but she felt that she too was his prisoner, his caged bird.

He would meet her at Number 89 Avenue de Saint-Cloud, the royal kennels, to show her the dogs training up for the royal hunt. Amid the yapping of puppies and the baying of thousands of hounds he would pull her behind the chestnut trees planted to keep the sun off the dogs in summer and kiss her hungrily.

His raw meat, she thought, his lap dog.

She would meet him at the royal menagerie on the edge of the Parc and look at the elephants, the dromedaries, the two fine lions, the wolves, the screaming peacocks: all his caged creatures, caged as he was. All of them denied their freedom just as she too was denied her freedom.

She longed to unlock the doors and let all his animals out, though she never dared say so. She thought Louis looked through the bars as a fellow prisoner, as if he felt as the animals felt: as if the only thing he wanted in the world was to escape, to be free of Versailles, which he so disliked.

Sometimes he did escape, to perform a circuit of his other palaces. Sometimes they escaped together, on one occasion to Fontainebleau, where Morfi had her own suite of rooms for the duration of the visit, an annual affair of six weeks in the autumn.

At Fontainebleau Morfi had celebrated her fifteenth birthday: floating in a boat on the lake, walking in the gardens, riding in a carriage through the forest. He had given her magnificent presents: diamonds, a gold clock, a gold snuffbox with his portrait on the lid and a mechanical bird inside made of emeralds and studded with lapis lazuli that so delighted her that she threw off her gold-embroidered shoes and danced on all the chairs.

Back at Versailles, Louis showed her, when the Queen was out of the way, his own private apartments – the 'Rats' Nests' high under the roofs, where he had built tiny libraries, a workshop with a lathe where he turned ivory, a still-room and a bakery where he made chocolate, sweetmeats and pâtisserie. Here he could forget etiquette and escape the crowds of spectators and be plain Louis Bourbon instead of King of France.

There were evenings when Morfi sat at the King's private dining-table and ate pheasant-egg omelettes cooked by the royal hand; he would relax and smile and talk interminably of his day's hunting, and they would drink coffee grown in the Potager du Roi at Versailles and brewed by Himself in his private kitchen.

Towards midnight, with a few courtiers, he would take Morfi's hand, lead her out on to the roofs, and make the *promenade digestive*, a tour of the whole château behind the parapet: with the view of the Parc, the dark outline of the plantations, the smell of lilac trees, the distant creak of waterbirds, the pale luminosity of the Pièce d'Eau des Suisses, the Grand Canal – faint, misty, with voices carrying across the water. They would look down into courtyards still humming with activity, into the candlelit windows of the sleeping château.

Sometimes Louis would pick up his chickens, talk to them in his husky voice, and pull eggs from their nests. The new cockerel would crow and they would listen to all the noises of Versailles by night: the bells of the potato-coloured church with domes like onions, the croaking frogs, the neighing horses in the royal stables, the crickets, the fish plopping in the fountains, the distant cheering of the 250 royal pages – still awake playing some game – and breathe in the heady scent of the royal flowers.

Morfi did not breathe in too deeply. Though the air was heavy with the scent of flowers it was for good reason. While there were a quarter of a million plants in the gardens and 9,000 orange-trees in tubs, it was also true that the château had no drains and no running water. The flushing water-closet was a luxury enjoyed only by Louis and the very wealthiest; 10,000 courtiers and 5,000 servants were chasing 250 bathrooms and too few dry closets.

Comtesses, Marquises, footmen and the general public would cease to resist the call of nature, feel disinclined to make the expedition of hundreds of yards to queue for the communal privies in the courtyards – that stank and swarmed with flies – and relieved themselves into the nearest vase of flowers, or behind a damask curtain, or out of open windows.

Morfi's nostrils were often full of the odour of stale urine, the stink of ordure. She would look out early in the morning only to see the night-soil cart parked below her window and the under-footmen struggling with the accumulated excrement of 15,000 people.

Versailles stank, and the quarter of a million flowers and the 9,000 orange-trees and all the scent in France could not hide it.

Close by the château stood the royal abattoir, doing a roaring trade, whence the squeals of pigs and the bellowing of cattle having their throats cut reached the royal table. The King's band did not play during meals for nothing.

In summer the smell was much worse. On the edge of Versailles was the midden, where the refuse was dumped and forgotten. On hot days when the wind blew in a certain direction the stench blew back through the open windows of the great Galerie des Glaces and came home to roost among genteel gatherings of Ducs and Princesses playing tric-trac in gilded salons.

The women did constant battle with their fans.

Morfi escaped, from time to time, in search of fresh air. She learned the hours when Himself was ensconced with his ministers, devoting his attention to the running of the kingdom of France and Navarre – approximately one hour each day, during which he said little. She learned the times of public eating, the days when he hunted, the grim dates when he disappeared to Marly or Saint-Germain without her. And then she would stop waiting for him to visit her and walk out of her gilded cage.

She told him, 'I cannot bear to be confined to the château all day like a captive.'

She would glide into the streets of Versailles to watch ordinary people doing all the things she could no longer do.

She walked along the Avenue de Saint-Cloud under the trees, looking in at windows where families were eating meals together, laughing, quarrelling and singing, and she wanted to live an ordinary life as well.

She wandered round the pale green polluted waters of the Pièce d'Eau des Suisses and watched the women of Versailles washing their linen, calling to each other and shrieking with laughter, hanging their small-clothes on the bushes to dry, and splashing their grey sheets in the filthy water – quite illegally, for the lake was reserved for the washing of the Queen's laundry – and she longed to be part of the ordinary world.

She drifted into the Place Dauphine to watch free men and women climbing into public coaches bound for Paris, being taken away from Versailles.

She lingered in the Place du Marché Notre-Dame looking at the chickens tied upside down by their feet, still kicking, waiting to be sold, and she thought of herself tied upside down and kicking just like them.

She thought of the normal life she had lost. She lived a false life, a prisoner's life. Her life had no purpose.

There were times when she woke in the middle of the night, alone, and wished she had never set eyes on Versailles. She wished herself behind a second-hand clothes stall back in Paris, with a lover of her own age, an apartment of her own, children of her own, and all her life under her own control.

And at the same time she loved Versailles and never wanted it to end.

Everywhere Morfi went she was followed by rumour. Everyone knew who and what she was. Everywhere she was greeted by murmurs of 'Morfi'. She felt men's eyes glueing themselves to her breasts, unable to look away. She felt men staring at her back. She was pursued by ripples of applause in the courtyards and corridors. She did not mind. She smiled as she had been taught, constantly and at everyone.

She rather enjoyed herself.

She attracted more attention than Madame de Pompadour. She distracted the guards and footmen, which the Pompadour had only rarely done. She was serenaded by workmen's whistles that disturbed the services in chapel and interrupted the devotions of the Queen. She made courtiers rise from games of écarté and run to the windows to see her go by for themselves.

Morfi stopped to talk to peers, servants, anyone who would talk back. She liked talking. She was Irish. She became friendly with the Ducs, who tried to divert her favours from the monarch by offering her bribes. Morfi was everyone's friend.

On summer evenings when Versailles was *en fête* with a great reception and 300,000 guests filled the vast Parc, and the *bosquets* were illuminated and the fountains played, and coruscating displays of fireworks crackled over the château and rained sparks and rattled the windows, and the King's band played airs by Monsieur Rameau – Morfi would part the giant crowds as if by magic. She glided among the great and good, smiling, and was treated almost as if she were royalty herself.

Versailles began to murmur that surely there could be no limit to Morfi's rise; that she might very easily become the next Pompadour, with the rank if not the title of Duchesse, and her hands on the reins of France, and six châteaux of her own. The Queen complained. Madame de Pompadour, jealous of her own protégée, complained. They could not let it go on.

'She causes too much fuss,' the Pompadour said.

Louis grimaced, did not know what to do with his hands.

'She must live a more retired life,' said the Pompadour.

Louis frowned, scratched his head.

'She must be kept more secret,' said the Pompadour.

Louis turned his back, waved his arms at nothing.

'She must live more quietly,' said the Pompadour.

Louis paced up and down, stamped his foot on the parquet.

He banged the books on his gilded *escritoire*.

'She *cannot* live in the château any longer,' shouted the Pompadour, 'it is not safe for her to wander in the streets ... She must have a keeper ...'

Louis had to agree.

They took Morfi away into the town, into the quarter known as the Parc-aux-Cerfs, the Deer Park, where in the past the Kings of France had raised game for the chase: a quarter formerly bosky, full of trees, but now full of new houses, chaotic with bricks and dust, and for the last eleven years noisy with the construction of the giant, pale-yellow church of Saint-Louis.

Here, among ordinary people, Morfi could be more easily controlled. She could be hidden from prying eyes. Here the King might visit her incognito, or she might slip into the château unobserved. No one need know what was going on.

Rumours spread that Morfi was dead; that she had fallen from

73

grace; that Louis had turned her out and sent her home; even
that he had started kissing the Queen again.

Marie-Louise Murphy vanished.

VIII

Somewhere in the labyrinth of streets in the Parc-aux-Cerfs, lugubrious like an abattoir, was a small house owned or rented by Louis XV, which became the lodging of his Irish mistress.

A Madame Bertrand, stout, jewelled, the wife of a clerk at the Ministry of War, watched over her as 'housekeeper' and pretended when necessary that Morfi was her niece.

Morfi waited in her white and gold room for the monarch to arrive. She bathed regularly in a red copper bathtub with gold taps. She was attended by two liveried footmen who lodged in the attics. There were rooms for 'Madame', for a cook and a *femme de chambre*, and not much more.

Legend painted the Parc-aux-Cerfs as a vast and luxurious establishment crowded with naked women, the seraglio of the King of France: Louis' answer to the Turkish harem, a place where everything was permitted and anything might happen; a château in miniature, with large gardens and a naked and excited monarch chasing hordes of squealing girls in varying states of undress; an establishment that cost the nation millions of *livres*, a place devoted to excess, where scandalous goings-on made the neighbourhood from which it took its name notorious.

The truth was that only a handful of girls were kept here at a time, that they were often changed for fresh ones, and often moved their lodgings; that the house and its régime were simple in the extreme, and that all was discreet. Louis himself arrived in heavy disguise, pretending to be a Polish Comte, some relation of the Queen, and the girls were often unaware of his true identity.

Exactly where Morfi was kept was a mystery to most of Versailles. Some thought the house was behind Number 78 Rue d'Anjou, a small hôtel on the corner of the Rue du Hazard: a double-fronted snuffbox with two dormer windows in an upper storey.

Others identified the house as Number 14 Rue Saint-Louis, a

larger building of three storeys with a single-storey wing to one side, in a quiet street near the Potager du Roi.

Versailles discovered in due course that Morfi had not been sent away. Rumours circulated that she went to and from the château, that she spent part of her time in one residence and part in another, even that Louis never once set foot in any of the houses in the Parc-aux-Cerfs.

At eight o'clock precisely Morfi would wake to the grinding moan and crunch of Madame Bertrand's shutters being pushed open. She would hear Madame Bertrand's 'Uh-hu-ugh', as if the effort of throwing open the shutters made her cough the same way every day. She listened to the great bell of the new church reverberating and she prepared to face another day on which she would be required to do nothing but lie in bed and wait.

In Paris she had been kept busy, running errands, cleaning shoes, scrubbing floors, washing clothes. In the Parc-aux-Cerfs she longed for the noise of a hammer banging nails into the sole of a shoe. She missed her sisters' quarrels. She pined for all the pandemonium of the château. She had been plunged into a nearly silent world, cushioned, muffled, a padded life where nothing ever happened. Her life was empty, with only one thing in it.

She spoke to no one except Madame Bertrand and the music master who taught her to sing and play the harpsichord. The footmen, who flanked her when she went out, were more interested in each other. There was often no other girl to share her thoughts with, nothing to do but tapestry and needlepoint and wait for Himself.

Every time the stairs creaked she thought it was Him and her heart turned over.

Every carriage in the street was His carriage and made her run to the window.

Every step on the cobbles was the gold-heeled shoe of Louis XV, King of France and Navarre, on his way to see her.

Often he did not visit her for a week.

She occupied herself by cultivating leafy plants with yellow and white flowers in pots on her window-sill. She sowed by moonlight on Good Friday, sprinkled Holy Water supplied by the *curé* of Saint-Louis, added a pinch of salt and a pinch of excrement, and stuck a cypress branch into the soil.

In the fullness of time she pulled the greenery upwards and performed her miracle, holding the stems up with soft black earth clinging to them, and golden potatoes dangling from the roots.

'Mademoiselle,' warned Madame Bertrand, 'the flowers look like deadly nightshade.'

'The tubers,' warned Lebel, 'look like deformed hands and feet.'

'The *pomme de terre* is dangerous,' Madame Bertrand told her, 'you must not eat it, Mademoiselle – you will be very ill.'

'Food for animals,' sneered Lebel, 'food for peasants!'

They assured her that eating potatoes would bring scrofula, rickets, consumption and leprosy, but Morfi took no notice. She sat staring into the glowing embers of her fire, watching her potatoes turn black.

Madame Bertrand summoned the Premier Médecin du Roi, who smiled and said the *pomme de terre* never did anyone any harm.

Offered a taste, Lebel and Madame Bertrand shook their heads, horrified. Morfi laughed. It was common knowledge that the potato was perfectly safe to eat; that half the Irish nation produced families of six to ten children as a matter of course and lived on nothing else.

'Surely you don't eat the skin?' Lebel asked her, disgusted.

Morfi laughed again. 'The skin is the best part, Monsieur!' she said.

She flourished on her new diet, spent her days swathed in pink watered silk, waited on hand and foot, growing steadily plumper.

She no longer removed her own shoes. She no longer had the inconvenience of brushing her own hair. She occasionally bathed in ass's milk provided by Madame de Pompadour.

The *femme de chambre* dressed and undressed Morfi as if she were a doll, in much the same way as Louis Himself was dressed and undressed in public, as if she was incapable of doing anything for herself.

Each morning the miracle of cleaning her room was performed by the two liveried footmen who glided, smiling, towards her bed, hauled the silk sheets from it, tossed them into an immense wicker basket lined with green taffeta, flipped the mattress – covered in green morocco like a giant book and stamped with gold lilies – up into the air so that it brushed the ceiling, and turned it over. Her bed was remade, her *chaise percée* was spirited away and returned shining and scented, all in the space of five minutes, when the footmen would vanish, leaving behind them the odour of perspiration – *eau de l'homme*, as they called it.

Red roses and pink carnations were delivered daily and whisked away when they showed the first sign of wilting: at Versailles even the death of flowers was unthinkable.

Faint in the distance she could hear the sound of drums and trumpets carried on the wind: Rameau, always Rameau. In the night sky above her windows she watched the stars appear and occasionally fireworks burst among them. Sometimes she was part of the *fête*, moving among the crowd, masked, close to the King, unrecognized by anybody but Himself.

More often her shutters banged in the wind and the rain slapped on her windows like hands clapping, mocking her. She stared on to a blank wall stained with pigeon droppings, waiting. She lived in a perpetual haze of scent, a life of the completest luxury, listening to the ticking of her gold clock, thinking he would never turn up.

Then suddenly her life would start again. Monsieur Lebel would appear in her doorway, his eyes like boiled sweets, pocket-watch in hand, barking orders to the smirking footmen. Her room would fill with lilies, and the footmen seized her, stripped the clothes off her back, submitted her to the sponge, the scent spray, the instant coiffure, and threw her into bed. Sometimes she would squeal with frustration and shake all over at the indignity of their treatment. Sometimes they tickled her and made her giggle at the absurdity of it all.

Then Himself would be there, tapping his fingers on the door-frame, impatient to begin his own disrobing at the hands of Lebel, like a grown-up child who had not yet mastered the art of undressing.

Then silence, privacy, the creaking of bed-springs. Outside, the pigeons flapped and fluttered, performing their own mocking gyrations with an endless liquid bubbling ooh ooh ooh.

As he went out of the door he would turn and smile at her and murmur, '*Après nous le déluge*...'

And the doctor would appear, smiling, bearing a giant brass syringe in a red morocco case, followed by grinning footmen with bowls of cold water, bowls of hot water and more lilies and the softest towels she had ever touched.

Silence but for the commotion of pigeons flying upwards, the gurgle of water, the doctor's voice saying '*Au revoir, Mademoiselle... à la prochaine!*' His feet clumping down the stairs, the slam of a carriage door, horses' hoofs in the street. Silence. The giggling footmen on the other side of her door. A snatch of Rameau in the distance, always Rameau, for the Pompadour had decreed that the King's band should play the music of no other composer. The ooh ooh ooh of pigeons.

Morfi recovered her equilibrium. She prayed every night that He would love her for ever. That He would not send her away. That He would not die. That she would not lose Him. That they would not assassinate Him. Not tonight. Not today. Not tomorrow. Not yet.

Each morning a crate of celery would be delivered to the Parc-aux-Cerfs, courtesy of Madame de Pompadour, who understood the need for such things.

Morfi would descend the stairs every day to sit with the other girls at a table covered with a blue damask cloth embroidered with gold *fleurs-de-lis*. On the table stood a vase of celery arranged like flowers.

In stony silence, broken by the pigeons' ooh ooh, more vigorous, mocking what went on in the house, a steady crunching began: the champ of delicate jaws, the snap of celery sticks, the angry ripping out of celery hearts. The ooh ooh ooh of doves. The constant flutter of wings.

After the celery came black truffles, sniffed out by the royal truffle-dogs in the forests of Périgord.

After the truffles came chocolate in silver pots, chocolate laced with triple vanilla and ambergris.

And so it went on, day after day, meal after meal: raw celery, celery soup, braised celery, baked celery, celery pie, boiled celery, mashed celery, celery purée... until she flatly refused ever to eat celery again.

On and on: hot chocolate, cold chocolate, iced chocolate. But about chocolate she made no complaint. At night she dreamed of chocolate rabbits copulating in a chocolate Parc, and chocolate money, chocolate shoes, chocolate chickens, chocolate clocks and chocolate kings and queens in a chocolate château, all of it melting in the sun.

With their desires kindled for the day, the girls settled down to wait for the call of duty that often never came. They attacked their embroidery with suppressed fury, hammered madly at the harpsichord, or walked up and down stairs over and over again for want of anything better to do. They all sewed the same thing: the radiant face of Louis XV, after the portrait by Hyacinthe Rigaud. Sometimes they could not bear to look at it. Sometimes it was satisfying to jab at his sooty eyes with their needles.

On Sunday mornings Morfi walked through the deserted streets to the church of Saint-Louis to hear the endless sermons of Père Rancé, flanked by footmen so that the eager gentlemen of the town could not sit beside her.

On Sunday afternoons she sat lazily in her room, quill in hand, doodling on her blotting paper endless *fleurs-de-lis* that slowly turned into the royal *jeanchouart*. She would idly embellish it, making it larger, until it had changed back into a *fleur-de-lis*, adorned with curlicues and curvilinear arabesques and the whole sheet was thick with lilies, then she snapped out of her reverie and rang for chocolate, more and more chocolate, waiting and waiting, trying to make time go faster.

On Sunday evenings the Parc-aux-Cerfs echoed to the rattle of the dice-box, or Madame Bertrand brought out her ivory *tric-trac* set or her playing-cards, and sat with Morfi and the footmen, trying, in the absence of the monarch, to liven up her life.

Morfi was reluctant to touch playing-cards. 'It is like having my fortune told!' she said. But Madame Bertrand made her join in to find out what the future held.

With the four of hearts in her hand Morfi would cry, 'Unlucky!'

With a run of black cards she exclaimed, 'The spades and clubs mean death!'

When she picked up the four of clubs she sighed, 'The Devil's four-poster bed!'

Madame Bertrand smiled and shook her head.

Morfi would invariably end up with just one card in her hand: the queen of spades.

'Bad luck!' she moaned.

Or the ace of spades.

'*Death*,' she wailed. 'Death, death, death, there's no end to it!'

'Sssssh!' hissed the footmen. 'Death does not exist.'

And she would be reduced to turning her chair round three times in desperation, trying to change her luck. But it never seemed to make any difference.

Louis XV made his way to the Parc-aux-Cerfs when he could. With Lebel's help he smuggled himself out after dark, wrapped in a heavy cloak, disguised as a chaplain taking the last rites to a parishioner or as a masked reveller on his way to a ball.

He migrated along the Rue du Vieux Versailles, across the Rue de l'Orangerie, into the Potager du Roi, skirting the strawberry beds. He slipped out of the gate that gave on to the Rue Satory and headed straight up the road with a strawberry in his mouth and a peacock-blue condom in each pocket, to the house where Marie-Louise lay awake. She held her breath listening for the creaking hinges of the garden gate, for the tread of the royal shoes on the stairs, for the sudden squeak of the bed as he slid in beside her, and she gasped as his cold hands slipped round her waist and his hot breath murmured endearments in her ears.

At first it had been a shock to find she was not the only girl in the Parc-aux-Cerfs. It was an economy, he explained. It was cheaper to keep them all together.

Hope did not stay alive for all of them. They arrived, they settled in, they departed, depending on whether they pleased him. He weeded out the girls who failed the ultimate test, spirited them away to the provinces, had them quietly removed.

Madame Bertrand would be found from time to time disinfecting a vacated room, debugging sheets, burning pillows. Silk and satin dresses would be redistributed to whichever girl they fitted best. The girls squabbled over the débris of pots of rouge, diamond pins, gold earrings, embroidery silks.

Occasionally a girl would have some premonition of her dismissal and leave in broad daylight *with* her diamonds and treasures and a carriage full of dresses, amid tears and sobbing, but the management liked to accomplish changes under cover of night where possible.

In secret, as Louis preferred.

Other girls found that banishment from the Parc-aux-Cerfs was like being released from prison. Face powder flew everywhere, letters from the monarch torn in shreds were thrown like confetti, firecrackers exploded under Madame Bertrand's bed, and Lebel found himself tied up with coloured streamers. The girls bounced and turned somersaults on their beds, and carnival reigned until the disgraced mistress had descended the stairs.

Then the profound silence would return, broken only by the distant band, the relentless cooing of doves and pigeons, the ceaseless fluttering of wings, and the girl who was left – Morfi – would go back to her interminable waiting.

Again and again he would pad through the dark streets, unaccompanied, dressed in grey or black, hugging the walls. Carriages passed him, slowed down as a coachman recognized his bearing, thought better of it, rumbled on, huge iron wheels clanking over the cobbles. He sidled onward, darting into a doorway to avoid the watch, adopting the pose of a man urinating so that no one saw his face. He had his adventures.

He walked on. He had slipped free. By night, surely, he might do as he liked and be himself.

They had spent the entire day doing everything for him. He had had his pants pulled on for him by the Premier Valet de Chambre, his shirt tucked in by the Deuxième Valet, his shoes put on by simpering pages. He had done nothing but sit in a gilded chair, drumming his fingers on the arms. He grew fatter. He was born bored, was bored to death. He dreamed of an ordinary day in which he could work, cook his own food, and be an ordinary citizen.

Today he did his hunting by night. He laughed to think they had lost him. He toyed with the idea of not going back, imagined them out searching for him, draining the Grand Canal, looking for a body, dragging the *étangs* with nets, hunting for a murderer, digging up all the gardens in Versailles.

He thought of their faces at the levée, with no King to wake up, no King to dress, no King to eat boiled eggs. He was plain Louis Bourbon, no King at all, out of the strait waistcoat of the monarchy, and free. Damn the *fleur-de-lis*, damn France, damn Versailles, damn etiquette, damn everything, damn them all.

He slouched priapic across the Place Saint-Louis, past the potato-coloured church in the moonlight, past the shuttered Café de l'Espérance where he could never go, past the garden gate on the corner of the Rue d'Anjou, up the steps and lost himself in the arms of Morfi.

Like a soul released from Hell he was ever conscious of time, of the need to be back in his state bed before the levée, to return before his time ran out . . . but for now he could dream.

One night he caught her unawares, with her hair down, all her Irish family around her, and her mouth full of pâtisserie, imitating himself.

All of them: Madame Murphy, Victoire, Geneviève, Madeleine and Brigitte. All with their mouths full of truffles and strawberries, all of them dancing, singing, jigging up and down, oblivious to who was ascending the stairs.

The door swung open and the advance party of footmen froze. The Murphys froze in their picnic, then they were up in the air squawking like startled chickens, in a panic to escape from the room, shaking crumbs out of their dresses, wiping their mouths, patting their hair, trying to look as sober and demure as whores at a christening.

Louis stood in his black velvet coat, gold brocade waistcoat and laughing eyes as the Murphys crept past him, smiling, smirking, curtsying as they went.

Madame Murphy brought up the rear, weighed down by a wicker hamper.

'Oh, she's a lovely girl, *Majesté*,' she said, 'a lovely girl to be sure . . .'

'*Enchanté*, Madame . . .' the monarch murmured.

The door closed silently on oiled hinges.

'*Bon anniversaire!*' he said, and the bed sank beneath his weight.

Fresh girls arrived and departed, but Morfi stayed where she was and lasted longer than any of them. She was good at smiling, good at keeping Himself amused. She came to enjoy his company and decided she preferred to be indulged.

At the beginning of March 1753 Madame Bertrand found Morfi in tears for no apparent reason.

A few days later Madame Bertrand heard Morfi complaining that her bathwater was too hot and that her food was cold.

On the *fête* of Sainte-Félicité Madame Bertrand heard strange noises coming from Morfi's room.

'Mademoiselle,' she said, 'I heard someone vomiting! It was you?'

A muffled voice called through the door. 'It was not, Madame.'

On the *fête* of Sainte-Justine Madame Bertrand heard the noises again.

'I am sure someone is being ill!' she called. 'You are unwell?'

'I am not,' Morfi called, 'I am quite well, Madame.'

But Morfi was aware of a strange metallic taste in her mouth, as if she had been chewing forks.

She found herself reluctant to eat meat.

She began to detest the scent she wore.

She even found chocolate distasteful.

To a girl so carefully tutored in gynaecological matters the symptoms could mean only one thing.

At first she tried to conceal her pregnancy, afraid that Louis (who was away from Versailles) would not love her, afraid she had let him down. She did not want to be banished from Versailles. She could not bear to think of her mother's and sisters' taunts that she had ignored their most important lesson. She would *not* be sent back to Paris. She could still hear them calling after her: 'Don't get *pregnant*!'

But she was pregnant. She had let everyone down and she was sure that he would send her away.

She chewed parsley picked in the garden of the Parc-aux-Cerfs. She bruised and crushed parsley with the heel of a gold-heeled shoe. She squeezed out the juice and placed it as best she could in the mouth of her womb. She lay down, expecting the abortion to ensue at once. Nothing happened.

She kept chewing parsley till she felt sick in the afternoon as well as the morning. She did overtime on the rosary, said all the prayers she knew, and kept her fingers crossed.

She anointed herself with parsley juice for a fortnight. Nothing happened except that her taut stomach grew tauter.

She watched the steady thickening of her body, horrified by

the gradual change in her complexion. She vomited silently into her potato plants and swore the *femme de chambre* to secrecy.

She strapped up her waist, held in her stomach until she could hold it in no more, and prayed that Louis would not come back.

She stood each morning in front of her full-length looking-glass, wearing only her shoes, to observe the progress of her rotundity. She laughed at her grotesquely distended belly. Until Madame Bertrand interrupted her, found her standing there, and screamed, with all her suspicions confirmed.

The fourteen Médecins du Roi queued on the stairs, waiting to examine Morfi. They slid cold fingers into her vagina in strict order of seniority, solemnly declared her pregnant, ordered bland food and complete rest, and forbade her to bathe for fear of opening the womb.

Himself returned, pronounced himself delighted with the news and sent her diamonds. Morfi stopped eating parsley and complied with the doctors' directions for a time, but Louis stopped visiting her. She felt neglected and unwanted. She decided she did not want her baby.

She thought, Fifteen is no age to be a mother.

She danced about, went back to her half-run, half-walk. She refused to be confined to bed and glided about Versailles very fast. She went back to chewing parsley, hoping that the abortion might yet be engineered.

On the *fête* of Sainte-Clémence Morfi lingered in the Galerie des Glaces with the crowd, in spite of His reluctance for her to be seen in public. She waited on the appearance of the King, thinking to catch his eye, to remind him of her existence. Word spread that something was going on outside in the Parc.

The Court of Versailles, idle, bored, thundered in heavy shoes across the parquet to the great windows to look.

Morfi forgot that she had been trained never to run and ran with them.

The parquet had been polished that morning so that it shone, reflecting all the glory of Versailles. The courtiers and livestock of Versailles had, as usual, defecated even in the grand gallery, which stank of ordure and urine like the rest of the château. Morfi found herself sliding on some parquet-coloured *immondice* across the floor.

She flew, out of control. She lost her balance, seemed to float, and her voluminous skirts of carnation silk taffeta flew out behind her. She fell, and her basketwork, crushed, creaked on the parquet beneath her. She lay on her swollen stomach, groaning, weeping with rage, surrounded by exclaiming courtiers. She tried to stand up and failed.

The strong hands of Vicomtes and Ducs bore her up, carried her to a sedan-chair, and directed the chairmen to the Parc-aux-Cerfs. It was not the swiftest of conveyances for a pregnant woman who had taken a fall. She was jolted along feeling faint, hot and ill, more worried about her twisted ankles than her baby.

Back in her white and gold room, in bed, with Madame Bertrand and Monsieur Lebel in grave attendance, waiting and waiting for the doctors to appear, she began to bleed.

She bled bright pink blood.

Then bright red blood.

Then dark red blood.

Then brown blood, accompanied by severe pains in her abdomen.

She dared not ask what was going on, but lay moaning, hoping it was what she thought it was.

After an hour Morfi was delivered of a clot of raw liver that was as far as her baby had developed.

She breathed a sigh of relief, glad to be rid of it.

The next morning solemn footmen bore – too late – rolls of Aubusson carpet towards the Parc-aux-Cerfs, to cushion the blow of any future fall.

Morfi lay in bed, weeping, her sprained ankles bandaged, hating herself, longing for Himself to visit her, wishing that she had not managed to get rid of the child.

Himself did not come. He sent a message to say he was sorry to hear of the accident, that he was occupied, that he would visit her as soon as he could.

She felt as if he was busy arranging for her to be sent away from Versailles.

On 14 May the news spread through the excited château that Mademoiselle Murphy *had* been sent away.

*

In July it was confidently reported that Mademoiselle Murphy – who had not been dismissed – was expecting a child.

She was quite recovered, and quite without any taste of metal in her mouth, without any attacks of vomiting in the mornings, or at any other time.

Towards the end of July Louis brought her a new pair of shoes, made of pink satin embroidered with gold wire. She smiled, delighted. Then suddenly she was screaming at him.

'Don't!' she wailed.

He looked blank, surprised, uncomprehending.

'Never put shoes on the table!' she cried. 'It's unlucky!'

Louis grinned, shook his head, as if to say *crazy*.

She did not smile back at him. He had given her new shoes at Noël, and to give shoes at Noël was unlucky.

She was careful to spit into her right-hand shoe before she put it on, even at Versailles, even in the presence of the King.

He laughed at her. Morfi with spit in her shoe! But after a time Louis began to spit into his own shoes.

'You can never tell!' she said. 'It might be lucky.'

Louis nodded. 'You never know,' he said, 'when your luck might run out.'

In August the news was again that Mademoiselle Murphy was pregnant. But in spite of the Premier Médecin and thirteen assistants poking her body about she remained slim.

By October, with Louis and the Court away at Fontainebleau, she found that Lebel's tobacco smoke irritated her.

She no longer wished to drink claret.

Her skin was drying up.

She had developed ugly spots round her mouth.

Her nails kept breaking and she noticed a curious tingling sensation in her breasts.

She was aware of vague flutterings in her stomach, as if she had swallowed half a dozen of the white butterflies that haunted the roses below her window throughout the summer.

Her nose bled often, her face was fuller, and she found on the warm days that her ankles would swell up.

One of Louis' requirements was that she wore no rings. Rings were cold, rings were a nuisance, they scratched him, he said. He made her take them off as soon as he arrived. Now she noticed that her fingers were so swollen that it was impossible to take the rings off. She tugged at them in vain.

As the weeks passed and she waited for Louis to return, she observed again the steady swelling of her stomach.

She watched the colour of her face, predicting from her rosy cheeks and the swelling on the right-hand side that she was expecting a boy.

She listened to her blood ping and splash in a silver bowl, reassured by the doctor's story of a Duchesse who had been bled ninety-eight times and lived to tell the tale – convinced that bleeding would result in the speedier delivery of her baby.

She walked about, when she had to, with a cushion strapped to her back and a cushion strapped to her front, in case she fell. Much of the time she dozed in bed, listening to the doves and pigeons, to the jingle of spurs and tramp of feet as sections of the Armée Royale executed manoeuvres on the far side of the Avenue de Sceaux. Later she remarked on the drumming of tiny feet against her stomach wall, and Louis would put an ear to an upturned wine-glass on her domed belly to listen.

The Court circulated rumours about Morfi's origins, her progress, her pregnancy, reporting now that she came of noble Irish stock, now that she was the daughter of a mere shoemaker, and that her mother sold old clothes.

It was also reported that the Pompadour expected to be summarily dismissed as soon as Morfi's son drew his first breath.

On 1 January 1754 Louis sent Morfi a gold bracket clock with the figure of Orpheus on the top, and Versailles buzzed with the imminent *accouchement*, and with her appointment as *maîtresse en titre*.

By Easter Versailles had grown tired of waiting for news, and Morfi had not been seen for months. The news circulated again that she was dead, bringing a distraught Madame Murphy hurrying to Versailles dressed in black, hammering on the door of the royal brothel in her grief.

As the confinement drew closer, Morfi began to worry about the provision of clothes for her baby, and could not sleep for the kicking of feet inside her.

'We shall have to buy a cradle . . .' she told Madame Bertrand.

'Of course!' said Madame Bertrand, bustling out of the room.

A week later they had the same exchange and Madame Bertrand made the same speedy exit.

After another week Morfi said, 'I shall have to purchase a wicker basket to put him in . . .' There was no doubt in her mind that he would be a boy. Names ran through her head: Seamus, Fergus, Paddy Bourbon . . .

'Of course!' cried Madame Bertrand. 'Do not worry, everything will be taken care of, Mademoiselle.'

Morfi, increasingly breathless, relaxed and put her trust in the 'housekeeper', who knew the way things should be done, and was in complete control of the situation.

Madame Bertrand knew very well what was going on and what was going to happen. There would be no need for a cradle in the Parc-aux-Cerfs, for the child would be born elsewhere. The King's children could not be born in a *maison de tolérance*. The baby would not stay with Morfi for five minutes. A cloth would be stuffed in its mouth and it would be taken away. They had agreed to tell her that the child was born dead. It would be sent off to a wet-nurse, who already had her orders and was sitting knitting clothes for Morfi's baby twenty leagues away.

In May the rumours grew insistent. On 21 May the birth of a son was confidently reported, and it was said that the Pompadour had offered to bring up the child.

'A strange offer,' Morfi said to Madame Bertrand, 'from a woman who already has a daughter of her own.'

Madame Bertrand rattled her gold bracelets and headed for the door.

'*I* should think,' Morfi told her the next day, 'I am quite capable of bringing up my son myself.'

Madame Bertrand smiled, hummed, and busied herself with banging open the shutters.

In June they removed the expectant mother to new lodgings in the Avenue de Saint-Cloud, cooler, tree-lined, noisier, a place of stagnant pools and dead cats, but away from the Parc-aux-Cerfs, where the screams of a woman in labour would make the neighbours ask questions.

Morfi settled down in a vast bed hung with green damask, in a room filled with lilies and giant tapestries depicting the Seven Wonders of the World, waiting.

Madame du Hausset arrived to take charge of everything, presiding over the *accouchement* like a fairy godmother.

On 19 June Alexandrine Lenormand d'Etioles, daughter of Madame de Pompadour, died aged ten, leaving her mother shrieking and groaning with grief.

On 20 June Marie Murphy's contractions began. She draped the crimson velvet *pantalons* of the child's father round her neck in order to lighten her labour pains.

A sword lay hidden under her bolster to keep the fairies away until the baptism.

Madame du Hausset indulged her patient's superstitions, but drew the line at placing the King's tricorn over Morfi's loins in order to speed up the delivery.

As it happened, her baby slid out with little difficulty. She glimpsed something purple, wet and slippery, with its eyes tight shut. That was all she saw of it, for the doctors cut the baby free at once and took it into the next room.

She did not hear her baby cry.

She was not given the baby to hold.

Madame du Hausset went silently about the business of cleaning the mother up, assisted by Madame Bertrand.

When Madame du Hausset brought hot water Morfi asked her, '*Why* did they not tell me this would happen?'

Madame du Hausset did not reply.

'When shall I be able to feed the baby?' she asked.

Madame Bertrand bit her lips.

'When shall I be able to see my son?' Morfi asked. 'Is my baby *dead*, Madame?'

Madame du Hausset gave no answers, said nothing but, 'It is better this way.' She went on sponging blood from Morfi's body and tears from her face.

'I would like to know,' Morfi said, '*s'il vous plaît.*'

The *accoucheuses* were silent, exchanged glances and frowns.

'Did you think,' said Madame du Hausset at last, sighing, 'that they would let you keep a child in the Parc-aux-Cerfs?'

Morfi said nothing. She had hoped so.

'Did you think,' said Madame Bertrand, 'that kind of house is a fit place to raise the children of Louis Quinze?'

Morfi was silent. She did not see why not.

'Did you really think,' said Madame du Hausset, sponging

furiously, 'that *sa Majesté* would permit his daughter to be brought up in a brothel?'

Morfi thought, I have had a *daughter*.

Madame du Hausset left the house in the Avenue de Saint-Cloud a few days later, smiling broadly, clutching a gold snuffbox studded with diamonds, her reward for supervising a difficult operation.

When Louis finally visited the young mother, back in bed in the Parc-aux-Cerfs, his prune-like eyes glistened and his face shone. He carried an aigrette studded with diamonds, the sort of thing he presented to the mothers of all his bastard children. Not too expensive a gift, and not too cheap: a token of his regard, something to keep her happy, something to keep her quiet.

As if, she thought, his unwanted, old-fashioned jewellery might make up for what he had done.

She refused to look at the aigrette.

She refused to look at Louis XV.

His smile gradually faded.

'We love you, Mademoiselle,' he said, and she knew he did not.

She refused to speak to him, lay with her face turned away, thinking he could not possibly mean it.

There was a long silence.

'What did you think would happen?' he asked. 'We could not let you keep her! It was better that you never saw her.'

'What is her *name*?' she asked.

He paused, as if he did not want to tell her.

'She is called Agathe-Louise,' he said.

'Agathe-Louise *what*?' she asked, hardly daring to hope that she might be a Murphy, wondering if she had given birth to a Bourbon.

'Agathe-Louise de Saint-Antoine de Saint-André,' he said.

She looked at him as if she thought it could not be true, as if she thought it was an absurd mouthful.

The Pompadour had made it up, laughing.

Morfi kept looking at the wall, tears welling up in her eyes, thinking he was too much of a coward to give his daughter his own name.

'She will be well cared-for,' he said. 'She is doing well. The sisters in a convent will look after her . . .'

She looked hard at him, as if she wondered about going at once to rescue her baby, as if she might steal away with her, away from Versailles for ever. As if, at least, she might be able to visit her.

Louis paused. 'We think it is better that you do not know where,' he said.

Tears rolled down her cheeks.

'Smile!' he said. '*Smile*! You have done well!'

Morfi could not smile. She did not want to smile. She had nothing to smile about.

'*Au revoir*, Mademoiselle,' he said.

Morfi did not reply. She turned her face back to the wall.

The door closed silently behind him and the warbling of the doves and pigeons started up, mocking her, ooh ooh ooh ooh.

IX

Morfi spent days squeezing useless, unwanted milk from her swollen breasts. In October Himself went as usual to Fontainebleau, leaving Morfi behind to celebrate her birthday alone. She lay awake all night thinking of him in the arms of some other girl.

On 24 October it was whispered in Versailles that the King was tired of Morfi, that she had died in August. But Versailles had no details relating to her death and seemed not to know where she was buried.

Madame Murphy hurried once again to Versailles, dressed in black, to attend her daughter's funeral, and once again her tears turned to laughter when she discovered her daughter alive and healthy.

Marie-Louise thought she might as well *be* dead; that the château of Versailles was her tomb; that Versailles was not Heaven but Hell on earth.

Louis visited her occasionally, but he seemed preoccupied and distant. Morfi was a shadow of her real self: silent, withdrawn, wondering what he would do with her. He could not keep her here, she thought, for ever. She would not survive in the Parc-aux-Cerfs without fulfilling some of his expectations.

She thought of her father saying 'No such word as can't,' and snapped out of her lethargy.

Himself began to visit her more regularly.

Far from Mademoiselle Murphy deposing the Pompadour, the latter had her own ideas as to how she might dispose of the *petite maîtresse* when necessary.

It was the Pompadour who would last for ever, the Pompadour who had earned the permanent place in the King's affections.

At some point, Louis and the Pompadour agreed, they would have to make Morfi an honest woman. She might flatter herself with the almost exclusive possession of the royal heart and the royal bed, but she could never ride in the King's carriage; she could never dine with him in public. She could not receive open visits from courtiers. If she had been presented at Court she might enjoy all these privileges, but she could not be presented.

If she were married – as the Pompadour was – such a presentation might be engineered, but as an unmarried mother, a girl taken from the streets, it was unthinkable.

For the moment they put the problem of what to do with Morfi in the back of their minds, and things went on as before.

In the Parc-aux-Cerfs the gate creaked at midnight, the stairs groaned under the royal shoes, and Morfi's bed-springs squeaked with an insistent rhythm that made Madame Bertrand think all was well.

Agathe-Louise de Saint-Antoine de Saint-André was entrusted to the care of the sisters of the Couvent de Sainte-Périne at Chaillot, half an hour's carriage drive from Paris. With her went an annuity of 8,000 *livres* from the King, who allowed the nuns to understand that she was the daughter of a highborn gentleman of Paris whose name could not be divulged.

Agathe-Louise was the identical copy of her father. Her baby-blue eyes gradually changed to the glittering blackberries of Louis Bourbon. She had his luxuriant auburn hair, the same round smiling face and alert gaze, well known from coins and portraits of the early part of his reign. It was not difficult for the sisters to work out who Agathe-Louise really was.

Her affairs were mysteriously regulated, like those of the numerous other royal bastards, by Monsieur Louis Yon, who sent her long and illegible letters throughout her childhood.

Monsieur Yon visited her on rare occasions, but when the other girls went home for their vacation Agathe-Louise would stay at Chaillot with the sisters, rising at five-thirty, framing every action with prayers, following all their rigorous régime.

The nuns were her family. Chaillot was her home.

Mademoiselle Murphy willed herself to forget she had ever given birth to a daughter. It was only when she woke in the middle of the night that she wondered whether Agathe-Louise was alive and what would become of her. For all her asking Madame Bertrand, Lebel, and Louis himself, she received no information. Whenever she raised the subject of her daughter, Louis would

94

look the other way or talk about hunting. She learned, eventually, not to mention Agathe-Louise to anyone.

In the New Year of 1755 there were presents from Louis: among them a watch studded with diamonds and with his grinning portrait in the back, which Morfi carried wherever she went. She continued to attract attention and gossip. It still seemed likely that she might supplant the Pompadour and move back into the château in glory.

At Versailles, they said, you could never tell what would happen. Miracles occurred daily. Men might fly; machines might talk: even an old-clothes woman's daughter might assume the rôle of left-hand Queen of France.

Morfi began to attract the courtiers the Pompadour alienated: the people put beyond the reach of her favours; those who could no longer cling to the points of her ever-rising star.

A brace of Vicomtes, a handful of Barons, half a dozen Marquis made sure that Morfi knew who they were. They acknowledged her existence, gave her the customary salutation, and treated her with all the semi-respect due to the King's unofficial mistress.

Courtiers who stood to gain from the Pompadour's downfall sent Morfi flowers. Sycophants who had nothing to lose and everything to gain from a double back-somersault in the system of patronage flattered her and smiled warmly in her direction.

Among them was the beautiful and foolish Madame d'Estrées, the dangerous wife of the Maréchal d'Estrées, commander of the army on the Rhine.

Madame d'Estrées, full of wise advice and kind intentions, so sophisticated, so expert at needlepoint, showed Morfi how to untangle her knots and how to butter up the Marquises. Dear, kind Madame d'Estrées, without a brain in her head, wanted only one thing in return: for her husband to be given command of the entire army of France instead of the Prince de Soubise.

Madame d'Estrées waged a bitter war all of her own against her sworn enemy: the Pompadour, who had given her patronage to the Prince de Soubise instead of the Maréchal d'Estrées. It was Madame d'Estrées' plan for the Pompadour to be ousted by Morfi, and thus to have in her control someone who would promote her husband to the most glorious position in France, to the pinnacle of his career.

Madame d'Estrées showed Morfi how to handle the King. She knew what held his attention. She knew what made him smile. She knew the private Louis so much better than Morfi did.

The Irish mistress was in danger of running out of things to say. She was nervous that she had annoyed him. She was scared that she might fall from favour, or be pushed.

'I never did kiss the Blarney Stone, Madame,' she told her friend.

The Maréchal's wife, ever resourceful, visited Morfi twice a week, full of ideas and amusing stories. She began to put words into Morfi's mouth. Before she knew what was happening, Madame d'Estrées was assuming control. It was easier to let her do the thinking.

'Ask him,' said Madame d'Estrées, 'how many children he has . . .'

'Ask him,' she said, 'how often the servants are paid . . .'

'Ask him,' she said, 'how he's getting on with his old woman. That will make him laugh . . .'

Marie-Louise Murphy found herself, the next night, asking Louis XV exactly that.

She said, *'En quels termes en êtes-vous avec la vieille coquette?'*

How are you getting on with your old woman?

How are you treating your old wife?

What terms are you on with the old flirt?

But Louis did not laugh. He was speechless. He wondered what she could mean. How was he getting on with his old Queen? The Queen of France, his wife, who never spoke to him when she could write a letter instead? The Queen, who lived under the same roof, the mother of his children, to whom he was still loyal.

Or did she mean Madame de Pompadour? The old flirt. His old tart. His old whore. The Pompadour, with whom his sexual relations had ground to a halt?

Legend related that Louis, always one for not replying but turning on his heel and disappearing, flew into a rage. They said he shouted at Morfi and smashed china on the floor of her room; that he demanded to know who had told her to ask him that question; that he was certain she could not have thought of asking it by herself.

Legend said that Morfi wept and confessed that it was Madame d'Estrées; that Louis stormed from the room and that Morfi never saw him again.

History recorded that Louis XV recalled the Maréchal d'Estrées from his command and replaced him with the Duc de Richelieu, and that Madame d'Estrées was banished from Versailles.

Madame de Pompadour spent an afternoon closeted in her golden salon with the Prince de Soubise, discussing the problem of what to do with Marie-Louise Murphy. She put in motion the mechanism for removing a royal whore from the royal harem with the minimum of fuss.

'We must not alienate her,' she said, 'she knows too much. She must not become our enemy . . . She must be properly rewarded . . . She must be sent as far as possible from Versailles . . .'

Morfi was too dangerous to leave drifting about the château without a keeper, without a husband: a woman seeking, perhaps, to exact her revenge.

The Prince promised that he would find someone, and began his quest at once.

Marie-Louise sat alone in her room, thinking, If Madame d'Estrées put the words into my mouth it is Madame d'Estrées who will be sent away, and not me . . . It is not my fault . . .

She wondered what she had done wrong, what had upset Louis. She did not understand.

There were other reasons for removing her. In the end, Louis tired of her. She had not the high civilization of the Pompadour. There were other girls. At eighteen Morfi would be past her prime. If they postponed her marriage much longer they might have her on their hands for ever.

Morfi thought, Could he not forgive just the one mistake? Could they not let bygones be bygones?

They could not. There were worse things. Louis now refused to be shaved on Sundays in order to avoid the toothache. It was an Irish superstition deriving from his Irish mistress.

He now crossed himself on the mouth when he yawned. 'To stop the devil jumping inside,' he said.

97

He now wore a blue thread round his neck as a prophylactic against all disease. 'For good luck!' he said.

He spat into his right-hand shoe before he would allow the pages to ease his foot into it. The pages would giggle. The spitting interfered with the solemn ritual of the levée.

He had picked up the mannerisms of Morfi's speech, her Paris slang, the vocabulary of the gutter.

She had taught the monarch to whistle by putting two of his fingers in his mouth.

He now crushed his eggshells at the Grand Couvert. 'So the fairies cannot turn them into boats!' he murmured.

There were more important things to be considered. Morfi could not be his prisoner for ever. She had been confined long enough. There was the matter of Agathe-Louise. They could not take *two* babies away from Morfi. The business of Madame d'Estrées was the excuse they had been looking for. It was time to give Morfi her liberty, whether she wanted it or not.

As dawn broke in the Parc-aux-Cerfs, Louis ran his fingers over the translucent pink of her ears.

'We want you to be happy,' he said.

'I *am* happy,' she said.

'Nothing can last for ever, Mademoiselle,' he said.

'What do you mean?' she asked.

'We mean,' he sighed, 'Versailles will come to an end . . . one day you will leave us . . .'

Her heart turned over on itself as the horror of horrors came slowly to life: the spectre of dismissal.

She looked at her gilded ceiling with its floating cherubs. She looked at the lilies in vases of Sèvres porcelain. She looked at all his gold-embroidered clothes thrown on the *fauteuil*. She looked at the crimson hangings of her sumptuous bed, at her red-painted fingernails. Then she looked at him: at his dark unshaven chin, his dark skin against the pale sheets, at the bristles on his head. He looked like any other man, like a convict returned from the galleys. His black eyes were glassy, like polished buttons. She looked at the hands that had never done a day's work, the great hands that stroked her skin, calmed her down and excited her at the same time; the hands there was no use for in the world apart from signing his name on a piece of parchment; no use for them apart from the exploration of her body. She looked at him and asked her question.

'When?' And then she said quickly, 'If you tell a lie your face will turn black and split open.'

His bleary eyes wandered lazily all over her body, lingering on her perfect nose, her lustrous eyes, her delicate hands, her roundness hidden between the sheets, her yellow-gold hair on the pillows. Then he looked away: at the landscape of a wolf tearing apart a sheep, at a still life of dead birds, at his gilt coat-buttons in the half light, at the absurd red and gold shoes that pinched his feet, at his tight red velvet *pantalons*. His mind drifted away.

He could not even put on his own clothes. He was never allowed to be alone, but must spend his day in a crowd. He had no wish to give orders, no desire to rule. He had everything a man could want, and yet without his freedom he was not happy. He was in chains, bound hand and foot to France. He was a prisoner.

He looked at Morfi again, formulating the answer in his mind. Tonight. Tomorrow. Wait and see . . .

He could not decide what to tell her. He did not know the answer. All he knew was that it was finished. He found himself brushing some wetness out of the corner of one eye. He avoided the unpleasant, as always. He sidestepped the awkwardness of it all.

'Lebel will tell you, Mademoiselle,' he said, 'we have yet to make up our mind.'

He could not bear the hysterics that invariably followed such an announcement. He should have kept quiet. It was better to wait till the last minute.

He sprang out of bed quicker than she had ever seen him move before and fell about trying to put his *pantalons* on the right way round, still incapable of dressing himself at forty-five.

When he had gone and the door had slammed and she had listened to his heavy feet on the stairs, his shoes on the cobbles walking away, it occurred to her that he had not said *au revoir*.

The sun hit her shutters and the fluttering wings started up, the intermittent liquid warbling ooh ooh ooh of the pigeons.

Maréchal de Camp the Prince de Soubise spent hours scanning

his list of eligible bachelors. He sent out scouts with details of the 50,000 *livres* reward and the 200,000 *livres* of dowry, a fabulous sum of money.

'You might think,' the Prince said to Madame de Pompadour, 'that hundreds of young men would come forward.' But he had difficulty finding even one young man to fulfil his requirements: a man young enough to be attractive to a girl of seventeen, noble enough to keep his bride in some style, and poor enough not to mind about her dubious provenance or care about her former occupation.

The Prince, a personal friend of Louis XV and the Pompadour, had become – without displaying much sign of talent – a general, a Minister of State and an ally of the royal family. Thanks to the Pompadour's patronage he now commanded a division of 24,000 soldiers. He owed his friends a good turn.

It was the Marquis de Lugeac who discovered the tall, dark young man, impossibly handsome, with brown skin and laughing eyes, without fear and without blemish, who owned nothing but his regiment and his genealogical table.

The Marquis, colonel of the prospective husband's regiment, looked him over with a new eye. He had been a sub-lieutenant at twelve and a half, a captain at fifteen, an aide-major at sixteen. He had distinguished himself in the War of the Austrian Succession. He was intelligent and brave, the descendant of Crusaders and *abbés* and gendarmes of the royal guard. All he lacked was money.

The Marquis called the Major to his tent and asked him searching questions about his private life, wondering whether he would fulfil the Prince's requirements. There was, he thought, only one thing that mattered.

The Marquis told the Major to take down his *pantalons*.

The Major hesitated, frowned, thought of the money, and obeyed orders.

The Marquis raised an eyebrow, grinned, smacked the Major on the back, and sent him off to Paris, to the Hôtel de Soubise in the Rue des Francs-Bourgeois.

The Prince de Soubise sat in a white and gold room wearing mouse-coloured velvet. He looked smug and felt pleased with himself. He asked the Major dozens of intimate questions, stared him in the eye, and decided he looked honest enough. There was only one thing that mattered, he thought, knowing what the Pompadour had told him about Mademoiselle Murphy.

'Let's take a look at your *zizi*,' said the Prince.

The Major hesitated. The corners of his mouth twitched.

'Come on,' barked the Prince, 'don't be shy.'

The Major lowered his *pantalons* a second time.

The Prince de Soubise raised both eyebrows, smiled, and sent the Major on to the Maison de Cèdre, Paris residence of Madame de Pompadour, with a note that read 'I think she will be quite satisfied.'

Madame de Pompadour, in a riot of sunflower-yellow silk, smiled at the Major, ogled him through her gold-handled lorgnette, asked a lot of questions, and decided she liked the look of him. She liked the look of the bulge inside his white *pantalons* and sent him on to the Premier Médecin du Roi.

The Pompadour's instructions were simple: 'Make sure he has all the necessary equipment.'

The Premier Médecin peered down the Major's throat. He felt behind the Major's ears and asked him to remove his uniform.

He groped about in the Major's armpits, looked into his eyes, prodded his stomach, poked about in his groin, grabbed him by the private parts and told him to cough.

The Major did as he was told.

'Any aches or pains?' asked the Premier Médecin.

'Any problems down below?'

'Waterworks all right, Monsieur?'

The Major assured him there was nothing wrong, and the doctor pronounced him in excellent health and fit for active service of the most strenuous kind.

'Don't worry, Monsieur,' the Premier Médecin said. 'She's as pretty as a picture!'

Neither the Marquis, nor the Prince, nor the Pompadour mentioned to Jacques de Beaufranchet anything about his prospective fiancée's past, except that she was a young lady of a certain position who needed a handsome husband as soon as possible.

The Marquis de Lugeac reassured the Major. 'Don't worry!' he said. 'We'll let you take a look at her first – she's not a hunchback.'

Jacques de Beaufranchet nodded. For 200,000 *livres* of dowry, he thought, he would not mind if she was a one-eyed amputee with no teeth. He asked no questions, clicked his heels, and saluted his colonel.

A private view of the bride was arranged in Versailles, at which the Major was able to see his prospective fiancée without being seen himself.

'Never fear,' smirked the Marquis de Lugeac. 'I am told she goes like a pair of lobster claws . . .'

The Major grinned, raised his eyebrows, and said yes on the spot.

In the spring of 1755 Victoire Murphy was married with great pomp to a Monsieur de la Vabre, whom no one had heard of, but who seemed to have a substantial fortune.

At the wedding feast Brigitte Murphy, still unmarried, with her younger sister marrying before her, was obliged to dance barefoot in order to counteract her ill luck in not yet having found a husband of her own.

'By rights,' Madame Murphy told her, 'you should dance in the pigs' trough, but we are now people of quality . . .'

The Irish relatives sang Irish songs and stamped and clapped and whistled as Brigitte danced a jig across the tables.

The de la Vabres smiled politely and kept their feet still.

In the summer Madeleine Murphy was married to a Monsieur Bourlier, a lawyer to the Parlement, and acquired a solid fortune. The Murphy sisters turned out in their finery to witness the event, at which the entire Irish population of the Palais-Royal was present.

Brigitte danced barefoot again, wearing emerald-green silk taffeta and false pearls, with her hair flying and her pock-marks hidden under the thickest layer of face-paint.

The Irish stamped, and banged their fists on the tables.

The family of Monsieur Bourlier wore fixed and glassy smiles.

When the Irish relations asked Madame Murphy how she had managed to fix such brilliant matches for her daughters, she smiled broadly but revealed nothing. She had transformed herself from plain Peggy Murphy, old-clothes woman, into Madame Marguerite de Morfi de Boisfailly. She had given up rags and prostitution and keeping chickens and now lived in the smart and salubrious Rue Saint-Maur, where she received respectable visitors, wore diamonds, and spoke perfect French all day.

She had Brigitte still on her hands, but she was resigned to the fact that she would never be rid of Brigitte.

'Brigitte is too ugly,' she said, 'she will never be married.'

But before the year was out Brigitte surprised everyone, left her false pearls behind, and was seen wearing the real thing. She gave up being an artist's model and left Paris in a blaze of glory.

'Who would have thought it possible?' Madame Murphy laughed to herself.

But Madame de Morfi de Boisfailly's greatest social achievement of the year was the marriage that was arranged in the autumn.

On 25 November 1755, in a notary's office near the Châtelet, a marriage contract was signed. The Prince de Soubise and the Marquis de Lugeac were present. A lawyer represented Madame Murphy as witness of the bride. A representative of the high and mighty chevalier seigneur Jacques Pelet de Beaufranchet, Comte d'Ayat, Comte de Beaumont, Comte de Grandmont and other places, Major in the army of France, was present.

It was a marriage contract about which the occupants of the royal brothel in the Parc-aux-Cerfs at Versailles were wholly ignorant.

The witnesses signed their names and the ceremony was over. It was a strange business. Usually the whole family gathered for the signing of a marriage contract. In this case neither bride nor groom, nor any member of their families, was present. All the parties concerned were represented by others.

In the Parc-aux-Cerfs Marie-Louise Murphy spent November, season of enemas and emetics, much as usual, resigned to fate leading her where it would. She bathed twice a day. She ate her artichokes and truffles and drank cup after cup of chocolate, as much out of habit as out of any need to excite herself.

She passed the time sewing, languidly playing the harpsichord, pacing up and down and waiting. Waiting for Himself to turn up. Waiting for something to happen. But he did not turn up and nothing happened. She was waiting for an end of it all, or a new beginning.

She lay in bed watching the light grow in the cracks between her shutters, watching the pigeons circling, watching the window of her prison.

She sewed green flowers, pink leaves, blue faces, yellow skies, red cats, and black babies that made Madame Bertrand frown and worry.

Some days, against all her rigorous training, Morfi would throw a screaming fit. Madame Bertrand pretended not to hear, but reported the screams to Monsieur Lebel and urged haste in the matter in hand.

At night they tied Morfi's legs together to prevent her from sleepwalking.

In the end she went out fighting. On the evening of 26 November she noticed that her gold watch studded with diamonds had stopped. She wound it up, and asked Madame Bertrand to tell her the correct time.

Her candle let fall a torrent of hot wax into the open back of the watch. She tried to remove the wax with her fingers, with a knife, with the end of a quill. She succeeded only in making a worse mess, and bent the works. She held the watch over the candle flame to melt the wax, but managed only to blacken the inside.

The watch was useless. It refused to tick. She felt as if her time had run out, as if there was no time left. She went to bed cross, and slept fitfully.

She had spent the day drinking chocolate and watching the doves, more bored than she had ever been.

She woke in the dark, lay warm in bed listening to the grinding of wheels in the street, to relentless footsteps, to the thump and scrape of something being dragged across the floor below her. She lay thinking that this time the noises in the night were for her.

At four in the morning Lebel and Madame Bertrand burst through her door, filling the room with candles, and pulled her roughly out of bed. They dressed her in silence, breathing hard, as if there was no time to be lost.

'What is happening?' Morfi asked, as if she could not have guessed.

There was no answer. They laced up her dress. She listened to their fierce breathing.

'What are you doing?' she demanded. 'Why are you doing this in the middle of the night?'

'We are going to Paris,' snapped Madame Bertrand, 'and don't talk, don't ask questions, Mademoiselle, you will wake the other girls.'

She let them pull her about for a while till she was fully awake, till they tried to lead her out of her golden room. Then she turned over the gilded tables. She swept the golden bottles of scent off her toilet table in a cloud of face powder and flying glass. She pushed over the Sèvres vases full of lilies in a crash of broken china. She pulled down the yellow silk curtains. She smashed the gilt-framed pictures on the walls. She knocked over the candles. She bombarded Lebel and Madame Bertrand with missiles. She cowered in a corner, threatening her keepers with a gilded chair.

Madame Bertrand thought, This is why he would not tell her.

Marie-Louise broke everything that would break except the gilded mirrors, and then, suddenly, she was tired of seeing her reflection. She longed to be old, to die, for no one to want to look at her ever again, so that she would be left alone. She smashed her fists into the mirrors. Spider cracks sped across the glass.

She bit and fought and scratched. She spat and hissed like a wild cat. She screamed abuse. She let loose all the obscenities saved up from her Paris childhood, words they did not know she knew.

They tried to tie her up, to tie her down, to strap her to a stretcher and carry her bodily into the street.

The other girls peered round their bedroom doors, hung over the banisters to watch Morfi go, amused by her wailing.

'The banshee!' they laughed. 'The bansheeeeee-ooo-ooo-ooo.'

Morfi was uncontrollable. Blood appeared on her mouth. Blood spread across her hands. She tore at Madame Bertrand's elegant coiffure, scratched at Lebel's face: a wild animal from the royal menagerie.

Madame Bertrand shouted to the other girls as she wrestled with Morfi on the staircase, 'She has been taken ill! She is mad.

She must go to the doctor. She is Irish!' As if that would explain her behaviour, as if that explained everything.

Eventually they managed to hold her down, prised open her jaws, forced a funnel between her teeth, and administered a sleeping draught that she sprayed and spat, screaming with rage and frustration, all over Madame Bertrand, into Lebel's face.

They forced her into the waiting carriage and drove her away into the night.

Her dress was ripped to shreds. Her hair was torn. She had bitten her lips and tongue. Her nose bled. She had lost control of her bowels. She knew she had left Versailles for ever.

Marie-Louise Murphy, scorched by the Sun, burnt by sitting too long in its powerful rays, slept.

When the carriage reached Paris four hours later it was still dark and Morfi still slept, crumpled in a corner with the blinds down. Outside it was snowing.

Madame Bertrand smacked Morfi's face, pummelled her into consciousness. Quite calm, quite resigned, Morfi was compliant. They carried her like a doll into a house she vaguely remembered: the Pompadour's Paris residence. They plunged her into a golden bath, soaped and rinsed her, dried, powdered and perfumed her, all at high speed. They sat her in a gilded chair and plastered her wounds with miracle-working creams.

An army of footmen and maidservants worked in silence, commanded by a brusque Madame Bertrand, today in her element, cool and efficient, thinking of her royal reward.

Morfi took every opportunity to bite hands that strayed too near her mouth. She lost no chance to scratch faces that bent too close to her fingernails. Today she hated everybody, and herself most of all. She grabbed a pair of scissors and tried to slash her wrists.

Madame Bertrand slapped her face and ordered her hands to be tied to the arms of the chair. Tears rolled down Morfi's cheeks.

She was pulled into a crisp rustling dress of cloth of silver, the most exquisite dress, the most beautiful dress she had ever seen.

Without warning she vomited blood all over it, and dismayed at the ruin she began to wail.

Alarmed, Madame Bertrand summoned the doctor.

But no, the doctor said, sniffing, it was not blood but chocolate, undigested chocolate.

They whipped the dress over her head and produced a second dress of white and silver silk that was more beautiful, more expensive; the Pompadour's wardrobe was full of such things.

They transformed her tangled hair into a mountain of a coiffure, brushed and cosseted her till she looked worthy of the 200,000 *livres* of dowry.

Madame Bertrand began to paint Morfi's face for her – something she had never done before, applying rouge to her cheeks to hide the damage.

'*Pourquoi*?' whispered Morfi, hoarse from screaming. As if she could not have guessed.

'*Les noces*!' said Madame Bertrand, smiling.

'*Moi*?' Morfi asked.

Madame Bertrand nodded, smiling again.

'*Qui*? *Qui*?' Morfi demanded.

'*Une surprise*!' said Madame Bertrand.

Morfi wanted to know at once. She was suspicious. It could not be Louis she was being taken to marry. She did not want to marry anyone else. She felt sick, and faint, and worried.

In a different carriage, looking like the Queen of France, with Olympian Dew on her wrists and behind her ears, with her silk whispering, Morfi had herself under control, curious to know who would be her husband.

Madame Bertrand squeezed her hand, fierce and kind and firm. She fixed a pearl choker round Morfi's neck in spite of her violent protestations.

'But pearls are so unlucky, Madame!' she wailed.

'Nonsense!' said Madame Bertrand, 'pearls are a sign of love, a sign of fidelity – a present from *sa Majesté*!'

Morfi sighed, hopeless, helpless.

'This is all for your own good,' said Madame Bertrand, warm at last. 'You will be happy at the end of all this. You will be pleased to escape from Versailles. You will thank us all in two years' time.'

Morfi kissed her on both cheeks, said she was sorry, and cried again. She wailed, 'Oh Madame Bertrand, what am I to do at all? I do not want to be married. I will not have this man I have never seen. I do not want him. I will not be told what to do!'

Madame Bertrand comforted her. 'But he is a nice man,' she said, 'a gentle man. He is a soldier! You will like him!'

Morfi went to her wedding with the suggestion of a black eye to come, her fingers twisted and swollen, and her wrists raw where the ropes had burned her. Beneath the face-powder her scratches began to ooze blood.

Snowflakes settled in her hair.

At nine in the morning of 27 November 1755 Paris was still dark. Workmen trod through piles of slush in the streets. The church of Les Saints-Innocents flickered with hundreds of candles, lit up for a wedding to which no guests had been invited. The *curé* waited at the door for a bride dressed for a summer afternoon.

It was a strange time for a wedding; an odd wedding, for no relatives of either the bride or the groom were present. An even odder wedding, for the bride had never seen the groom. A blind wedding.

They had kept the place and time secret, to keep away the dancing Irish: to marry Marie-Louise Murphy de Boisfailly, younger daughter of Daniel Murphy de Boisfailly, Irish gentleman, deceased, in some dignity.

None of Morfi's Versailles friends appeared. Fair weather friends, she thought, ashamed of her now, wanting to be rid of her as quickly as possible.

Just the Marquis de Lugeac, just Lebel and Madame Bertrand saw her through the service, to make sure she behaved herself; just the King's pander and the mother-abbess of the royal brothel.

'The King has ordered you to marry,' Madame Bertrand warned her at the church door. 'You cannot refuse.'

Morfi held his scribbled note crumpled in her hand throughout the ceremony, raging inside but maintaining her seraphic smile. She would not let him down, she thought.

Louis had written, 'We decided you would prefer a surprise.'

She screwed the paper tighter and tighter in her fist.

Afterwards the Marquis de Lugeac kissed her hand and called her Comtesse. She realized he was addressing her, and laughed. She laughed when she discovered her name: *Madame la Comtesse de Beaufranchet d'Ayat*, and she laughed again when she found she was Comtesse de Beaumont and Comtesse de Grandmont and other places as well. Then her face was stinging with rice thrown by the smiling congregation of three, and stinging as all her wounds opened up again.

She climbed into her husband's carriage and was hurried away into the blizzard, without the remotest idea where she was being taken. She smoothed the King's message and read it over and over again.

She was forbidden to return to Versailles.

She was forbidden to set foot in any town.

The dowry came with endless instructions and conditions.

If infringed, all future payments would be withheld.

She thought, I am still his prisoner.

Having removed Marie-Louise Murphy from the Parc-aux-Cerfs, Louis wished he had not. Her portrait still hung on his wall. He missed her. He dreamed about her.

Louis had a penchant for sisters. In the past he had made sisters of his mistresses into mistresses themselves. It was a standing joke at Versailles. Sisters often had similar qualities. Sisters smelled the same. A sister was a mirror image. Sisters fascinated him. They often had the same voice, the same turn of phrase. Often he liked the sister better than the original; often he preferred the reflection to the real thing.

Louis had seen Brigitte Murphy before. She had visited the Parc-aux-Cerfs. He knew all about her. He liked the idea of Brigitte.

On her way to Versailles Brigitte thought about *Cendrillon*. She thought of the Prince not realizing he had chosen the ugly sister. She thought of the slippers of fur, of the toes and heels cut off, of the trail of blood, of the birds telling the Prince he had picked the wrong girl.

Brigitte laughed. She was twenty-eight, ten years older than Marie-Louise. Her face was pitted with the smallpox. Her legs quivered with rolls of fat. She rubbed her beautiful hands together, smoothed cream into them to make them smoother. The carriage hurried her through the golden gates into the City of the Sun as she adjusted her mouse-skin eyebrows.

*

Louis did not care what anyone thought. He would do as he liked.

'I have heard all about you, Mademoiselle,' he said. 'I wanted to see for myself . . .'

Brigitte smiled her most perfect smile.

'I like your hands,' Louis told her. 'I like your voice.'

Brigitte's tenure of Number 4 Rue Saint-Médéric, Versailles, was brief. She was back in Paris with her mother by Noël, but her fingers had earned her a pension.

By Noël Brigitte had had enough of men and was content with the thought of being *Mademoiselle* for ever.

'False pearls before real swine,' she told her mother, laughing.

When Madame Bertrand returned, exhausted, to Versailles after the wedding she dealt at once with the usual burning of pillows, the delousing and fumigation of Morfi's ruined room.

She shed tears on seeing Morfi's dresses trampled on the floor. She resolved this time to have the girl's belongings sent on to her.

Madame Bertrand rearranged the furniture so that it did not remind her of Marie-Louise. She opened drawers and found the sprigs of mint she had tied round her wrists to ward off stomach disorders. She discovered the rabbit's foot on a gold chain that was supposed to be round Morfi's neck bringing her good luck.

She gathered up the bundles of letters from the King, tied with pink ribbon, in order to return them to him for burning, as instructed.

As she opened the door of Morfi's armoire to see what was hanging inside, she was startled by a rumbling noise, and an avalanche of what appeared to be wooden balls bounced and drummed on the parquet all round her.

She sprang out of the way until the bombardment had stopped, then bent down to see what Morfi had left behind.

It was a deluge of potatoes, her winter supply.

'Madame Pomme de Terre,' Madame Bertrand said to herself, laughing aloud.

X

The wedding breakfast was held in a purple-and-white striped tent lit by a thousand candles. A large company of gentlemen had assembled, all dressed in coats of purple velvet edged with silver braid, waistcoats of ivory silk, and purple shoes.

The ladies were all dressed in purple velvet and white fur against the cold. They all wore the same heady scent. They all smiled at the new Comtesse de Beaufranchet d'Ayat.

It was a surprise: Louis himself, the Pompadour, all the royal family, all the nobility, all her friends from Versailles raised their glasses of *vin de champagne* to wish her luck.

The Comtesse's eyes wandered over long tables covered with white linen cloths and piled with pyramids of fruit, pyramids of pâtisserie, pyramids of truffles, pyramids of celery, and row after row of silver chocolate-pots.

The *garçon d'honneur* grinned under his silvery wig and banged a silver hammer on the table for silence.

'I would like to say,' he began, 'I would like to say how much we all appreciate the very great pleasure and the very great happiness the Comtesse has given us all, over the years . . . the repeated pleasure . . . the extraordinary happiness . . .'

There was a general murmur of agreement from the rows of personages: a murmur of assent, which became a chuckle, then a ripple of laughter, then gales of merriment. All the gentlemen had enjoyed her favours, a stolen kiss behind a damask curtain or in some dark corner of the château.

Tears of laughter poured down the faces of Madame Murphy de Boisfailly and her four daughters (they had invited the family after all), and the bride herself smiled, forgot her convent manners, laughed, guffawed, howled with laughter.

The *curé* of Les Saints-Innocents allowed his eyes to twinkle; *abbés* and bishops permitted their shoulders to shake. They laughed as if they would never stop. The purple velvet shoes thundered on the parquet and the Comtesse could see the gold *fleurs-de-lis* embroidered on all the toes going up and down on the floor. Jewelled fists banged tables. The banging grew louder. The drubbing of gold heels was faster, louder, more insistent, with a rhythmical clapping until the Comtesse woke up.

There was no wedding breakfast, only the regular rumbling of carriage wheels, the clatter of hoofs, the violent rocking of the coach, and the rhythmical creaking of springs like mocking laughter.

The journey had to begin at once, before her next tantrum blew up, before her next screaming fit, before her next wild outburst of swearing, before she disgraced herself and all Versailles in public.

The carriage had rolled out of Paris with the handsome Comte smiling at the prospect of all the money and possessions he needed in order to live comfortably for the rest of his life. Hundreds of old shoes roped, by Lebel, to the back of the carriage were bounced and dragged through the black mud and virgin snow, now defiled and mixed up behind them.

At the barrier leaving the capital the customs officers stopped the coach in order to exchange the usual incivilities.

'*Avez-vous quelque chose à déclarer?*' demanded the official.

'*Nouveaux mariés,*' said Major le Comte d'Ayat, grinning.

They were required to open every box. The official turned over jewels, prodded countless *objets d'art*, poked at everything. He was suspicious that the Comtesse could not remember her name. He was suspicious of her cuts and bruises. He attempted to confiscate all her treasures, under the opinion that she was making off with the better part of the Crown Jewels.

The Comte told him to mind his manners, and the coach rumbled on until it met a sea of cattle, all skin and bone, thundering along the road to the beast market in the capital. Stranded in the middle of the herd the coach was bumped and rocked, pierced through by long horns. The horses reared. The interior padding was ripped.

When the cattle had passed there was nothing on the road but cow-dung mingled with the snow, the endless lines drawn by carriage wheels, endless hoofprints, and the stench of excrement.

She thought, So this is the country.

In her mind there was only outrage that they had chosen a

husband without consulting her. She ignored the Comte d'Ayat as much as she could, and sat wondering about his dark, lowering eyebrows, afraid that he had the evil eye.

When she asked where they were going to, where he lived, he said, 'The Auvergne, Madame, we shall be there by Noël.'

The Comtesse laughed. 'I might as well go and live on the moon,' she said, and they drove on in silence.

At an inn some leagues along the road to the Midi, in the middle of nowhere, they supped in silence on a dozen larks. The bride attended to her wounds. The groom wondered what he had let himself in for. Exhausted by the fight, exhausted by travelling, the Comtesse slept.

On a second coach that fell further and further behind them travelled the magnificent trousseau. Dozens of red morocco trunks teetered on the roof, all embossed with the gold *fleur-de-lis* and crown of France, or bearing the arms of defunct members of the royal family. They contained, amongst other things, a hundred dozen chemises, a hundred dozen pairs of white sleeve-length gloves, fifty pairs of pearl-embroidered shoes. There were baby clothes fit for princes, silk monogrammed handkerchiefs, and two hundred Court dresses in all the colours of the rainbow; all marked with the *fleur-de-lis*, as if He had unloaded on her all the unwanted linen, all the old-fashioned outgrown clothes of the female members of his family, all the contents of the attics of Versailles – vast quantities of things she would never need.

Two weeks passed: the carriage broke its axle, was repaired, creaked along heavily, rarely achieving more than one league in an hour. Snow fell. Torrential rain hindered their progress, reducing fordable rivers to impassable floods. Guides hired to see them through difficult country lost their way. She began to think they would never arrive, that the Auvergne did not exist, but towards Clermont the Comte grew animated and pointed to the grey mountains on the horizon.

'Volcanoes, Madame,' he said. 'The volcanoes are home.'

The Comtesse made a face.

Towards Châteauneuf the carriage rocked through a district of deep gorges and tree-clad hillsides, with torrents of water crashing down. Snow had drifted everywhere. Cliffs cast shadows across the road. Woodpeckers knocked and drilled, echoing in the stillness. She watched an eagle circling slowly overhead on silent wings.

The carriage crawled up a narrow road with hairpin bends, rising out of the valley of the Sioule. At the top the Comtesse was surprised to see open fields and a panorama of the volcanoes, and the snow brilliant under deep blue skies. She saw the spike of a church, a straggle of hovels that was Ayat-sur-Sioule, and aloof, apart, in the distance, her husband's château.

She was struck by the deafening uproar of the rooks and the overpowering stink of manure.

The Château d'Ayat had four round, fat towers, squat, with roofs like pointed hats, like something out of a story. Later she wrote to tell her mother about the courtyards, fish-ponds, alleys of walnut-trees, fruit-trees, granges, stables, kennels; about the salons and bedchambers, the chapel, the library. She told Madame Murphy the château had everything a château was meant to have, in miniature. She did not dare reveal that her new home was crumbling and possessed of every ancient inconvenience.

The Comte showed his wife proudly over his ancestral dwelling, but the more bare, empty rooms she stepped into, full of dust and cobwebs, the more her heart sank. The Comte had great plans for renovation. The château would be transformed, he said. But as it stood, the château leaked, echoing to the steady drip of rainwater into metal buckets. The windows let in the wind. The flagstones oozed moisture. Roof tiles slid to the ground without warning. Everything was battered by time, tarnished, worn, broken or about to break.

The bottoms were falling out of the chairs. The tapestries were full of moths. Chickens wandered in and out of dark rooms and perched on the dining-table among candelabra that had once been silver but were now encrusted with wax, blackened by smoke, and daubed with chicken shit.

She missed the gilt mirrors she was used to and had expected to find. There were none. The Beaufranchets were country people, ordinary people, who appeared to live in only one room.

She asked for croissants, but there were no croissants in Ayat. There was no chocolate. There was no water supply. She missed her red copper bath with gold taps. She missed the constant hot water of Versailles. She missed the Versailles pâtisserie that melted in her mouth.

She had longed for a return to ordinary life; she seemed to have found it.

It was here that the Comte's aged parents lived: the high and mighty chevalier seigneur Monsieur le Comte Amable de Beaufranchet and his wife; an old couple who dressed always in black because it was cheaper to be in permanent mourning 'for distant relatives.'

The family fortune had run out. They had frittered away their capital on equipping their sons for the army, on gambling, on wine, until their debts exceeded their income. There was little left but the château and its farm, and a few parcels of land that brought in the miserable sum of 800 *livres* a year.

Hedged in by complicated traditions and laws which forbade the nobility from earning a living, they were too proud to sell their land. They were too grand to do anything about paying their debts, too poor to effect the simplest repairs, too set in their ways to do anything differently.

In the absence of money to pay farm labourers the Comte Amable walked behind his oxen himself and ploughed his own fields, wearing – as was the noble's privilege – his rusty sword. His boots were caked with mud, his face was gaunt, hollow-cheeked, weather-beaten. He changed his shirt once a month like a true Auvergnat. Many of the peasants who paid him their seigneurial dues were better off than he was.

The weather-vane, symbol of the seigneur, stood on top of the stables, bent by the wind into a grotesque shape. In the stable was one horse. Beside the fire lay one dog. The Beaufranchets clung to their noble status and shrugged their shoulders. They had always been people apart. No one visited their château without good reason. Ayat was cut off by snow for nearly six months of the year. The Beaufranchets kept themselves to themselves.

In the circumstances, 200,000 *livres* of dowry was just what the family needed, and Marie-Louise Murphy was the solution to all their problems. They swallowed their pride over her lack of noble birth and welcomed her with open arms.

'Every so often,' the old Comte told his wife, 'it is good to manure the fields.'

They put the traditional cockerel under the bridal bed together with *oeufs en neige* in a chamber-pot, and could not stop smiling at her.

The new Comtesse found it difficult to smile back.

At Noël the villagers came after dark dressed in black and white costumes, with flambeaux, drums, bagpipes, hurdy-gurdy and reedy wind instruments to serenade the new Comtesse. They danced the whirling dances of the Auvergne, sang haunting songs, and tramped in out of the blizzard to stand in front of the fire.

She thought, The bagpipe is the Devil's music.

The peasants smiled shyly at her and stroked the sleeves of her Versailles dress covered in pink roses. They touched her face as if they thought she was a vision. They addressed her in their impenetrable dialect and spoke words of welcome that her husband had to interpret for her.

'She is not a vision, Messieurs,' the Comte d'Ayat told them, 'she is real.'

For weeks after her arrival there were deliveries by cart and wagon carrying the remains of the trousseau: boxes of Sèvres porcelain smashed during the crossing of swollen rivers; trunks stuffed with clothes that were too small for her; gilt mirrors shattered into fragments.

Exotic fowl in crates had frozen to death on the journey.

Chinese jars packed in straw shivered intact for a few seconds, then collapsed into piles of dust.

She found bricks packed in straw, but what had been in their place it was impossible to guess.

The wedding presents that did survive intact served only to remind her of Versailles, but she did not want to be reminded of her past, or of Himself.

Chiffoniers and commodes with gilt decorations became rabbit hutches, chicken houses, ferret cages.

'I do not want my house full of golden furniture,' she said.

But she could not forget, and at the same time she wanted all of Versailles still to be going on, and bitterly resented what Louis had done to her.

*

The Comtesse resisted her husband, fought him, threw everything in her room at him, making him wish he had never agreed to marry her, and that he had never been born.

'You have tricked me in making me come here,' she told him.

The Comte prevented himself from retorting that he had himself been tricked into marrying her.

He lectured her calmly on the subject of the ideal wife.

'You must have no wishes or desires separate from your husband,' he said.

She screamed at him and threw food. She never touched a knife and fork without wanting to kill herself.

'In all reasonable matters,' he said, 'submission to a husband's wishes is obligatory.'

She hurled china.

She flung her furniture out of the windows, followed by the bedding and all her clothes. To the dismay of her mother-in-law, she walked about the freezing château naked.

She screamed, 'I do not want to be married to you.'

'You are married to me,' he said calmly, 'you are my wife.'

'I hate the country,' she screamed, 'I want to live in Paris with my family.'

'The King has forbidden it, Madame,' said the Comte, shrugging his shoulders, beginning to understand why.

He could get nowhere near her. They slept apart, for she would attack him in the middle of the night. He tried to reason with her. 'I could love you if you would let me . . .' he said.

'I will not let you,' she moaned.

'I would give you anything if you would talk to me,' he said.

'I do not want anything from you,' she wailed, 'you have nothing that is not already mine. I will not talk to you.'

The Comte took legal and medical advice, and considered removing his wife to an asylum for the insane. He thought about sending her back to Versailles.

She tore her clothes off in front of the doctor, screaming, 'I am not Madame d'Ayat, I am the King's whore . . .'

The doctor rode away shaking his head, saying that there was nothing he could do, that only time would tell.

The Comte remained calm, mild, the perfect gentleman that the Pompadour had made sure he was. On one occasion the Comtesse split his lip. She repeatedly tried to scratch his face.

'It is worse than war,' the Comte confessed to his father, but he never retaliated and would not be provoked. He did not administer the slaps, punches and kicks that other husbands gave their wives. He caught her hands as they flew at him. He deflected her blows where he could.

'I understand, Madame,' he said gently, 'I want to help you.'

When she attacked his face for the third time in three days and ripped his wig to shreds, he decided to leave her to her own devices. He had, in any case, to rejoin his regiment.

When the Comte d'Ayat's fellow-officers saw his slashed face, his black eye, his broken nose, they laughed at him.

'Ah,' they howled, '*le nouveau marié!*' They could not stop laughing.

Left alone, too far from civilization to run away, the Comtesse had no one to witness her anger except her ageing parents-in-law, against whom she could feel no malice. With no one to fight against she calmed down. She realized she was among friends, that Ayat was home, that she would not be recalled to Versailles.

She had been thrown out of Paradise like a fallen angel.

After a week of sulking in her room with nothing to eat but bread and water, she went to sit with her mother-in-law, whom she found making soup with a vat full of pig's blood.

She appeared one morning and said to the old Comtesse, 'Today I am going to kill myself.'

'You can do what you like,' said her mother-in-law. 'You are not a prisoner.'

She contemplated throwing herself over the cliffs into the gorge of the River Sioule, then she thought of her father saying 'No such word as can't'.

She began to make an appearance at mealtimes.

Her mother-in-law said, 'To talk politely will not burn your tongue.'

The new Comtesse settled down, shooed the chickens out of the château, began to make conversation and to remember her convent training.

She looked out day after day on to a frozen landscape. She listened to the howling of wolves, the snow sliding off the roofs, the drip of water into buckets, the almost total silence.

At night she watched the yellow eyes of wolves close to the château, reflecting the light of her candles. She dreamed dreams of soap and hot towels, dreams of Versailles, dreams of everything she had lost and left behind her.

In the outbuildings she came upon a row of dusty wine bottles on a window ledge, each one full of some liquid, each one with a bright-green snake coiled up in it.

She found stiff crows nailed to barn doors, their wings spread-eagled, their eyes pecked out.

Towards the end of winter a courier was discovered frozen to death in a snowdrift, a near-skeleton dressed in a mangled scarlet uniform, his face eaten by animals. In his pocket was a letter from Versailles, an illegible mass of sodden paper sealed with the *fleur-de-lis*.

She prayed to be free of the dark world of the Auvergne, to escape from peasants with tongues too big for their mouths, whose *patois* she could not understand.

When the snow thawed she walked in the slush along the pot-holed lane to the church. Behind the creaking door she found the Beaufranchet tombs in their seigneurial chapel. She paused at the fourteen gilt and woodwormed Stations of the Cross, prayed for all the Murphys and for herself in particular. She disturbed the *curé*'s chickens roosting in the rafters. She shooed chickens from the head and arms of a life-sized crucifix that was festooned with cobwebs.

White cows mooned in the lee of the church. Dogs wearing spiked collars to protect them from the wolves set up a frenzied barking at her approach. Chickens fluttered laughing into the air. Ancient faces stared at her from cracked windows.

She saw no one but the villagers, met no one of consequence. There was no polite society in Ayat. There was no carriage traffic, for Ayat was not on the road to anywhere and had little contact with the outside world. She returned to the château, disappointed.

Sometimes, desperately bored, she chased a chicken round the courtyard, wrung its neck, and walked across the cobbles with the corpse hanging limp under her arm. She dragged a rickety chair out into the winter sun and sat plucking feathers, frowning with concentration, happy to have something to occupy her hands.

When the Comte returned to Ayat in February 1756 he found his wife tractable and co-operative.

In her sleep she murmured 'Louis' in his ear, and he would shake her awake to tell her, 'My name is *Jacques*, Madame.'

The Comtesse turned the pages of an *Histoire de France* and engaged in polite conversation about strategy and the different types of artillery.

She reminded him, 'I am a soldier's daughter, Monsieur.'

Before the month was out she felt as if she had been chewing spoons. She did not mention to her husband that she already had a daughter. She had almost forgotten that Agathe-Louise existed.

In the frost the wolves came into Ayat looking for food. The men trapped them and made themselves wolfskin coats.

The peasants worked the land, minded sheep, felled pine trees, and eyed the Comtesse when they could.

On Friday nights they drank the local wine and fought each other: it was not unusual to lose a limb or an ear on a Friday.

On Saturdays they fought with their fists and cracked each other's skulls.

On Sundays they went to Mass to gaze at the Comtesse, hopelessly in love with her, and to hear Père Cromarias lecture on the works of Saint-Thomas d'Aquin and the number of angels who might dance on a pinhead.

When the *curé* spoke of *Notre Seigneur*, the villagers thought of the young Comte d'Ayat; when the *curé* prayed to *Notre Dame*, they thought of the Comtesse and offered up their prayers to her. They would genuflect to her sometimes, as if she were Our Lady herself and would save them all from damnation.

They stared and stared at her. In turn she stared back at them: the hunchbacks and grotesques, the maimed and the limping, the illiterate and the insane. In time her heart warmed to them and she gave away things she did not want, until most of the women and children of Ayat were dressed in some part of her trousseau, some garment worked with the *fleur-de-lis* or marked in the corner with a crown.

In the spring, as part of the seigneurial obligations, the peasants brought in procession to the château the tongues of the recently-slaughtered oxen.

The Comtesse smiled, accepted the offering with all the graces of Versailles, and regaled the visitors with the wine produced by her husband – Château d'Ayat – that took her breath away and was to her Versailles palate quite undrinkable.

She fed the smooth pink tongues to the dog.

Her stomach swelled and she kept her eyes on the muddy lane that led to civilization, whence news would come of her recall to the City of the Sun. But no letter came. The sun had gone behind a cloud.

The rooks woke her early in the morning; flies buzzed at the window-panes. She listened to the herdsman sounding his horn, to the jangling bells of sheep and goats being moved to greener pastures – and she stayed where she was.

In the summer the *curé* excommunicated all the wasps in the parish and the Comtesse wandered through the fields, heavily draped in black gauze to keep off the sun, followed by a cloud of humming insects attracted by her Versailles scent.

She lay sleepless on hot nights with the velvet moths fluttering on her breasts, her only company apart from the drumming of tiny feet against her stomach wall.

She thought, The moth is an omen of death.

In mid-September the peasants presented her with ox's testicles for the delectation of the château.

The Comtesse thought, No such word as can't.

She smiled, reached for a saucepan, and the dog went hungry.

On 30 October 1756 the Comte d'Ayat became a father. He hid his disappointment that the child was a girl and spat on her as his wife insisted, for luck.

On the day Louise-Charlotte de Beaufranchet was born the Comtesse heard the cock crow, and crossed herself at once.

This time she did not let go of her daughter. She refused to leave her alone in any room, even with an open Bible. She carried Louise-Charlotte everywhere and fed her herself, in spite of her mother-in-law's astonishment.

When the peasants brought the Comtesse the first lamb of 1757 she frowned and crossed herself again, but said nothing. The lamb was black.

The Comtesse prayed hard, Please God, not my daughter. But wherever she looked there seemed to be portents of mortality. She became convinced, on finding a wren inside the house, that Louise-Charlotte was going to die young.

When the Comte returned again to his regiment, swallows flew down the chimneys of his château, which his wife could interpret only as an omen of misfortune.

She fought against a constant invasion of wings: swallows, jackdaws, bats flapping round the rooms, unable to fly out of open windows. Swifts frequently beat their wings against the windows from outside.

'Birds are unlucky, Madame,' she told her mother-in-law. 'Birds mean death.'

In the spring of 1757, when Louise-Charlotte was four months old, her mother felt again the taste of metal on her tongue. The next day she saw a magpie on the roof of the stable.

'The Devil,' she whispered, and crossed herself.

She took every possible precaution. She was careful not to comb her hair after dark, not to look into mirrors by candlelight. But the bats effected an entry in the evenings and seemed always to fly into her candles and put them out.

She did battle with the natural world, told herself to take no notice, tried to keep her mind on pleasanter things, but she knew perfectly well that wings in the house were a sure sign of a death in the family.

Sometimes she ventured as far as Riom or Clermont in the new carriage, but obedient to the letter of her instructions she would wait on the edge of the town, forbidden to go any further.

Lawyers and doctors rode out to keep appointments with her beside the road. More often she would remain at home, resting.

The summer passed. Flies and wasps swarmed on the dungheap and the Comtesse's peacocks screamed like the damned. She grew stouter as the heat increased, and spent the afternoons lying down, fanning herself with a *fleur-de-lis*-covered fan, drinking bottle after bottle of lukewarm water.

Major le Comte d'Ayat, in the middle of rediscovering war and the horror of war, spent almost the entire year with his regiment, solving problems concerning the supply of rifles and ammunition, the digging of trenches and the pitching of tents.

In peacetime the Prince de Soubise's regiment never went outside in the rain for fear of catching cold or spoiling their uniforms. Army officers were permitted as a rule to take the whole of the long hot summer as leave, but such rules did not apply in time of war.

The Comte spent his evenings writing reports for the Prince and poring over ill-written dispatches. He read manuals on tactics till he fell asleep over his candles.

The result was that he was obliged to apply to the oculist by appointment to the army of France for a pair of green spectacles with thick lenses. He kept them in their leather case in the pocket of his uniform coat and wore them only when his eyes began to ache.

The Comte was handsome, tall, dark-haired, dashing. He had few faults, as Monsieur de Soubise and the Pompadour had been careful to find out, but one of those faults was vanity. The Major was vain. He did not like to be seen wearing his spectacles.

At Rossbach in Thuringia the Prince de Soubise was in command of some 50,000 men, whom he marched into Saxony, convinced that he was going to beat the stuffing out of Frederick the Great of Prussia, who had only 20,000 men under his command.

The Allied generals had not had the presence of mind to provide any food for the French army, which was followed, as always, by an equally large army of courtesans and hangers-on. There was nothing for them to eat.

The Prince had long since given his troops unlimited licence to pillage and plunder, but it was November. They were marching through enemy territory. There was no food in Merseburg or Weissenfels, nothing to eat in the hedgerows or sodden fields.

They drank the filthy water from streams beside the road. They chewed strips of leather from the horses' harness. They ate bark pulled from the trunks of trees. Some swallowed toadstools and began to vomit.

When they reached the village of Rossbach, where Frederick the Great lay in wait for them, they were in low spirits and had not eaten properly for three days.

The French troops marched doggedly towards the enemy with fixed bayonets and cannon ready to fire; and were mown down by hidden artillery. The unprotected flank of the French was overwhelmed by General von Seidlitz's cavalry.

The Prince de Soubise appeared incapable of co-ordinating the action of his men. He watched them being blown limb from limb, falling all around him, and he wept.

By late afternoon bad light stopped the battle. The Prussians had taken 7,000 French prisoners. The French dead numbered 3,000.

The Prussians had lost just 165 men.

All France mocked the hapless favourite of Madame de Pompadour, but the blame fell as much upon the King's mistress as upon her Prince. She had meddled in politics. She had dabbled in men's business. She had appointed men like Soubise to the highest command, choosing generals because she liked their faces, because they were amusing, rather than for their abilities. She was like a child playing at toy soldiers. She did not seem to understand that war was real.

On 5 November 1757 Major le Comte d'Ayat was ravenously hungry, in spite of instructions that officers should be fed first.

His stomach was empty.

It was a misty afternoon. The Major had put on his spectacles. They fogged up. He was annoyed because he was hungry; an Auvergnat is fond of his food. He could not see the enemy. He could not concentrate on the enemy. The smoke of battle made matters worse.

Bullets whistled past his ears. Horses screamed and died beneath their riders all round him. The ground exploded beneath his boots. His horse bucked and reared, out of control.

The Major whipped off his spectacles, put them in his inside pocket, and decided he could see well enough without them.

Some said that the Comte d'Ayat, tricked into marrying the King's mistress, mocked and teased about it by his fellow-officers, rode into a bullet deliberately.

A rumour circulated regarding the paternity of the Comte's first child: that the father was not the Comte d'Ayat but Louis XV himself.

It was not the truth that mattered: it was what people believed to be true. What mattered was what people were saying. It was of no consequence that the new Comtesse had not set foot outside the Auvergne for two years and had been nowhere near Versailles since her marriage.

The Comte would have been mown down whether he had his spectacles on or not, and the paternity of his children had nothing to do with it.

Jacques de Beaufranchet lay motionless and bloody. The cavalry rode round him and over him, until there was nothing left of his face, and his body was pushed deep into the muddy field of Rossbach that should have been full of cabbages.

At Ayat-sur-Sioule there was no word from the Comte. The Comtesse was unaware that he had been at Rossbach, let alone that a battle had been fought there.

She felt a vague sense of unease, as if something was wrong. The omens worried her.

Heavily pregnant, she gave orders for all the cockerels in Ayat to have their throats slit, so that she should not hear a cockerel crow on the day her son was born.

On the afternoon of 5 November she noticed that the ticking in the château had stopped, and remarked to her mother-in-law, 'The frost has got the clocks!'

A rumour passed through Riom about the fate of the Prince de Soubise's regiment, but the Comtesse was too far off the beaten track to hear anything but a garbled repetition of something that sounded wildly improbable. She did not believe it possible that the army of France could have been defeated.

The *Gazette de France* arrived in Ayat a month old, wrapped around dead fish, and there was no guarantee that anyone in the village would or could read it. Newspapers were, in any case, full of news that was wrong, full of lies.

It took a letter from the Marquis de Lugeac, circumlocutory, couched in obscure French, to alert her to the fact that the Comte's campaign had not been a success.

It took a personal courier from the Prince de Soubise to make her realize that the Comte was missing.

It took the return of a fragment of faded red uniform, a bloodstained sword, a bloody gold epaulette, a pair of tarnished spurs, and a gold signet-ring – taken from other corpses – to convince her that Jacques de Beaufranchet would never return to Ayat.

She had not loved him. She showed no emotion, just as she had been trained in her convent; just as she had been taught by her sisters. She felt as if her body did not belong to her; as if her brain was no longer in control.

She sat on a dilapidated chair, quite still. She looked out through the flaws in the greenish glass of her window on to snowy fields with white cows standing in them, breathing out clouds of breath as if they were on fire.

She listened to the wind whistling, the howling of the wolves, the hissing of logs on the fire. She thought of the banshee. She felt cold. Then she felt sudden pains in her stomach and spent the next twelve hours delivering her baby herself, shrieking instructions to her mother-in-law between contractions.

When the doctor and the midwife reached her through the blizzard, she held a son tight in her arms.

'You must call him *Jacques*,' said her mother-in-law.

'I will not, Madame,' she said. 'His name is *Louis*.'

She clung to him as if he were the only thing she had left in the world. She was careful not to wash his right hand lest she washed away his fortune.

She took him upstairs and stood with him on a chair so that he would be sure to rise in the world, and she had him baptized at once, lest the Devil took up his residence inside him.

The Prince de Soubise condescended to be the child's godfather, and he was formally baptized as Louis-Charles-Antoine Pelet de Beaufranchet; he was at once Comte d'Ayat, Comte de Beaumont, Comte de Grandmont, and Comte of other places.

The entire female population of Ayat shuffled down the lane to the château in huddled groups, muffled against the biting wind, to keep their vigil round the coffin of the young seigneur.

The widow Beaufranchet, aged twenty, plied them with traditional plates of *petits pois* consumed at funerals in the Auvergne. They chewed toast soaked in sugared wine, prepared according to her mother-in-law's ancient recipe. They sang solemn litanies, chanted interminable prayers, sang the most mournful songs of the Auvergne, and told the dead man's story, which went on throughout the night, amid flickering candles and the clack of wooden knitting-needles.

The Comtesse realized she had hardly known her husband, and was left thinking that he might after all have been a man with whom she could have lived on very friendly terms.

The women joked, kissed her babies, and tried to cheer her up. In the morning they shuffled back along the lane with the coffin to the church, two stout women supporting the Comtesse lest she was overcome with grief and collapsed. Snow fell out of a dark sky and blew in drifts across the lane.

The wind howled, buffeting the belfry and drowning the words of Père Cromarias, and the widow's cheeks stayed dry.

In the absence of a body they buried a coffin filled with rocks, and with them the tattered fragments of red uniform, the tarnished spurs, the gold epaulette, and a pair of gold-rimmed spectacles, splintered, spattered with dried blood, none of which items had belonged to Major le Comte d'Ayat but purported to be all that was left of him.

He was twenty-six years old.

Not knowing how her husband had died, she imagined his dark skin cut to ribbons, his limbs hacked off, his face blown away.

She dreamed his death each night, and he appeared to her, standing at the end of her bed in the moonlight, wearing his uniform, with bloody tears rolling down his cheeks, like a miracle-working statue.

She laid a place for him at table for a month, as custom prescribed, in case his ghost came back.

Sometimes he would sit opposite her by candlelight, quite motionless, and she would look into his black Auvergnat's eyes and talk to him about the weather and the design of rifles, and jiggle the new baby on her knee.

XI

For the first forty days of her bereavement the widow d'Ayat was required to sit in a room hung with black draperies, with the mirrors covered by black cloths, the pictures under black veils, and to dress herself from head to foot in black.

'As black as Lucifer,' she said.

Imprisoned anew, she took on the grim mood of her surroundings – but black became her. Men she had never seen before found their way to Ayat to inspect her, with a view to becoming her second husband.

Her mother-in-law, dressed as always in black, was hysterical.

'Now is the time to shed your tears,' she told the young Comtesse. 'You must weep now, while the neighbours cannot see you.'

'There are no neighbours, Madame,' said the widow.

'Weep!' cried her mother-in-law. 'Gnash your teeth!'

But the Comtesse could not produce any tears. Her eyes were dry, her black lace handkerchief was unused, and the black veil over her face was superfluous. She had been trained not to fall in love, and for death to mean nothing at all.

After forty days she emerged from seclusion wearing a black crêpe bandeau round her forehead, like a nun's headdress, to begin the second stage of mourning, which would last another twelve months.

When her melancholy came upon her she would walk into the overgrown gardens and tear the blooms off all the flowers. She walked with her children into the fields and watched the sheep and rams frantically coupling, and she screamed until she lost her voice.

She spent evening after evening burning wedding presents on a bonfire.

Unable to sleep, she made herself consume the feet of a turkey – the only remedy for insomnia that ever worked. But the more turkey feet she ate, the more she dreamed of Versailles.

Sometimes in the hot summer of 1758 she went absentmindedly to bed leaving the doors open, so that she woke to find the cockerel perched on the end of her bed crowing, and chickens in every room, sitting on chairs, perched on doors and cupboards.

She thought of Versailles, of her childhood in Paris, and wanted to go back.

In the end it was the children's needs that made her snap out of her depression. She thought, The children are all I have.

Louis-Charles de Beaufranchet grew fast. His hair was like straw. His baby-blue eyes did not acquire the sparkling blackness of the Auvergnat, or of Louis Bourbon, but stayed blue. He was the mirror image of his mother.

In the absence of a father the Comtesse spat on Louis-Charles herself, hoping that did not counteract the magic.

'For good luck!' she said, and kissed him.

Lying in his wicker cradle near the window of his nursery, Louis-Charles was serenaded by the tumult of birds building nests in the trees around the château. Other babies uttered *Par-Par* or *Mé-Mé* as their first words. The new Comte d'Ayat's first utterance was the guttural cawing of the rooks.

How Monsieur François-Nicolas Lenormand de la Gravière came to hear about the widowed Comtesse d'Ayat was a mystery. He was thirty-six years old, owned the estate and château of La Gravière, and held the lucrative post of receiver of taxes at Riom, the hub of Auvergne civilization, famous for its lawyers.

The tying-up of the dead Comte's affairs was complex. The widow was hit by legal complications: her dowry, paid out of the interest on certain Crown offices (and not costing Louis XV or Versailles anything), was payable to her husband, not herself.

She spent hours talking to lawyers in the Rue de l'Horloge at Riom, breaking the order forbidding her to set foot in any town, in an attempt to disentangle the labyrinth of legalities she did not understand.

It was in her lawyer's offices that she first saw Monsieur de la Gravière. She noticed his black eyes, his smart grey coat, and made polite conversation about the weather, and taxes, and estates and tithes, and the upkeep of buildings and the upbringing of children.

A week later de la Gravière turned up unexpectedly at Ayat in pursuit of the payment of some bill. He sat down and talked about the weather, and finance, and the education of children, and about his wife's recent death.

The widow said she was sorry to hear the sad news.

Back in Riom de la Gravière told his intimate friends, 'I intend to marry money.' He rubbed his hands together in anticipation of fabulous riches, and grinned.

In the autumn of 1758 Louise-Charlotte, aged two, fell ill. Doctors made regular journeys between Riom and Ayat but Louise-Charlotte grew weaker.

Monsieur de la Gravière appeared again and recommended the best doctor in Clermont, who had much experience of children's complaints.

Louise-Charlotte made a dramatic recovery.

De la Gravière kept on appearing. Some said he was a relation of Jeanne-Antoinette Lenormand d'Etioles, Madame de Pompadour: that the Pompadour herself had put him on the trail of the widow d'Ayat; that his appearances were not the result of chance but of careful calculation; that the Pompadour had her fingers in this pie as she had her fingers in every pie, stirring things up – seeing whether she could not arrange a second marriage for Morfi and enrich her kinsman at the same time.

As if she thought Morfi incapable of finding a husband for herself.

As it turned out, the marriage – arranged or not – was the right thing for the widow to do at the time. At Ayat she was falling into grave difficulties from which she could not extricate herself. She lacked advice. She was encumbered by the Beaufranchets' debts. By marrying Lenormand de la Gravière she would fall on her feet. Or so she thought. Or so he said.

She wrote to her mother, still living in style in Paris, 'It is a business arrangement . . . no one marries for love any more . . . Love is out of fashion.'

Louise-Charlotte fell ill again, and mother and daughter spent the winter struggling through the snow to visit the doctor. They kept bumping into Monsieur de la Gravière by the church of Notre-Dame de Marthuret at Riom, where they prayed for a miracle before the statue of the Virgin with the Bird.

Monsieur de la Gravière smiled constantly. His black eyes were full of laughter. His grey coat was always spotless. He always asked after Louise-Charlotte's health.

Negotiations began and Madame d'Ayat wrote to Versailles for permission to remarry. She must still ask His permission, as if she were still chained to him – just as Lebel was chained to him at night – in case he should require anything. As if he thought that one day he might like to have her back at Versailles, as if he was not finished with her yet.

She continued to hope and pray.

De la Gravière continued to rub his hands together and dream of a golden future. In return for rescuing the Comtesse from the disorder of Ayat and sorting out her financial difficulties, she would unlock a flood of money that would pour down on them for the rest of their lives. She had expectations from Versailles. They had promised to look after her.

She told de la Gravière, 'When I can lay my hands on the dowry all will be well.'

On 6 February 1759, with Ayat under snow, Louise-Charlotte died of a fever, aged two years and three months.

The following day the people of Ayat trudged with the coffin through a blizzard, silent, wrapped in furs, stamping their feet, weeping, to bury her. The Comtesse regaled them with the traditional plate of *petits pois*.

In order that the château might be safely reinhabited, the Comtesse drove a flock of sheep into the house to sleep there for three nights.

She sat in the black-draped *salle à coucher* with her parents-in-law, all of them dressed in black, surrounded by the bleating flock, weeping for the loss of her second daughter.

On 18 February, after eleven days of mourning, the Comtesse d'Ayat was in Riom once more – to sign a marriage contract.

Madame Murphy de Boisfailly wrote from Paris, 'I will not travel a hundred leagues just to sign my name to a piece of parchment.'

The following day the Comtesse ceased to be a Comtesse and was married, in black, at the church of Saint-Jean, in the shadow of the great black cathedral of Riom.

She held Louis-Charles de Beaufranchet, aged fourteen

months, firmly in her arms. He was also dressed in black, and he cawed distinctly throughout the service.

François-Nicolas Lenormand's eyes glittered like coals. His first wife had borne him two handsome children: the robust Jean-Jacques, now aged four, and Marie-Antoinette, a frail two-year-old. The labour of giving birth to the daughter had killed his wife.

The new Madame de la Gravière found herself a mother of three, with a new daughter to replace the one she had lost.

She embraced her new family warmly.

Versailles had written giving permission for the marriage to go ahead. Then, for some reason, the permission was withdrawn and the remarriage was expressly forbidden.

Rumour thought that the Pompadour was pulling strings; that Louis wanted Morfi back in her old apartment; that he was willing to end her exile; that he had a long list of Ducs and Vicomtes, infinitely richer than de la Gravière, who were falling over themselves to marry her instead.

Morfi could do better than marry a mere tax official, a man with no title, a man no one had heard of. He was not good enough for her.

But the letter refusing permission did not reach Morfi till she had been married a fortnight.

'I cannot be unmarried, can I?' she exclaimed, wondering what was wrong with Monsieur de la Gravière that she should be forbidden to marry him.

Versailles explained nothing. A shadow fell over her new beginning and she was obliged to pour out the truth about her past.

Monsieur de la Gravière sat frowning, as if he did not know all about it already.

He paid her debts all the same: tradesmen's bills, servants' wages, doctors' bills, and the costs of transporting the widow's goods to her new home.

She settled down in the grey-black château of La Gravière, near Varennes-sur-Morges, to the north of Riom, surrounded by black volcanoes. There was also a grey-black town house in Riom itself.

She was perfectly happy. She had become a tax inspector's wife. She found the idea quite amusing.

Madame de la Gravière exulted in her new freedom to wander the streets of Riom and buy things. She was delighted to accept the invitations of her husband's acquaintances: the lawyers, doctors and higher clergy of the town, and in turn she entertained them herself, with no expense spared.

Monsieur de la Gravière, who had grown thin after the death of his wife, began to eat seriously.

The new Madame de la Gravière threw her energy into looking after the children. She passed on to them all the beliefs and traditions of old Ireland.

She had a piebald horse brought to the door to cure Jean-Jacques of whooping cough.

She cured Marie-Antoinette's warts by smearing them with clay from the boots of the men who carried coffins.

She anointed all three children with bull's blood to keep their skin free of freckles.

To Louis-Charles she said, 'If you keep touching your *zizi* all the dogs will follow you down the street.'

At first the de la Gravière children resisted her and refused to do anything she told them.

They put worms in her *café au lait*.

They filled her embroidered shoes with ants.

They dribbled in her wine when she was not looking.

They pinched Louis-Charles and stuck pins in his clothes so that he cried from morning to night.

Later they transferred their affections from the dead Madame de la Gravière to the living one, and got used to her.

François-Nicolas Lenormand de la Gravière smiled a great deal and made a fuss of his new wife. He brought her flowers, ribbons, and jewellery, and watched to see how she would react.

She was grateful for his gifts, but her husband's presents were not Louis' presents. His jewels were not the King's jewels and looked cheap in comparison. She found herself reluctant to wear anything but the diamonds given to her at Versailles.

Monsieur de la Gravière was offended. He began to put on weight.

He watched to see who his wife smiled at in the street, and saw her smile at everybody. He saw her waving to the apprentices in the Rue de l'Hôtel des Monnaies, and took offence.

He intercepted a glance with the Mayor outside the Hôtel de Ville, and narrowed his eyes.

He saw her passing a note to one of the magistrates by the Palais de Justice, and interrogated her about it.

She spent much of her time with her lawyers, trying to resolve the problem of her finances. Her husband grew jealous.

Monsieur de la Gravière's appetite increased. He ate three heavy meals a day and kept eating between meals. He began to grow stout. He refused to take down the gilt-framed portrait of his dead wife.

He liked to spend money. He liked the idea of owning land. At the same time he was subjected to a campaign of hate by various Riomois he had harried for late payment of their taxes.

Madame de la Gravière sometimes woke to find a crow nailed to her street door so that the bird sprang up and flew into her face, spurting black blood on to the doorstep and splashing the hem of her dress.

Parcels of ordure were delivered to her husband by mysterious couriers.

Passers-by spat and crossed the street as her husband approached, throwing him evil glances and muttering threats.

De la Gravière grew fatter and his wife became reluctant to be seen in his company.

They tolerated each other, but when Madame de la Gravière did something her husband disapproved of he made use of his fleshy hands. He struck out without warning and pummelled her with his fists. He smiled less, drank more wine, and had the waistband of all his *pantalons* extended.

Eventually Madame de la Gravière retaliated in the traditional way and retreated to her own bedroom.

In response to his repeated knocking she wrote a note saying, 'I do not love you, Monsieur.'

Out towards Varennes-sur-Morges the Lenormand's country estate stood amid straight lines of poplar trees in a remote and unhealthy district.

Madame de la Gravière was bored by her new home. She froze

in winter and stifled in summer. She found herself hoping the volcanoes would erupt and take La Gravière with them, and put an end to the monotony of her existence. But the volcanoes were already extinct.

On dull days there was nothing in view but the grey shadow of the volcano and dripping poplar trees. She would stare into space with nothing to occupy her except her memories and a new kind of despair.

La Gravière was built of grey stone. Inside it was painted grey. The people she met all seemed to wear grey clothes. She seemed to live under a perpetually grey sky. She ate grey meat off grey plates. Even her body began to look grey.

In April grey blossom appeared on the trees and she would ride in her carriage through the mist to Riom, built exclusively of dark grey Volvic stone. She walked in the streets paved with dark grey lava cobbles from the grey volcano. She prayed before the grey-black Virgin of the Bird for help.

The grey fountains on the street corners ran with silver-grey water. The town was full of grey horses, grey dogs, fat clergymen in grey coats, and thin nuns in grey habits that the wind whirled upwards, turning them into giant grey pigeons that could not get off the ground.

She told her husband, 'I am tired of the provinces. I long for Paris.'

She refused to speak to de la Gravière till he agreed to do something to relieve her boredom.

He shrugged his shoulders, tugged at his dove-grey silk coat, blew the grey slime out of his nose into a silver-grey silk handkerchief, thought of the money, and sat down to write to his supposed kinswoman, the Marquise de Pompadour.

Nine years passed, during which Madame de la Gravière waited regularly in the shadow of the grey-black cathedral as the great clock struck noon, as if she were expecting a priest to hear her confession.

She was seen in the Rue Saint-Louis, always on the same spot, at four in the afternoon, wearing pink silk, as if she were waiting to be taken to dance in the highest society.

She was observed standing in the Rue de l'Horloge at six in the evening, dressed in flame-coloured silk, looking into the windows of a watchmaker's shop, as if she were thinking about the time.

In the mornings a white carriage with white horses would pause by the Fontaine des Lions and a woman would climb into it and be driven away along the Rue de l'Hôtel de Ville.

In the afternoons a brown carriage with brown horses paused by the Fontaine Ballainvilliers in the Rue Saint-Amable and a woman stepped inside and was driven fast towards Mozac.

In the evenings a black carriage with black horses stopped by the Fontaine du Refuge near the Palais de Justice and the same woman was hurried away to the east of the town.

Anyone following the movements of Madame de la Gravière would have known that she left her house three times a day on foot; that she returned in a carriage that put her down not outside her own house but at the end of the street; that none of the carriages was her own – which was grey, with grey horses – and that her children were, more often than not, left in the exclusive care and control of their nurse.

News of Versailles, news of Louis himself filtered through to her, embroidered and exaggerated: news of victories, news of defeats, news of an assassination attempt, news of births and deaths, death after death.

She was unmoved by news of the death of her mother, and received it with all the sang-froid demanded by her convent education.

She thought, A mother never dies anyway. A mother will always be there, looking over your shoulder. A mother is sewn up with you, inside your skin.

She lay awake at night thinking about Madame Murphy, wondering how her life would have turned out had she not gone to Versailles and she woke up in the mornings with her pillows wet with tears.

'Death,' she told her children, 'does not exist. We do not speak about death.'

But in April 1764 she heard that the Pompadour herself had died of pneumonia, and that her body had been smuggled out of the château like a parcel of refuse, and that Versailles had become a dull place in consequence.

Madame de la Gravière found the news hard to believe. She

felt as if the Pompadour was still alive, still her 'protector', still seeking to keep her away from Louis. She felt that the Pompadour could never die either. She imagined the sweet smile of her rival. She thought of the steely, determined heart beneath the façade, and she felt a strange burden lift from her shoulders.

She dreamed again of Versailles, a golden Versailles made of money.

François-Nicolas Lenormand de la Gravière dreamed of money every night. He did not lack the will to rise in the world. In 1745 he had been granted noble status. Now he had married a Comtesse. He had more money than he could easily dispose of; he lacked only a title.

In 1765 he purchased the substantial Château de Flaghac, some leagues south of Riom, in the middle of a different wasteland not far from the hamlet of Saint-Georges-d'Aurac.

He dispatched elaborately engraved cards to inform his acquaintances that he should be known and addressed in future as Monsieur Lenormand de Flaghac.

The new château could be seen from the highway to Lyons, an imposing mediaeval fortress with five turrets like witches' hats and a steep hipped roof of grey slates that rose above the trees and glittered in the sun. It was four storeys high, sturdy, threatening, sinister, secure against all intruders. It was surrounded by a moat full of giant carp.

With the château came the estates of Flaghac and a standing army of hereditary servants. There were barns and granaries, stables, cowsheds, lodgings for grooms, coachmen, maids, valets, gardeners, labourers, and their wives and children: all of them in the service of the seigneur.

Madame de Flaghac hated the château. It was too big, too old, too cold. It was further away from the civilization she hankered after. It was not Versailles.

'The countryside is out of fashion, Monsieur,' she said. 'I cannot imagine why you want to live there.'

Monsieur de Flaghac showed his teeth. It would keep her away from the temptations of Riom. At Flaghac he might keep her under control.

'Wait and see, Madame,' he told her. 'When they find that I

live like the nobility they will grant me a title to go with the estate.'

Meanwhile he basked in the glory of being the proprietor of a vast domain. He enjoyed the obeisance of his peasants, who knelt at the château gates and bowed as he rode by in his carriage. He was rid of the stigma of being a tax official. When the title was conferred he would give up paying tax as well.

To his Riom friends de Flaghac confided that he had found a more lucrative source of income than tax: his wife. He had discovered a vastly more interesting ladder of advancement: the Court.

'Madame de Flaghac has the entrée,' he told everyone. 'We are going to Versailles.'

He dreamed dreams in which gold coins fell slowly out of the sky, like snowflakes.

Louis appeared to have forgiven Morfi for whatever she had done to upset him. He was anxious to do what he could to help her in her misfortune. He still appeared to feel for her the old affection.

Madame de Pompadour no longer stood in her way; Louis had made it known that he would like to see Morfi again.

Strange things began to happen in the de Flaghac household. Madame de Flaghac bore no children to her new husband. It began to look as if her child-bearing days were finished. Then, suddenly, she was experiencing tingling sensations in her breasts, suffering odd cravings for peaches and strawberries. She felt as if she had been licking knives and began to vomit in the mornings.

Monsieur de Flaghac knew very well that he had not climbed into his wife's bed for nine years.

In October 1767 she celebrated her thirtieth birthday, hiding her distended stomach beneath a blush-pink silk dress and sitting on a pink *chaise-longue* in the town house at Riom, which she refused to leave for a draughty château where medical attention was difficult to obtain in an emergency.

'I shall remain here,' she said, 'till the child is born.'

At Riom on 5 January 1768 Madame de Flaghac was delivered of a daughter. Within the hour the *curé* of Saint-Jean hurried through the snow to baptize her, lest she should die, lest the fairies should spirit her away, lest the Devil should claim her soul first.

Officially, Marguerite-Victoire was the child of François-Nicolas Lenormand de Flaghac, but both he and his wife knew perfectly well that the father was Louis XV's Comptroller-General of Finance, the Abbé Terray.

A rumour circulated at Versailles that the former Marie-Louise Murphy had been sighted ascending the grand staircase, and that she had resumed her former position.

XII

After the fall of Morfi and her sister, Louis XV had installed a succession of temporary mistresses in the Parc-aux-Cerfs. The rumours piled up. It was said that he knelt in prayer with them before he jumped into bed. The Duc de Croÿ wrote in his journal the untruth that Louis had enjoyed the favours of ninety different beauties in his premises in the suburbs of Versailles.

With the appointment of Madame du Barry as the Pompadour's official successor, Louis sold his properties in the town and the harem of the Parc-aux-Cerfs was no more. He had no need of it. He told his confidants that La du Barry did things for him that no woman had ever done before.

That, Versailles retorted, was because La du Barry came to the château straight from the brothels of Paris. With Madame du Barry at his side Louis had no need for Morfi. She had grown. She had grown up. She was not *La petite Morphise* any more. The old bond between them had melted away. Morfi had changed, Louis had changed, Versailles had changed.

Louis was ageing rapidly. Lebel was dead. Even Boucher was dead, found in front of an unfinished canvas of Venus, brush in hand.

Louis introduced Madame de Flaghac to his Minister of State and commended her to him. The Pompadour – almost the last thing she did – had suggested and encouraged the liaison: the Pompadour, to whom the Abbé Terray, like so many others, owed his rise to power, and under whose protection he had become Intendant-Général des Bâtiments and Directeur des Beaux Arts.

'I have no heirs,' moaned Terray to the Pompadour.

'No one else but Morfi will be able to love the Abbé,' mused the Pompadour.

'How fitting, how amusing,' laughed the Court, 'that the Pompadour should introduce her rival to the most repulsive man in Versailles.'

The Flaghacs did not leave the Auvergne for nothing. It was

not for nothing that in 1771 they dropped their provincial life and came to live in Paris in the height of fashion and luxury.

Madame de Flaghac's smile returned, the old smile. She wore her hair piled high, plastered with gum Arabic, tallow, hog's grease and powder, adorned with exotic feathers, and studded with diamonds. When she dined by candlelight she glittered and twinkled like a fallen star put back in its element.

Rumour hinted that Madame de Flaghac had become the mistress of the Abbé Terray. For once rumour was right.

Terray, the cold, calculating Minister of Finance, was by common consent the most hideous-looking man of his time. His face was a grey-green. He frequently went unshaven, giving him the appearance of a bandit. He was tall, gaunt, rugged, sinister, terrifying, horrible, a clergyman of dubious celibacy.

His clothes looked as if they were second-hand: the sort of garments peeled from corpses fished out of the Seine; the kind of clothes once sold by Madame Murphy de Boisfailly. The Abbé was thin, a walking skeleton, but beneath his clothes he was made of iron, a sleek animal with dappled markings and rippling muscles. He was strong, tireless, and possessed of voracious appetites.

Madame de Flaghac tried not to think about his appearance. Her training told her to lie back and dream of Ireland: that this was work, not pleasure – the means to a roof over her head, food in her stomach, clothes on her back, and a comfortable old age. It made no difference that the roof was a château, the food oysters and champagne, that the dress cost 30,000 *livres*, or that her old age was made comfortable by diamonds and Old Masters.

She ignored the smell of garlic and onions that hung about the Abbé's clothes. She hardly noticed the fact that he only rarely washed. She smiled at him as she smiled at everyone else, imagining an Ireland that she had never seen: green and cool, under a relentless drizzle.

The Abbé had little time for endearments, but he did not beat her or tie her up. He did not draw blood or reduce her to screaming for help. He was kind enough in his way: offhand, remote, insistent on doing exactly as he liked.

He would fall into a profound sleep on top of her. His mouth hung open, revealing his blackened teeth. He snored, and his breath engulfed her in a dark wave. She kissed him all the same and thought about diamonds.

Sometimes, squashed and suffocating, she would have to smack him awake. His black eyes would glimmer open, showing the faintest flicker of a graveyard smile. On they would go, the Abbé's *jeanchouart* working away at her dark places throughout the night, tireless, inexhaustible, as he murmured of stocks and shares and the balance of payments.

They would talk about money and mathematics and high finance and of nothing else, and he taught her how to make her fortune increase and multiply.

'He's no oil painting,' she told Brigitte Murphy, laughing. 'It's like being kissed by death. I have to pretend he doesn't exist.'

Monsieur de Flaghac, fully aware of what was going on and fully approving of how much he was being paid for it, turned a blind eye.

'It is the fashion to sleep with your neighbours,' de Flaghac told her. He was not bitter. He had mistresses of his own to keep him happy. His girth had become grotesque and he was not in the best of health. He wandered about the house, sighing, subject to the blackest of depressions, and kept predicting his imminent demise.

Though he seldom had real need for it, he bought himself a three-wheeled wicker wheelchair and creaked from room to room of their apartment, making calculations on small pieces of paper, thinking of what he might buy next, of how he might further enrich himself.

The Abbé Terray began at once to pull the strings for his mistress that Monsieur de Flaghac had not managed to pull on his own. Money poured into the Flaghacs' bank accounts. Money piled up in their apartment. Money kept falling into their hands.

In the autumn of 1771 Madame de Flaghac was richer by 150,000 *livres*, a colossal sum, enough to purchase another château. She ran about waving a banker's draft, unable to contain her excitement.

In the spring of 1772 she received a gift of 50,000 *livres* from the King himself.

Later that year, the post of Receiver-General of Taxes of Paris was created for the benefit and enjoyment of François-Nicolas de Flaghac. Out of the income of the office a pension of 12,000 *livres* a year was to be paid to his wife. The pension cost neither Louis personally, nor the royal coffers, nor the Abbé Terray, nor the state, anything at all. The job carried no duties of any kind.

Before the year was out Madame de Flaghac received a further payment of 150,000 *livres* from the Abbé.

Money kept on flowing. There were further six-figure sums, further participations in profits, none of which cost the Treasury anything. Madame de Flaghac was quite pleased to have been introduced to the Comptroller-General of Finance. She began to spend in earnest. She threw money up in the air. She spent money like water, and changed her diamonds three, four and five times a day.

Just before Madame de Flaghac's thirty-fifth birthday her step-daughter Marie-Antoinette was married with great ceremony to a nephew of the Abbé Terray. A dowry of 150,000 *livres* went with her, paid by the Abbé Terray, who was gradually becoming one of the family.

Shortly afterwards the de Flaghacs moved house – to the Rue Notre-Dame des Champs in Paris – and it was quite by chance that the Abbé Terray was to be their next-door neighbour.

There were two separate gardens at the rear. The Abbé Terray went in and out of his own front door, with a *concierge* in his livery to open the door for him. The de Flaghacs had their own front door and their own *concierge*, but behind the façade several interior walls had been knocked through, creating one household.

The Abbé came and went in his clerical costume, preserving the odour of sanctity in which he was supposed to live. As soon as he crossed the threshold he would rip off his wig and clerical bands and run up the gilded staircase four steps at a time in search of his mistress, tearing his clothes off as he went, and leaving a black trail behind him.

On an upper floor Madame de Flaghac sat in a gilded boudoir filled with dozens of gilded clocks, most of them presents from Louis XV. There were clocks with gold cherubs wearing gold wings. There was a gold clock with the figure of Aurora drawing back the cloak of night. There were clocks with shepherdesses, clocks with Orpheus blowing a trumpet; a clock with the gold figure of Time abducting Youth in the form of a naked girl; and a clock with gold satyrs' masks edged with gold sunbursts and female figures representing Time – as if Morfi had got all the Time in the world, as if she had abducted Time herself.

The clock room pulsated with the heavy tick and whirr of Time, with the clocks regulated to begin striking at five minutes to the hour and finish at five minutes past, so that there were ten minutes of pandemonium; as if all the devils in Hell were let loose on the hour every hour; as if Time had gone berserk.

It was here that the Abbé Terray came to flex his muscles and slake his lust, and to hear the Comtesse confess her sins before she committed them.

'*Ego te absolvo*, Madame,' he said, grinning, making the sign of the Cross from his side of the yellow-green sofa, and they would begin to wrestle and talk of the rate of exchange and higher mathematics.

'Why,' Brigitte Murphy asked her sister, 'do you let yourself behave like this? Why do you do it?'

Madame de Flaghac laughed and shrugged her shoulders. 'Why did I ever do anything?' she asked.

She looked out of her window on to smartest Paris.

'Do who can,' she said, laughing, 'dance who knows how.'

She would concentrate on the time to take her mind off the Abbé's face. She steeled herself to be indifferent to his ghoulish looks, trained herself not to mind his haggard eyes and shifty glance: the sinister, evil face of the satyrs on her clocks.

The Abbé Terray yawned. She put her hand over his mouth.

'Cover it up, Monsieur l'Abbé,' she said, 'or the Devil will jump inside.'

He laughed his terrible, caustic laugh, like gravel rattling in a snuffbox. 'Ah,' he said, 'the Devil is inside already!'

The Abbé revealed to her glimpses of the icy heart that was impervious to affection. He told her of his overriding ambition: the acquisition of the pink hat with pink tassels. He told her about the bribe of half a million *livres*, now in preparation, which would ensure that the miracle took place; of his cool faith in his ability to achieve whatever he wanted.

'Give me time,' he told her, 'and I shall be *Son Eminence le Cardinal Terray* . . .'

She kissed his ring in anticipation.

'Anything is possible, Madame,' he said, *'le Bienheureux* Joseph Terray . . . *Saint* Joseph Terray . . . wait and see.'

She fed him peppermint pastilles to sweeten his breath. She thought of the money, more and more money in return for bearing the Abbé's child.

She dandled Marguerite-Victoire on her knee among the golden clocks. She stood with Marguerite-Victoire on a gilded *fauteuil* to ensure that she would rise in the world. She left Marguerite-Victoire's right hand unwashed so that she would be fabulously rich.

She made the Abbé spit on Marguerite-Victoire's perfect face.

'For good luck!' he said, smiling horribly at his daughter.

In the dark the reptilian features of the Abbé fixed themselves into a humourless grin. His cold lips kissed Madame de Flaghac among the thump and tick of clocks. His lizard tongue darted in and out. His large aquiline nose snuffed at her skin. His iron muscles worked at her like an automaton. He mounted her with the impassivity of a dog, priding himself on the regular performance of the machine that was his body, oiled like clockwork, on the hour every hour throughout the night, amid the clamour of timepieces, their chimes regulated to coincide with the rhythmic yip-yip-yipping and the steady panting that reached the ears of Monsieur de Flaghac, sweating and sleepless on the floor below them.

'Making love to your neighbour's wife . . .' the Abbé murmured, laughing. 'No other love is fashionable . . .'

Following her return to civilization Madame de Flaghac applied, together with Brigitte, for letters patent granting them the status of nobles.

Brigitte Murphy de Boisfailly was still a Mademoiselle, too ugly for any man to contemplate for long, too proud to look at any man herself now that she had been looked at by the King. Brigitte had ideas above her station.

'We shall be nobles together,' she laughed, 'two shoemaker's daughters!'

Madame de Flaghac had a more serious purpose. Louis-Charles was in need of the right start in the army.

'There is no question about it, Monsieur,' she told de Flaghac, 'he will be a soldier like his Papa.'

The only place for an officer to begin his career was at Versailles, as a royal page; and to gain admission to the École des Pages candidates must prove 400 years of nobility. That was no problem for the Beaufranchets, but the Murphy family, the distaff side, was an unknown quantity, its history lost in the bogs and mists of Ballymollymore.

The Murphys, wandering about Europe, had left their past behind them. They had no documents, no proof of who they were.

It was not unusual for the Irish on the Continent to have mislaid their ancestors, and alternative procedures existed to cater for them. It was the accepted custom for six noble gentlemen of Ireland to make an affidavit of their opinion on the matter of whether such and such a family was or was not a noble family at all.

Madame de Flaghac concentrated her charms and energy on persuading Colonel Conway and Captain Madligor of the Régiment de Clare; and Captain O'Sullivan of the Régiment de Dauphin; and Captain Fagan of the Régiment de Soubise; and Captain MacMahon of the Régiment de Fitz-James; and a Lieutenant-Colonel Conway – among them five Chevaliers de Saint-Louis and two Chevaliers de Malte – to make the solemn declaration:

'... That they know well the house of O'Murphy or O'Murrough-oue de Ballymollymore to be one of the most ancient noble families of Ireland ... and that Denis Ogue O'Murphy and his son Daniel were recognized by a number of the Irish as having honour in the Brigade ...'

Madame de Flaghac submitted proofs that the Murphys were a family who had lions on their coat of arms and sent a document tracing her father's descent from Denis Ogue O'Murphy, son of Denis O'Murphy, son of Morgan, son of Edmond, son of Thaddaeus, son of Morgan, son of Amrot, son of Thaddaeus, son of Charles O'Murroughoue de Ballimollimore, who flourished in the year 1388, longer ago than anyone could remember and conveniently spanning the requisite 400 years.

'Who would dare to suggest that we made it all up?' she asked Brigitte, her eyes flashing with anger. 'Of course it's the truth.'

Thus Louis-Charles, Comte d'Ayat, put his foot on the first rung of the ladder of promotion, and thus his mother became a noble and rode about Paris with her own lions and her husband's stars legitimately emblazoned on her carriage doors. The carriage was painted pink, and inside it Madame de Flaghac sat dressed in pink to match, unable to stop smiling.

Much of the time she left her children to their own devices. They grew, they learned their lessons, they kicked their heels at Flaghac or in Riom, and rarely came to Paris.

When Madame de Flaghac was available they learned a smattering of English. When she was not available, they would peer through a hole in her bedroom door to see what it was she did with the Abbé Terray and the distinguished gentlemen who came from Paris to visit her, who they were told to call 'Mon Oncle' – though they knew very well that the rich visitors were not their uncles at all.

All Madame de Flaghac's clothes were shot through with gold thread. Many of her possessions were made of solid gold or decorated with gold. She wore diamonds all day and slept in them, glittering by moonlight.

Louis-Charles and his stepbrother would climb up into the towers of the château and explore the attics. They rummaged in trunks, fought with rusty swords, flipped through the wormholed pages of books of maps, and unfurled flags captured in forgotten battles.

When Jean-Jacques went off to the École Militaire at Effiat, leaving Louis-Charles without a companion, he perfected the fine art of playing with fire and aimed his pistols at anything with wings.

When Jean-Jacques returned for his vacation he was full of his exploits and full of new tortures. He twisted Louis' translucent ears and tweaked the hairs on the back of his neck, and made his eyes water. Jean-Jacques had learned to wrestle and performed holds that instantly reduced Louis to begging for mercy.

Helpless with laughter, Jean-Jacques force-fed his stepbrother with mud and goat-droppings. He decanted cow's urine into a wine bottle, poured a glass, and choked with laughter when Louis sniffed, mimicking his stepfather, rolled a mouthful round his mouth, swallowed, and declared it an excellent vintage.

Jean-Jacques sliced worms into Louis' food and rolled on the floor in hysterics when Louis announced that he had dined very well.

The sun beat on Flaghac and dried the fields into dust-bowls. The boys caught and dismembered lizards, rode the cows bareback, and shot the apples off all the trees. They lined chickens up on the wall surrounding the château and shot them one by one into oblivion amid flying feathers, frantic squawking, and fountains of blood.

Louis-Charles spent most of his time killing things. Before he learned to love he learned to hate. His mother decided that the time had come for him to be sent away to learn how to kill the enemies of France, to stop murdering her table-fowl, and to learn how to be of some use in the world.

She sat down and wrote to Versailles. She wrote to the Prince de Soubise, enclosing the proofs of noble status and requested him to pull the strings he had promised to pull on behalf of his godson.

Louis-Charles continued to give himself target practice. He lined up ten of his mother's finest golden clocks, aimed at the dials inscribed LEROY A PARIS, and shot them to bits in ten magnificent explosions.

When his mother saw the débris she screamed.

'*Je tue le temps . . .* ' Louis-Charles said, laughing.

Later Monsieur de Flaghac demanded, 'Why do you not take the pistols away from him?'

'Why,' she said, 'he will join the army soon! I cannot take his guns way. Would you prefer that he grew up playing with dolls and dressing in his mother's clothes?'

Monsieur de Flaghac banged the inkwell down on his *escritoire* and glared at her, thinking of wasted money.

'He is a man!' she shouted, angry. 'He will be a soldier like his Papa!'

Monsieur de Flaghac shut the top of his desk with a crash.

'Boys will do these things!' she screamed. 'You must learn to forgive!'

Monsieur de Flaghac summoned his stepson into the library all the same and beat him till he howled and bled.

More than anything, more than shooting, the young Comte d'Ayat's passion was for equestrianism. From an early age he had thrilled to the snorting of horses. He had learned to ride as soon as he could walk, with large cushions strapped to his back and stomach, and a pillow tied on his head with a string that went under his chin, in case he fell off. When he did fall off, his mother put him straight back on his pony and made him carry on riding round in circles.

At four he told his mother, 'I want to be in the cavalry.'

At six he was riding unaided, without cushions.

At eight he rode with the hunt and was smeared with blood at his first kill in the woods near Flaghac.

At ten he could make any horse dance, could ride bareback, back to front, upside down, standing up, and was an accomplished trainer of horses. He could tell the good from the bad.

'You have the eye,' his grandfather d'Ayat told him, smiling.

By the time the thirteen-year-old Louis-Charles set out for Versailles he had bandy legs from spending all day in the saddle. His bedside reading was the *Manuel de Cheval*. His dreams were full of horses. It was natural that he should take up lodging in the attics over the royal stables and spend his idle moments engaging the men who bred the King's horses in serious conversation about prolapsed foals, the ovulation of mares, and the relative fertility of equine spermatoza.

On the afternoon of 21 June 1771 Madame de Flaghac delivered her only son to Versailles. She kissed him on both cheeks, wept, clung to him, and left him in the gateway of the Petite Écurie du Roi.

'*Au revoir, mon petit*,' she said, 'don't let the Murphys down.'

Louis-Charles sweated inside a red velvet coat and velvet *pantalons*, a cloth of gold waistcoat, a cocked hat with white plumes, and a sword with a silver hilt. His mouth and pockets were full of liquorice lozenges. He felt proud and stupid at the same time.

He shook in his buckle shoes because he was afraid of doing the wrong thing. He was afraid of what would happen. He looked up at the faces of his fellow-pages peering out of the windows, watching the arrival of the newcomer.

The Governor of the Pages received him warmly, introduced him to his colleagues, and recommended him to their friendship. There were 250 of them, all dressed in red and gold, all destined to become officers in the Bourbon army.

The Comte d'Ayat was soon installed in the Hôtel des Pages, near the royal kennels, with his ears full of the baying of a thousand hounds. The smell of dogs and horses made him feel at home.

He kept chewing liquorice.

In the stifling attics above the stables a kind of anarchy reigned. Long after the Governor had retired to bed, the pages lit candles and crowded into one of the yellow-painted dormitories, wearing their nightshirts, breathless with excitement to watch d'Ayat perform the Initiation.

Their perfectly-spaced eyes watched him with a not unfriendly stare; their noses were perfectly straight, the product of 400 years and more of noble breeding. Their bristly scalps crackled under their fingers.

Sweat trickled down d'Ayat's face on this hottest of summer nights. His knees shook. He had sucked so many liquorice lozenges that his tongue was black. He felt as if the stubble on his head was standing on end. He took deep breaths and sat down at a table, wearing his uniform as instructed.

The senior page brought a large wine-glass and placed it in front of the Comte with the utmost gentility, like a waiter in the best eating-houses.

'*C'est la tradition*, Monsieur,' he said. The glass was full of a yellow liquid that might have been lemonade or white wine, but which d'Ayat knew was neither.

The pages began a rhythmical chanting, whispering first, then growing louder: '*Bois! Bois! Bois! Bois! Bois . . .*'

The Comte grinned, and sniffed eagerly at the wine-glass. He slurped a mouthful, as if he had drunk this stuff before. He rolled it round his mouth as if it were *vin de champagne* and swallowed. He paused, thinking, in the deathly silence. Then he stood up, clicked his heels together, tipped the pint of urine down his throat, and banged the glass down on the table.

The pages cheered, delighted. D'Ayat smacked his lips, grinned, shook his head once, and held out his glass for more. There was laughter, then a silence in which someone giggled.

The pages began to stamp their bare feet rhythmically on the wooden floor. The senior page put a silver knife and fork and a white napkin in front of d'Ayat as if he were going to serve him a meal.

D'Ayat tucked the napkin into the collar of his uniform and held the knife and fork point upwards in his fists on the table, waiting. His fists shook. His black tongue flickered in and out, lizard-like.

The senior page brought a silver plate that winked in the candlelight, with something on it that d'Ayat did not want to look at or think about. It steamed slightly.

'C'*est la tradition*, Monsieur,' the senior page murmured apologetically as he put the plate down.

D'Ayat shut his eyes and concentrated on his breathing. He knew that his career depended on whether he passed the test or not. He took deep breaths, kept himself calm.

He thought, A Beaufranchet can do anything. There is no such word as can't . . .

His hands felt cold, as if they were someone else's hands; as if they were going to disgrace him.

Other pages had at this point, he knew, shed tears, howled, fled, complained to the highest authorities, or written letters begging to be taken away. D'Ayat was determined not to join their number.

The pages began to chant: '*Mange! Mange! Mange! Mange! Mange!*' Their faces glowed in the candlelight.

D'Ayat coolly plunged in with the knife and fork and ate his way through what was on the plate with something approaching glee. He belched, wiped his mouth on the edge of the napkin, and asked if there was any more.

There was immediate uproar, screams and howls of delight. D'Ayat heard, muffled, in a daze, the noise of the rooks at Ayat. The senior page was shaking him by the hand, slapping him on the back, and the 250 pages cheered and stamped, hoisted d'Ayat shoulder-high, threw him repeatedly into the air, and d'Ayat knew what it was to fly.

The Governor turned over in his sleep, relieved that d'Ayat had passed the test.

The Comte managed not to vomit until he was out of the room. He managed not to let his tears flow till he was back in bed with the sheets over his head.

Jean-Jacques had trained him well, had briefed him properly, and Beaufranchet d'Ayat went down in the history of the École des Pages as one of the finest fellows they had ever known.

He wrote to tell his mother that he was doing well.

When his training was complete the new page would rise each morning, dress in his red velvet suit with gold embroidery and attend the King's levée, waiting for the moment when he should remove Louis XV's right-hand slipper so that the Gentlemen of the Bedchamber could ease the royal foot into the royal shoe.

Later, d'Ayat would let off steam astride a demented horse that was unused to the sun and almost uncontrollable. He would render his mount docile, make him dance in the sand of the riding school, and describe *fleur-de-lis* patterns with his hoofs, to the envy of the other pages.

In the evenings d'Ayat would play billiards and wait for the *coucher*, when he would ease the right-hand royal foot into the right-hand royal slipper and be free of his duties for the day.

When d'Ayat showed off too much, a dozen pages would tear off his uniform and hold him, according to tradition, under the eight taps that filled a large marble basin in the pages' dining-hall with ice-cold water. They kept d'Ayat there, naked, howling, squealing with laughter and rage, until he wriggled out of their hands like a wet fish and escaped in search of a towel.

He wrote to tell his mother that he was doing very well.

The Comte returned to Flaghac for the vacation able to swipe the tops off his boiled eggs with one wave of his fork. His mother was astonished.

'It's just a trick,' he told her, 'everyone can do it.'

He spent his first morning at home pulling the wings off butterflies.

He spent the afternoon cutting the heads off all the chickens until the farmyard was the scene of bloody massacre.

He spent the evening catching fish in the streams that flowed behind the château. Instead of beating the fish to death on the stones, he watched them twitch and flip somersaults in the dust until they died.

At dusk he went out with a parcel of gunpowder and blew up the largest tree in his stepfather's Parc, lighting up the sky with an explosion that broke half the windows in the château.

'That boy,' said Monsieur de Flaghac to his wife, looking out into the dark, 'one day that boy will be a general.'

Nevertheless he gripped his stepson's right arm, twisted it round behind his back, marched him into the library, and shouted at him for ten minutes. Then he told him to let down his *pantalons*, and beat him with a stick till his bottom was striped red, white and blue and the Comte was panting with rage.

'That will teach you, Monsieur,' shouted de Flaghac, sweating, 'to blow up my trees without my permission.'

'That didn't hurt,' said the Comte, putting his tongue out at his stepfather. He turned on his heel and left the room, slamming the door behind him.

Later in the week a grinning Jean-Jacques arrived at Flaghac and demanded a full report of the proceedings at the École des Pages.

'*Well*,' he said, 'what *was* it?'

'Dog,' said the Comte casually, his stomach churning at the memory. 'Hot dog.'

'*Merde!*' whispered his stepbrother. He smacked the knee of his *pantalons* with the flat of his hand and howled with laughter.

D'Ayat hit him, and they spent the rest of the day fighting.

The Comte d'Ayat returned to Versailles fired with a new zeal for his studies. He vowed to return to Flaghac and blow up the entire château and everything in it, including his stepfather.

He spent much of his spare time loitering beside the abattoir of Versailles, listening to the music of the pigs having their throats cut. He watched the steaming blood flood across the cracked pavements into the drain that eventually reached the blue waters of the Grand Canal. He thrilled and shivered at the sight of the butcher's knife glinting in the sun. His heart beat faster when he heard the screams of death.

He thought, soon it will be the real thing, war and the glory of war, when I shall kill things myself, and not just chickens.

Death was in his blood.

He wrote to his mother, 'I long to be in the army: death is the only thing worth living for.'

XIII

The Comte's half-sister, Agathe-Louise de Saint-Antoine de Saint-André, now nineteen years old, was still imprisoned in the convent at Chaillot. She rose and retired early, thrived on a diet of relentless prayer, and had the insatiable appetite of a Bourbon.

Every year, on her birthday, she would receive a present from Monsieur Yon, acting as an intermediary for her father. But Agathe-Louise was still ignorant of who her father was.

'I have never seen my father,' she complained to the sisters. 'I do not know his name. I do not know him. We have never met.' She would not look at his presents and refused to open them.

Agathe-Louise thought often about her mother, the family she might have had, the home she might have lived in, the brothers and sisters she might have played with. She wondered *why* she had been sent to live at Chaillot. She asked the nuns if, in fact, the boring Monsieur Yon was her father. She asked endless questions but never received any answers.

She counted the long years of her confinement: five, ten, fifteen years and she was still locked up. She felt forgotten, neglected, unloved. She wondered if she might not be doomed to spend her entire life among the sisters of Sainte-Périne, who spoke merrily of the day when Agathe-Louise too would take the veil and become a nun herself. Agathe-Louise told the nuns, 'I will *not* take the veil. I do not want to be a nun. I want to be married.'

She was rarely allowed outside, save to glide with the other girls – all of them dressed in black – in a crocodile towards the Seine. When they reached the river they would wrinkle their noses, turn round, and glide home again. The stout door of the convent closed behind them and they would not be seen in public for a week. There was at Sainte-Périne a *concierge* who opened the door to visitors, but he was over eighty years of age. Monsieur Yon and the *concierge* were the only two men Agathe-Louise had ever spoken to.

*

While the girls seldom went out, members of the public did make their way inside the convent walls. The Sunday morning Mass was open to the girls' relatives. Visitors were encouraged: they gave generously to the charitable causes supported by *la Mère Supérieure*.

Agathe-Louise stood out on Sundays as the girl who never had visitors. Other girls received the quadruple kiss from their parents, were hugged, made a fuss of, and given interesting presents. But Agathe-Louise wandered about on her own, looking lost.

Agathe-Louise had never been kissed. Kissing was discouraged at Sainte-Périne as the gateway to impurity, the road to Hell.

As the girl with no relatives, Agathe-Louise attracted the notice of the du Barry *père* and *fils*, Comte and Vicomte respectively, who were both particularly fond of kissing young girls. The du Barrys had gone to Mass at Chaillot with the sole purpose of casting their eyes over the young ladies and fixing up young Jean-Baptiste with a wealthy wife, and with a view to stabilizing their rocky finances for the future.

The Roué du Barry, rake and adventurer, brother-in-law of Madame du Barry, the King's latest mistress, was in a perpetual state of penury. His plan was to arrange a grand marriage for his son, to acquire a grand dowry, and to live more grandly himself as a result. They had spotted Agathe-Louise looking forlorn, and made enquiries about her.

'She looks,' drawled the Roué, ogling her through his gold lorgnette, 'as if she could do with a nice young man to give her a kiss . . .'

The Vicomte du Barry smirked. 'She looks,' he replied, 'as if she could do with a young Vicomte to fall in love with . . .'

They judged that Agathe-Louise, with no official parents to stand in their way, would be easier to carry off than the daughters of conventional high society. She was better endowed than most girls. She was herself the daughter of a royal mistress – there could surely be no objection to such an alliance.

Jean-Baptiste du Barry *père* left Jean-Baptiste du Barry *fils* to get on with the wooing.

*

The Vicomte became a regular communicant at Chaillot on Sunday mornings. He would bang on the street door wearing a gold stuff coat lined with sable and tell the *concierge* he was a cousin of Mademoiselle Tour de Poitrine (a girl who did not exist). The ancient *concierge* would reveal the gaps between his teeth and open the door for him.

Throughout Mass the Vicomte kept his ice-blue eyes fixed on Agathe-Louise She was herself supposed to be practising humility of the eyes, as taught by the nuns, but she was her mother's daughter, and her father's. She was weary of staring at the broken parquet floor. She was tired of gazing at the cracked spine of her missal. She preferred to look about her. Her eyes fell repeatedly on the grinning face of the Vicomte du Barry, who had never been taught humility of the eyes or humility of anything else.

Agathe-Louise began to watch for the young man with the charming smile and the gold stuff coat, who always seemed to be looking in her direction.

She began to smile back at him, her black eyes shining.

Agathe-Louise asked her colleagues, 'Who can the young man be?' But the girls did not know who he was.

'If no one knows him,' Agatha-Louise mused, *'how* has he managed to squeeze past the *concierge*? If he knows no one, why has he come here?'

'Oo la la!' said the girls, 'he comes to see *you*, of course.'

It was common knowledge that Agathe-Louise was the heiress to a considerable fortune, even if her identity was a secret and her name was false. It was no secret who her father was; no secret except from Agathe-Louise herself. All smart Paris knew the King was her father, but Agathe-Louise had never seen Louis XV and had never handled the coins with his portrait on them. She did not know what the King looked like.

Eventually the Vicomte du Barry manoeuvred himself into a position where he could address Mademoiselle de Saint-André.

'Jean-Baptiste du Barry!' he said, bowing. 'My family call me Adolphe. I am *Lolo* to my friends.'

Agathe-Louise smiled her most perfect convent smile. She was charmed. She told him her name and fell in love on the spot.

She began to think of Lolo du Barry all day. She dreamed about him all night. She had no idea who Madame du Barry was. She did not realize that the grotesque old man with rouged cheeks, dribbling lips, and outlandish clothes with golden roses all over them was the outrageous Roué du Barry.

She had no idea that the Roué had anything to do with her Lolo.

The du Barrys pulled all the strings they could, desperate to get their hands on the King's bastard daughter before anyone else.

The Roué applied urgently to Madame du Barry for her support in winning the King over to their cause.

Louis was amused and laughed aloud. Then he was interested, not inclined to say no, and perhaps would have given his consent to a union between Lolo and Agathe-Louise.

But Monsieur Yon was incensed by the idea and wrote dozens of indignant letters. It was he, Monsieur Yon, who had watched over Agathe-Louise and cared about her all these years, and he would have his say in who she married.

The Vicomte du Barry had no money and no reputation, except the appalling reputation inherited from his father. Surely, Monsieur Yon reasoned, Mademoiselle de Saint-André, daughter of the King of France, had a right and a duty to look higher than this disreputable family of rakes and prostitutes with a bogus title.

The Vicomte meanwhile had discovered Agathe-Louise's window and was to be found at Chaillot every night standing below it, throwing gravel at the glass until her pale face appeared.

There was the dashing Lolo du Barry, sword at his waist, jingling his spurs, flashing his white teeth, flexing his muscles for her, removing his flowing white shirt so she could admire his rippling torso in the moonlight, blowing her extravagant kisses, and talking to her in his slightly husky voice.

He wrote to her every day. He told her that he loved her and could not live without her. He asked her to be his wife.

Agathe-Louise wrote to tell Monsieur Yon that she would be very pleased to become the Vicomtesse du Barry, and asked him to make the necessary arrangements as soon as possible.

*

Under the influence of Monsieur Yon the King cancelled his tentative approval and broke off negotiations with the du Barry family.

The Vicomte's letters and visits to Chaillot stopped abruptly.

Agathe-Louise was told nothing. She could not understand why Lolo had stopped visiting her and stopped writing to her.

She wrote in desperation to Monsieur Yon, asking him to find out if the Vicomte had been taken ill, begging him to tell her what had become of Lolo du Barry.

Monsieur Yon sent back a curt note.

Agathe-Louise stopped smiling. She stopped talking. She refused to eat. She would not brush her hair. She grew thin and made herself ill, mourning for her lost marriage. She refused to get out of bed. She grew thinner. The lustre went out of her black eyes. She wanted nothing but to be married and to escape from the prison of her convent. She feared she might spend her whole life behind locked doors.

She thought, Marriage is the only escape. Marriage, or I shall leave Sainte-Périne in my coffin.

The nuns jammed a metal funnel between her teeth and force-fed her. She wept and screamed and spat and sprayed food all over her bedclothes. She attacked the sisters with her fingernails.

'You must pull yourself together, Mademoiselle,' Soeur Fidelitas told her, 'or no one will want to love you.'

Agathe-Louise lay in bed praying that Lolo du Barry would walk through the door, but her prayers were not answered.

'No man ever loved a girl who would not brush her hair,' Soeur Caritas warned her.

Agathe-Louise scribbled another note to Monsieur Yon.

'I love Lolo,' she wrote, 'I shall never love anyone else.'

This time Monsieur Yon did not reply.

Agathe-Louise spent her days weeping. She was unable to sleep and the sisters of Chaillot began to fear for her sanity.

A month later the news reached Agathe-Louise by chance that the Vicomte du Barry had been married to a Mademoiselle de Tournon, a girl of great beauty who had no money. It was said that the King had given her a handsome dowry.

Agathe-Louise tore her hair, wailed all night, and fell into a new decline. The sisters of Chaillot began to fear for her life and made the decision to send for her mother.

When, as a matter of urgency, a new suitor was found, Agathe-Louise seemed to forget her failed romance and made a rapid and remarkable recovery.

'He is a nice young man,' Soeur Fidelitas told her, 'he is a soldier, you will like him.'

Agathe-Louise was introduced to the young man, and did like him. All was done through the proper channels. Monsieur Yon graciously gave his consent. Louis XV gave his approval – and then, out of nowhere, Agathe-Louise's mother appeared.

Her *mother*, whom she had never seen. Her *mother*, who she had thought was dead, whom they had repeatedly told her was buried twenty years ago. Her *mother*, who in all her life had never so much as written her a letter. And now she was standing smiling in the doorway, waiting to talk to her, wanting to come to her wedding, with her arms full of expensive-looking presents.

Agathe-Louise was curious to see her. At the same time she did not want to see her. She received Madame de Flaghac coolly, astonished that she was wearing a dress the colour of ripe tomatoes. But all the presents her mother showered on her now she was to be married did nothing to make up for twenty years in prison, twenty years of being locked away, twenty years of being forgotten.

Agathe-Louise asked a lot of questions that her mother did not particularly want to answer.

'Who is my father?' she demanded.

'Why have I never seen him?'

'Who is Monsieur de Flaghac?'

'How many sisters do I have?'

'What have you been doing these twenty years?'

Madame de Flaghac spread her hands helplessly and answered Agathe-Louise in the vaguest of terms, but she kept on asking about her father.

'What is his name?' she demanded. 'Is he Monsieur de Flaghac? Is he Monsieur de Saint-André? When shall I see him?'

'What is a croissant?'

'What is a pineapple like?'

'What is it like to see the sea?'

Madame de Flaghac explained as well as she could. To the last question she had no answer. She did not know.

'I have never seen the sea either!' she said. The tears poured down her face. She put her arms round Agathe-Louise and they clung to each other, and the tears gradually turned into laughter.

On 29 December 1773 Mademoiselle de Saint-Antoine de Saint-André was married at the church of the Madeleine in Paris to Colonel René-Jean Mans de La Tour du Pin, Marquis de La Charce.

The bride's mother sat with her sister, Brigitte, both of them dressed identically in silver silk and silver lace, smiling, happy, the only relatives on the bride's side of the church.

Agathe-Louise was resplendent in a dress of cloth of silver, embroidered with silver, and a cloak of silver-lace. Her mother was alarmed to see that Agathe-Louise was wearing six strands of pearls, the gift of her father.

During the ceremony Agathe-Louise noticed that the Marquis de La Charce had spots on his face, and found herself thinking that Lolo du Barry did not have any spots but a perfectly clear skin.

She went to the altar in total ignorance of what went on beneath a man's *pantalons* or what would happen on her marriage bed.

'No one told me about *this*,' she declared to the Marquis in the middle of her wedding night.

'*Oo la la*,' she exclaimed in the dark, 'I did not know that this would happen.'

Although her mother had promised to visit and promised to write letters, she had had no chance to whisper in her daughter's ear. Agathe-Louise was, after all, a complete stranger.

In the New Year the smiling Marquise de La Charce was presented at Court, coruscating in canary-yellow silk. Her diamonds glittered. She had put on weight. Her black eyes sparkled again.

Louis XV, presented with the mirror-image of himself, was overcome with emotion, shed tears , embraced his daughter, and had to tell her who he was.

Freed from captivity, the Marquise gorged herself on all the forbidden fruits that never passed the portals of the Couvent de

Sainte-Périne: strawberries, avocados, pineapples, sugar-plums, truffles, chocolate, pâtisserie. She put on more weight. She discovered alcohol and spent the afternoons crashing into her gilded furniture, knocking over golden tables, breaking her wedding presents, smashing priceless Sèvres vases.

After a few weeks of marriage Agathe-Louise realized that she had no feelings for René-Jean Mans de La Tour du Pin.

'I do not love him,' she wrote to her mother. 'I shall never love him.'

The Marquis' spots had turned into angry boils. He did not often wash. His stubble scratched her face. She decided she did not care for what he liked to do in bed at night.

'I do not like his sticky fumblings,' she wrote to her mother. 'I do not like the Marquis' spit in my mouth. I do not like slime.'

She found herself hankering after a return to the regular routine, the calm, quiet, ordered life of the convent at Chaillot.

She sat in her boudoir drinking *vin de champagne* and dreaming of Lolo du Barry. At night she lay awake with the dead weight of the Marquis de La Charce on top of her, trying to fit his tongue into her mouth. She thought of Lolo. She thought that to be in bed with the Vicomte du Barry would be quite different. She dreamed that Lolo was jingling his spurs under her window, ready to run away with her.

The rich food made Agathe-Louise feel bloated and ill, and disagreed violently with her digestion.

The Marquis told his fellow-officers, 'My wife never smiles.'

Agathe-Louise began to grow so stout that her mother asked if she were not expecting a child.

Agathe-Louise shook her head.

'I do not wish to bear the Marquis a child,' she said. '*Never.*'

She stopped eating again, trying to grow thin, and grew hollow-eyed. Her husband ignored her. He had the handsome dowry. He was busy enjoying the laughing ladies of the Palais-Royal.

Agathe-Louise pined for Lolo du Barry for four more months and though her mother visited her every day she could do nothing to raise her spirits.

On 7 September 1774 Madame de Flaghac dressed Agathe-Louise in the cloth of silver wedding dress and rode with her in a coal-black carriage pulled by coal-black horses to bury her in the church of Saint-Sulpice, followed by a gliding procession of all the girls and nuns of the convent at Chaillot, the only family Agathe-Louise had ever known.

Madame de Flaghac and her sister, prostrated with grief, wept beneath black veils.

Agathe-Louise, drunk on champagne, had sprinkled her strawberries not with sugar but with arsenic and died horribly, retching, doubled up, shrieking, and alone.

The rumour spread that she had done it on purpose.

Agathe-Louise had not long profited from her meeting with her father: she spent the last three months of her life wearing Court mourning.

In February 1774 Louis XV had celebrated his sixty-fourth birthday. He was obese, tormented by dyspepsia. Latterly he gave up overeating, avoided pâtisserie, and submitted to a régime of Vichy water, but his good health had vanished. So had his reputation. He was no longer Louis the Well-Beloved.

In Lent the Abbé Beauvais preached vehement sermons in the chapel at Versailles against the vice and debauchery of the Court. He thundered on the subject of death, the subject that should have been unmentionable.

'Death is ever-present,' he shouted, 'death is coming closer.'

The Abbé disguised his remarks on Louis' own conduct as a commentary on the life of King Solomon. The Court watched the King turn pale. When the Abbé roared, 'Only forty days and Nineveh will be destroyed', they watched Louis tremble.

At the end of April Louis fell ill with pains in his head, nausea, aching all over. His eyes were like dried prunes.

The doctors diagnosed a simple fever, bled him, installed him on a camp-bed of crimson damask, and told him there was nothing seriously wrong with him. But whatever was wrong, it began to look increasingly like malignant confluent smallpox of the most dangerous kind: 'black smallpox.'

No one could say quite how Louis caught the disease except that he had caught it. It took him a fortnight to die.

Fourteen medical gentlemen waited on him – six doctors, five surgeons, three apothecaries – and a crowd of valets, pages and courtiers, amid complete chaos.

The King, depressed, put his tongue out fourteen times for the fourteen doctors. He had his pulse taken fourteen times, night and morning. It was not necessary to be a doctor to tell what was wrong with him: everyone knew what the illness was except the patient.

The first eruptions of the skin made their appearance and the news leaked out, echoing down the corridors of the château.

The royal house of France, alone of all the royal houses of Europe, had not bothered to have themselves inoculated against smallpox, and none of its members had had the disease.

On 3 May Louis asked for a mirror and discovered that the doctors had not told him the truth.

'At my age,' he said, 'one never recovers from smallpox. It is necessary to put my house in order.'

He sent Madame du Barry away and made preparations for his confession. His face began to turn black.

On 6 May Louis made his peace with his Maker. The princes, pocket-watch in hand, said his confession lasted just seventeen minutes. Drums beat the arrival of the *saint sacrement*, brought from the chapel in a procession of great solemnity. The clergy, bishops, the royal family, the ministers of state all followed behind, bearing lighted tapers, until the whole Court knelt in the King's chamber.

Louis was reported to have said, 'If God pays the honour of a visit to such a wretch as myself, the least I can do is to receive him with respect.'

He threw off his bedclothes, tried to kneel down, pulled off his nightcap, put his hands together with a piety that touched the hearts of those that saw it, and brought tears to their eyes.

His face grew blacker. His body began to give off a repulsive stench. The windows of the chamber were kept constantly open. Flies buzzed in circles, their buzzing often the only sound apart from the King's laboured breathing and the ticking of the clock.

The valets, bearers of food, emptiers of chamber-pots, and carriers of water, stayed at their posts. They tried not to breathe in, stood as close to the windows as they could, and dosed themselves with anything that might keep them alive. Nonetheless, fifty people in the château caught smallpox, and ten of them died of it.

The Comte d'Ayat, now sixteen years old and finding all his red uniforms too tight – who had been inoculated at his mother's insistence five years before – spent the first ten days in May squashing flies in the Chambre du Roi. He wrote to tell his mother the news of the King's illness.

D'Ayat moved fast among the whispered conversations. His rolled-up *Gazette de France*, now a fly-swatter, beat the air. The smack of his hand rang round a room full of courtiers who firmly believed that d'Ayat was witnessing the death of his own father.

Louis XV lay on his camp-bed surrounded by candles, his face a mask of bronze, his eyes encrusted with pustules, his mouth hanging open, breathing with difficulty.

The room buzzed. The gold clock ticked. The Bishop of Senlis intoned prayers in Latin. In the distance d'Ayat could hear laughter. Throughout the château there was general indifference to the King's slow fading-away, even a kind of hilarity. The setting sun was forgotten: they could only think of the sun that was about to rise.

They found the waiting rather tiresome.

In the evenings the Comte d'Ayat, half-suffocated, netted and trapped the bats that flew in through the windows. He swatted the moths that lurched drunkenly round the candles.

He sent regular bulletins to his mother at Flaghac.

He wrote, 'The *stink* is disgusting.'

He placed bets on how long the King would last out. He listened to the ticking of the clock, to the click of heels on the parquet. The King would die as he had lived, as he had been born – in public. He would die in the middle of a crowded room, friendless, with no one to hold his hand.

D'Ayat wrote to his mother that Louis had terrible visions, believed himself to be surrounded by the flames of Hell, that he kept throwing off his bedclothes and demanding Holy Water to be sprinkled over his body.

'He is nearly dead,' d'Ayat wrote. 'He is *rotting*.'

At the end there were some fifty courtiers on their knees round the camp-bed. Handkerchiefs held to their faces performed the dual function of wiping away real or unreal tears, and smothering the stench.

The King's face was blacker still, crusted. He was a black man in a white nightcap. The prayers droned on and on.

Through the windows d'Ayat watched the night, the blue-black sky with the stars bright in it. The moths circled, dived into the candle flames, sizzled and crackled; suicide moths that could not help themselves from flying into the fire, burning themselves up, incapable of doing anything different. The Bishop waved them grandly away but the moths kept settling on his book of prayers. Moths landed on Louis' blackened nose and flexed their wings on his barnacled hands.

D'Ayat thought, The moth is the soul leaving the body.

Morning came with the smack of the *Gazette*, the crowing cockerel, hours and hours of ticking. Then everyone held their breath, as if some miracle had happened, and the Bishop's voice, still intoning, stopped in mid-sentence, and someone stopped the clock.

At three-fifteen on the afternoon of Tuesday 10 May the very high, very mighty and very excellent prince Louis XV expired.

The fourteen doctors took the royal pulse one more time to make sure.

The Comte d'Ayat threw down his newspaper, now in shreds, and fled from the room like everyone else. He ran down the stairs into the Cour de Marbre and vomited on the cobbles.

The new King, Louis XVI, and Queen Marie-Antoinette, still in quarantine from the smallpox in their apartments, then heard the famous hubbub: a terrible noise like thunder, the drubbing of feet on the famous parquet of Versailles – the Court fleeing the stink of the old King to be first to salute his nineteen-year-old grandson.

Heavy red-heeled shoes pounded, scraped and scratched the floor. Some of the runners fell, some slipped, some were pushed; delicate ankles suffered sprains and fractures. A few white hands were trampled. The château echoed with shouts of *'Vive le Roi'*, making the Comte d'Ayat think of the pandemonium of the rooks at Ayat.

166

To his mother he wrote just three words: 'Himself is *dead.*'

The old King they buried simply, according to his strict instructions. They stuffed the body, too decomposed and too disgusting to embalm, into its coffin with a cement made of quicklime and vinegar and camphorated spirits of wine.

The smell refused to go away.

Two days later began the journey to Saint-Denis, by the simplest mode of transport available – as he had instructed – which happened to be the three carriages Louis had formerly used for hunting.

The coffin travelled in the first coach under a pall of black velvet embellished with gold. As the cortège left the château the people of Versailles shouted – as they usually did when they saw this carriage of all carriages – 'Tally-ho! Tally-ho!' and cheered him on his last journey.

D'Ayat rode with him among the pages, holding his handkerchief over his nose.

During the year the new King was vaccinated against the smallpox and the Comte d'Ayat discovered girls.

On Tuesday 10 May at three-fifteen in the afternoon all Madame de Flaghac's clocks began to chime, and then stopped altogether.

Her diamond-studded timepiece seized up. In the back of it, under glass, a precious souvenir lay coiled like a watch-spring: a pubic hair of Louis XV.

In a gold ring set with emeralds she had preserved bright orange wax from the royal ears.

Set in a gold locket glittering with sapphires, she had conserved the royal toe-clippings, brittle yellow moons to light up her firmament.

No Irishwoman could think of the stopping of clocks as anything but a meaningful concurrence of events. She knew in her heart before d'Ayat's letter arrived. Cold shivers rippled down her spine. At night she tucked herself tighter into her ivory silk sheets, against all the things that disturbed her sleep.

By the end of the week she could think of nothing but Louis. Himself. His image loomed up wherever she looked. He materialized in her head when she shut her eyes. She did not know how to get rid of him.

She saw the King making his way across the fields that surrounded her château. She passed him coming down the grand staircase. She watched him walking along the carriage-drive. She recognized his features on the face of every man she met, accusing her, as if he had come back to annoy and delight her, to be with her all the time, as she had always wanted.

His face leered at her from the coins in her weasel-skin purse until she flung them all away.

She saw his shadow move behind her. She saw him in the mirror as she arranged her hair. She saw him grinning over her shoulder, lowering his silk *pantalons*, ripping off his velvet coat, tossing his clothes all over the floor.

There was never anyone there: only the quiet closing of a door, a shutter blowing in the wind, the flutter of pigeons above the window frame.

She wept a little. She noticed that lines were beginning to appear on her face, that she was out of breath after running up the stairs.

Alone with her thoughts, she hid the damage to her face under miracle-working creams. She increased her expenditure on cosmetics.

She fled Flaghac for Paris and kept the twelve volumes of *La Sainte Bible* in gilt red morocco beside her bed, ready to throw if Louis XV, King of France and Navarre, came to haunt her again.

XIV

A month after the old King died the Comte d'Ayat removed
Louis XVI's right-hand slipper for the last time. According to
custom he went to take his leave of the monarch.

The new King barely acknowledged d'Ayat's existence. He
made a slight nod in his direction, though it might have been a
movement he would have made in any case: some tic, something
irritating him inside his collar; some trouble with his neck.

D'Ayat bowed his stiff bow and walked backwards out of the
Chambre du Roi thinking, He cannot even be bothered to say *au
revoir*. He made his farewells to the Governor of the Pages and
to his fellow men. He wiped the yellow-grey dust of Versailles
off his riding-boots.

He left the City of the Sun with polished manners, a skilled
fencer, a superb horseman, but with fewer morals, few scruples,
and with something indefinable smouldering inside him.

He made the usual transition into the army, as a sub-lieutenant
in the regiment of his godfather, the Maréchal de Soubise.

Madame de Flaghac had already written a dozen letters to the
Prince, urging him to treat her son like any other sub-lieutenant.

The Prince laughed as he read the letters. 'It was his mother I
was interested in,' he told his adjutant.

There were no favours and no favouritism. Soubise ignored
the Comte d'Ayat completely.

D'Ayat underwent the usual initiation rites, took everything in
his stride, and settled down to learn the art of death: the fine art
of killing.

He perfected the use of the bayonet. He became a crack shot.
He sat up late into the night studying the art of fortification and
the science of strategy. He wrote regularly to his mother, careful
to play the dutiful son, assuring her of his affection; not unmind-
ful of the question of her wealth and the matter of inheritance.

At nineteen d'Ayat was promoted to full lieutenant and

devoted the hours of darkness to the girls who haunted the Palais-Royal gardens.

At twenty-one he became a captain. He was scrupulous in obeying orders. His uniform was always spotless. He thought nothing of sleeping under canvas or under the stars. He did not mind standing out in the rain: he preferred to carry on building encampments, supervising the digging of defences, exercising his brain with problems of military engineering.

His fellow-officers found d'Ayat too keen. He was too pleased with himself. He was boastful. He tried too hard. He talked of horses all the time, which his colleagues found boring. On foot, he was a fish out of water. He should have been in the cavalry.

D'Ayat remained a captain for twelve years and found it hard to understand why his promotion never came.

Following the death of Louis XV the superfluous office of Receiver-General of Taxes of Paris created for Monsieur de Flaghac was suppressed and the 300,000 *livres* he had paid for it were refunded. The cascade of cash that had showered on the de Flaghacs suddenly dried up.

They lived rent-free next door to the Abbé Terray in return for services rendered. Madame de Flaghac, now thirty-eight, was received everywhere in the best society and was inundated with invitations. A police report of 1776 described her as the most handsome woman at Court, and as 'the vestal of all the ministers.' She was seen at Versailles going to and fro in the Rue de Surintendence between the office of the Comptroller-General of Finance and the office of another government official.

The Abbé Terray continued to pull strings. In due course François-Nicolas de Flaghac was made a Comte and his wife became a Comtesse again.

She celebrated her fortieth birthday by buying wonder-working lotions that were guaranteed to preserve her skin against the deleterious effects of old age and all the ravages of Time. She was at last presented at Court, in a black gown with a garniture of black gauze. She wore diamonds in her hair, diamonds in her ears, diamonds on her fingers, and a diamond girdle round her waist. She was still able to make Versailles gasp – a quarter of a century after her first appearance.

She kissed hands with smirking Ducs and winking Vicomtes.

She came and went by a front staircase instead of a back staircase. She spent her mornings in the jewellers' shops in the Rue du Faubourg Saint-Honoré in Paris, and increased her expenditure accordingly.

All thanks to the Abbé Terray. But in 1778 the Abbé died, before he could manage to become a cardinal. Hated alive and hated dead, he was buried at midnight to ensure that riots did not break out at his obsequies.

Among the Abbé's bequests was a dowry of 120,000 *livres* for his supposed daughter, Marguerite-Victoire de Flaghac.

Marguerite-Victoire, now aged ten, spent much of her time bent over the keys of her harpsichord. Her mother taught her how to smile. She taught her what would please men, and made her balance *Le Guide des Pécheurs* on her head in order to improve her deportment.

The Comtesse stayed on in the Rue Notre-Dame des Champs for some weeks but she kept catching glimpses of the Abbé Terray. The odour of garlic and onions lingered in every room. She threw Bibles, had the house exorcized, had masses said for the repose of the Abbé's soul, but he kept reappearing. When she could bear it no longer she bought an hôtel in the Rue Poissonière instead, where the ghost of the Comptroller-General did not follow her.

Here Marguerite-Victoire amused herself by collecting the black snails that crawled about the garden. She would put a snail on a silver plate full of flour before she went to bed, cover it with a silver meat cover, and leave it overnight. In the morning she inspected the silver trail left in the flour, which revealed the initial of the man she would marry. Her snails always traced a florid L that made her say 'Louis'.

'Louis Desaix,' she said to herself, 'Cousin Louis.'

Then, following family tradition, she would plunge the snails into boiling water and eat them for her *petit déjeuner*.

Her mother told her, 'The black snails are the spirits of the dead.' But Marguerite-Victoire took no notice.

The Comte de Flaghac kept rising in the world. He was appointed Maître d'Hôtel to the Comte d'Artois, the gambling, playboy prince, brother of Louis XVI. He purchased the office of

Treasurer of the Order of the Holy Ghost for 700,000 *livres*, a sum that dented his fortune hardly at all. He purchased the office of Treasurer of the Marc d'Or. His new offices brought him almost limitless wealth, and all the prestige that went with the first order of chivalry of the monarchy.

Three times a year he walked in procession with the Chevaliers of the Order of the Holy Ghost, wearing the brilliant costume embroidered with *fleurs-de-lis* and flames.

His head swelled slightly. He strutted in a new coat of mole-coloured silk embroidered with silver, and boasted of his achievements.

His head also swelled with something other than pride, and he was forced to visit the spa of Bagnères in search of the restoration of his health.

By 1780 he had recovered only indifferently and was still living on whiting, invalid's food. But the torrent of cash was flowing again and the Flaghacs regularly received substantial sums: 340,000 *livres* of rents, a further payment of 500,000 *livres*, another windfall of 150,000 *livres*. They did not always know what to do with the money. They bought several châteaux. In 1781 they had all their ceilings gilded, and purchased gold knives and forks.

The Comte de Flaghac spent a further year living on perch, sick man's fish. His doctors predicted that he would be dead in six months and advised him to make his will.

Flaghac ignored the advice, stayed often at Bagnères, and continued to build his empire. He bought estates here and there; he invested in money-making schemes; he thought constantly of ways of increasing his fortune.

The Comtesse was seen more often in Versailles, gliding back and forth between the château and a new apartment, where the Comte cruised from room to room in his wheelchair, employed half a dozen black footmen and ate off gold plates.

Meanwhile his stepson, the Comte d'Ayat, remained a captain. In 1782 the 'charming young man of twenty-five' was introduced to an Italian gentleman in his fifties, a Signor Casanova, at Fontainebleau, where d'Ayat was part of the royal guard.

He was the identical copy of his mother, with hair like straw under his wig, and blue eyes, not an Auvergnat at all. He wore a piece of blue thread round his neck. Casanova asked him what it was for.

'For good luck,' d'Ayat explained, 'it's an old Irish custom.'

Casanova asked whether he knew his mother's history. The Comte shook his head, curious to know why the Italian's eyes were laughing, and what he meant.

'I don't think it is my place to tell you . . .' Casanova said, smiling, but he reeled out the story all the same, full of mistakes, full of inventions, and he included his own speculations on the matter of the Comte d'Ayat's paternity.

Afterwards d'Ayat left him and walked into the gardens alone, his mind boiling. He picked up stones, flung them into the fountains, and wandered into the distance, thinking, with all his questions answered.

On 24 April 1783 François-Nicolas Lenormand de Flaghac was buried in his seigneurial chapel. His widow sat dry-eyed in Paris, ignoring the existence of death. She wore black for twelve months but refused to take off her diamonds.

In the Rue Poissonière she wandered from room to room, alone, thinking that she was at last free. The ghost of her husband stayed away from her.

Marguerite-Victoire's fingers danced endlessly over the black and white keys of her harpsichord while she thought about her cousin Louis Desaix, aged fifteen, bound for a military career.

Her mother noticed that Marguerite-Victoire had begun to smile like the Abbé Terray and told her to stop it at once.

The widowed Comtesse, free of the shadow of the Abbé Terray, free of the Comte de Flaghac, occupied her evenings entertaining the Maître de Requêtes, Monsieur Jean-Marie-Antoine-Claude de Valdec de Lessart. She encouraged her children to regard Valdec de Lessart as the gentleman who helped her with her finances, not as her lover. The affair was supposed to be a secret.

Valdec de Lessart was thirty-seven in the year the Abbé Terray died. He bathed regularly. He was fastidiously clean. He was handsome, warm, kind, well-intentioned, everything the Abbé was not. His face was smooth, unmarked by smallpox, still unmarked by worry.

He had plenty to worry about. He worried about his work. He

worried about finances, accounts, foreign exchange. He worked constantly, taking his career wherever he went, spending hours making calculations on minute scraps of paper as he lay in bed with the Comtesse.

His nails were bitten down, with nothing left to bite, but he went on biting them. The Comtesse laughed at him.

'If you bite your nails,' she said, 'your hands will fall off!'

She grew fond of him. It felt strange. It was not what she was used to. She cursed herself for having allowed it to happen, not knowing where it would lead, but not caring either. She grew attached to him. She watched her clocks, counting the hours till Valdec de Lessart would reappear, with none of the heaviness of heart she had felt in the Parc-aux-Cerfs. She thought about him constantly. She felt warm inside in a way she had only rarely, only momentarily felt warm before. She thought this must be what people meant when they spoke of falling in love.

She found herself serving Valdec de Lessart fried artichokes. She occasionally drank chocolate laced with triple vanilla and ambergris.

'*Lézard*, she said, kissing him, thinking he tasted nice, thinking of the past.

At the same time the Comtesse was locked in a bitter battle with Jean-Jacques de Flaghac over her late husband's estate.

'It was through me that Monsieur de Flaghac enriched himself!' she told her lawyers. 'Without me he would have been nothing but a tax official in the Auvergne all his life.'

She grew angry. 'It is my money, Messieurs!' she shouted. 'It is my earnings!'

Even so, she was not short of cash. The Court jewellers, Boehmer et Rouen, visited her once a week bearing velvet-lined trays of treasures: ropes of emeralds, ruby earrings, diamond tiaras, diamond necklaces, diamond pins, and strings of pearls.

The pearls she would never touch, but she was unable to resist anything else. She spent as if she had all the money in the world, as if there was no tomorrow, and plastered herself with wonder-working creams to preserve her body in eternal youth.

The Comte d'Ayat, aged twenty-six, still vegetated in the rank of captain. In 1783 he married Mademoiselle Marie-Anne Guyot de Mongrau, who came complete with the all-important dowry of 160,000 *livres*. She had a mane of black hair, a complexion like a china doll, the wild spirit that d'Ayat so admired in a horse, and a wild spirit between the sheets that excited him. He looked forward to making his wife dance in the way he made his horses dance: she was tameable, manageable, just what he wanted.

Her family he could not tame. The Guyots made it clear that they intended to pay the dowry by instalments, starting in 1794, the eleventh year of the marriage.

The Comte d'Ayat, red-faced with anger, spent a morning shouting at his lawyers, and an afternoon in grim negotiation with the Guyot lawyers, but he failed to talk them out of their determination to hang on to their capital.

He shrugged his shoulders at last and said, 'It does not matter much. My mother is a wealthy woman.'

The Comtesse de Flaghac remarked, 'To be sure, the Guyot de Mongrau have plenty of business sense . . .'

At the wedding breakfast there was a frostiness in the atmosphere. The Guyots glared and made remarks and looked down their noses at the Irish relations. All the food was eaten inside eighteen minutes, and the Murphy family was with some difficulty prevented from throwing the remains of the pâtisserie at the family of the bride.

When the Irish relatives brought out their fiddles and the Comte's Aunt Brigitte began to dance a hornpipe on the tables, the bride's family made their excuses and fled.

In 1784 the Comte d'Ayat was granted the privilege of riding in the King's carriage, and his wife began to sew tiny clothes embroidered with the *fleurs-de-lis* of the Bourbons.

The Comtesse her mother-in-law advised her to avoid eating potatoes at night if she wished her baby to be born with a small head, but her daughter-in-law was repelled by the idea of eating potatoes at any time.

In the following year Monsieur Parmentier the agriculturist presented the potato at Court and was rewarded with the honour of kissing the hand of Marie-Antoinette.

Louis XVI wore a potato-flower in his buttonhole for some days in an attempt to popularize the consumption of a vegetable that had for too long been regarded as fit only for peasants and animals to consume.

Louis laughed. The potato had made its début at Court thirty years before, the protégé of Marie-Louise Murphy. Now he was expected to see it as something entirely new. He chewed his *pommes de terre à la Parmentier* distastefully, unable to understand what all the fuss was about.

The rage was for striped clothes: striped *pantalons*, striped dresses, waistcoats and stockings, in honour of the King's zebra, lately arrived in the royal menagerie at Versailles. The rage was for anything new.

Madame de Flaghac accordingly wore stripes of pink and red. The Comte d'Ayat wore stripes of black and white, like the zebra himself.

The Beaufranchet baby was born, dressed in stripes of black and white like his father, and before he had had an opportunity to smile, was buried in them.

The old Comtesse's time passed quickly. She spent money, she hired servants; she entertained lavishly and frequented nothing but the best society. She supervised Marguerite-Victoire's further education; and then Marguerite-Victoire was eighteen, and her hand was sought by the Comte de Chousy, a cavalry officer whose family was high in favour at Versailles.

Given a choice, Marguerite-Victoire would have married her cousin Louis Desaix, despite his baleful looks.

'His face is not important,' she told her mother, 'I don't care what Louis looks like. I happen to love him. I shall never love anyone else.'

But Louis Desaix had not asked Marguerite-Victoire to marry him. He was more often than not abroad with his regiment. He was a penniless lieutenant with no title and no position in society.

Marguerite-Victoire was not given a choice.

'If you fall in love,' her mother warned, 'your heart will break.'

Marguerite-Victoire sulked, wept, and slammed doors for a month.

'You only get the one chance,' said her mother, 'and this is it, and you must take it.'

Marguerite-Victoire had to do as she was told.

'It is money that matters, Mademoiselle,' the Comtesse told her daughter, '*money*. And Louis Desaix has no money.'

Marguerite-Victoire shrugged her shoulders, calmed down, and in due course Louis XVI himself, Marie-Antoinette, and all the royal family signed their names to her marriage contract.

In the evening after the signing the Comtesse de Flaghac, wearing cramoisie silk taffeta and all the diamonds she possessed, was the hostess at a glittering reception in the Rue Poissonière. Some of her guests murmured at the oddity of the de Chousys' wish to be allied to a family of such recent nobility as the de Flaghacs, and to a family of such doubtful origins as the Murphys de Boisfailly. But the Flaghacs had their châteaux and their royal connections, and their fabulous fortune.

No one told the de Chousys that their prospective daughter-in-law was the illegitimate child of the much-despised Abbé Terray, but they were well aware of who and what Madame de Flaghac was and what she had been. They made no objection.

'Marguerite-Victoire has money,' said Chousy *père*, 'and nothing else matters.'

Marguerite-Victoire was her mother's daughter, not – the Comtesse was relieved – her father's, not the identical copy of the Abbé Terray. She was reputed to be the wildest girl in Paris, and the de Chousy fortune was one of the largest in France.

The Comtesse de Chousy's diamonds sparkled. Her face glowed. She knew that she did not love the Comte de Chousy and never would, but for the day of her wedding she pretended that she did.

Madame de Flaghac's diamonds glittered in the light of her crystal chandeliers. Her house was packed with the cream of the nobility. The pyramids of food on her tables had been prepared by the most fashionable chefs in Paris. Her hand had been kissed by the King and the princes and all the royal family. She had enhanced her complexion with red lead mixed with carmine to produce bright spots of colour on her cheeks. She had made up her eyes with lamp-black and used white lead to make her face whiter. She was dressed in the height of fashion, with ostrich feathers towering in her headdress. Her hands were still free of liver spots. She could have passed for thirty.

She thought, in the middle of her gilded salon, among the brittle laughter of the best society in Paris, receiving the homage of half the nobility, that she had travelled a long way since she left Rouen at the age of six.

Her eyes flashed and shone across the room from man to man, watching, moving from face to face, wondering where fate would take her next. But her gaze always returned to the figure of Valdec de Lessart, tall, handsome, distinguished, in a silvery wig and a flame-coloured velvet suit embroidered with silver braid, and lined with chocolate silk.

Rumours about the widowed Comtesse persisted. People whispered about her secret marriage to Valdec de Lessart. The Comte d'Ayat thought it more likely that she had refused to marry him. She did not want to be married to anyone. She would not surrender her liberty. Nothing was going to tie her down ever again. For the first time in her life she was free to do as she liked.

But it was true that she had fallen in love with Valdec de Lessart.

Tired of watching time ticking away she sold her gold clocks and put the proceeds into a property of her own, that no one could take away from her, where no one could tell her what to do.

The Château de Soisy was in the country, but near enough to Paris to be convenient for entertaining. It was not damp, or old, or cold, or too big.

It was built of honey-coloured stone, with a drawbridge, a moat full of goldfish, a *pigeonnier* full of white doves, alleys of poplars, and woods of Bordeaux pines. There were twin gatehouses, a ferryman's house, rooms with gilded mirrors and handsome parquet floors. There were white-and-gold salons full of gilded furniture and sumptuous beds hung with silver damask. There were flushing water-closets of the latest design. It was like Versailles in miniature. Her dream had come true.

There was so much box hedge that the Comtesse employed half the village of Soisy to clip it. In the kitchens and cellars she employed the other half of the village, in cooking, cleaning, labouring, fetching and carrying.

She paid 208,000 *livres*, in cash.

At Noël she distributed coals, logs, bread and meat to the poor. She gave money for the upkeep of the church. She was serenaded by singers with drums and bagpipes. She sent soup and linen to women in childbed. No one was turned away from her door. She sent her cast-off clothes to the village so they could be altered to fit the little girls.

The people of Soisy took her for an angel and came up to touch her to make sure she was real. They frequently knelt at the château gates waiting for her to make her appearance.

Two liveried footmen carried her about Soisy in a pink and gold sedan-chair with pink silk curtains and decorated with a Cupid and golden bows and arrows. She smiled and waved wherever she went. Everywhere people were charmed and fell in love with her.

Shortly after the purchase of Soisy the Comte d'Ayat's wife presented Madame de Flaghac with a new grandchild to replace the one that had died. They called her Anne-Pauline-Victoire. The Comte spat on her as the Comtesse his mother insisted he must.

'For good luck!' he said.

But the Comtesse d'Ayat was disgusted by the barbaric custom.

In July there was a tremendous storm of hail and thunder, the worst in living memory. The Comtesse de Flaghac ran frantically through the château slamming the shutters shut and turning the golden mirrors to face the walls.

In August the heat was so intense that it dried up the moat, revealing generations of discarded shoes and leaving the goldfish flipping about in thick, stinking mud until they died of exhaustion.

In September the cold was sufficient to make the Comtesse wear a heavy silk cloak and sit by a blazing fire all day. In the absence of Valdec de Lessart in Paris she invited Brigitte Murphy de Boisfailly to keep her company. They slept in the same bed to keep warm, as they had done throughout their childhood. They clung together for fear of the dark, for fear of burglars, for fear of being alone, for fear of thunder and lightning, for fear of ghosts, for fear of the banshee, for fear of death.

And in the morning they laughed at their fears and forgot about them.

The sisters settled down and made themselves comfortable. The Comtesse was presented with a second grandchild, Alexandre-Édouard-Marguerite de Beaufranchet d'Ayat. There was another severe winter, then floods, then drought, then another great hailstorm almost a year to the day after the one before. And then the Comtesse was fifty, and allowed herself to lie about her age.

On summer afternoons she walked in the pleached alleys past statues of Juno and Ceres, under blue skies, wearing her emeralds. She sat in her gardens smiling, under a red silk parasol, wearing her rubies, dressed in flame-coloured silk taffeta, accompanied by Valdec de Lessart, or by Brigitte, or with her grandchildren clinging to her skirts.

White doves warbled and flew endlessly upward. Peacocks screamed, butterflies settled on her jewelled hands. White cows browsed in her lush pastures. Scores of gardeners endlessly clipped her hedges into fantastic shapes: chicken shapes, turkey shapes, spherical potato shapes, *fleur-de-lis* shapes, and rows of fat green pigeons.

The Comtesse felt that nothing could interfere with her peace of mind, or her happiness, or her financial security. She filled her château with pink roses from the gardens and calmly contemplated the prospect of her old age spent in quiet and comfort, with Jean-Marie-Antoine-Claude de Valdec de Lessart – married to her or not – by her side.

XV

Madame de Flaghac's world turned slowly upside down. At first she took little notice of the riots. Then the Bastille fell. The Great Fear followed behind and her world fell with it, and she did not know what any of it meant, or where any of it would end, except that everything she had thought secure was threatened; everything she had thought safe was in danger.

She boiled the turkey feet night after night, and chewed and chewed before she went to bed, but still lay awake worrying, her mind full of horrors.

The Château de Soisy was stuffed full of gilt, gilded and silver-gilt *objets d'art* and priceless antiques. It had become almost overnight a liability, something she must dispose of as quickly as she could; something that endangered her life.

She had formerly felt in control of her future; now she felt it sliding away, slipping through her fingers. She dreamed that she was walking on ice, unable to stand up, falling through the ice into cold black water, deeper than she could imagine.

'It is not safe to be rich,' she said to Brigitte. They clung together more tightly at night, and sat in the dark behind bolted doors.

She spent longer and longer in bed, hoping the troubles might pass her by, would go away if she did not look, if she did not think about them, if she did not show her face in public.

'It is not safe to go out,' she told Brigitte. They kept the shutters locked and pretended the château was unoccupied.

Then the Revolution came as far as the gates of the château, threatened to break them down and make its way up her gilded staircase and into her white and gold salon, and lay its hands on her person and break her in pieces.

She could stay in bed no longer. She put away her dozens of silk dresses in all the colours between salmon-pink and brilliant red. Instead she wore simple clothes of mud-brown, sludge-green, and dust-grey. She splashed them with food, tore at them to make them look old, ripped at sleeves and hems, and turned herself into a woman of the people.

She smeared mud on her hands and rubbed coal-dust into her face. She went out, when she had to, wearing a battered straw hat and dung-coloured shoes, battered and scuffed, looking like one of her own servants.

The servants themselves wandered off to join the rioters in cities, to seek their fortunes in the revolutionary armies, as members of mobs, as looters of shops, and as spectators beside the guillotine.

People of the Comtesse's class left France or tried to cling to what was theirs for as long as they could, and then were swept away by the flood. The deluge. She thought of Louis. Now she dared not even say his name. Now she was afraid to use her own name. She dropped the particle so eagerly, so easily assumed: the *de* of de Flaghac. Then she abandoned Flaghac itself. She jettisoned *de Boisfailly*, the bogus appendage, a place that had never existed. She forbade anyone to use her title.

'Call me *Murphy*,' she told her acquaintances, 'just *Murphy*.'

She scratched her coat of arms off the pink carriage and painted it black. She went back to the life she had led before the arrival of the dream, before the nightmare of Versailles had overtaken her.

'I am not French at all,' she told her neighbours, 'I have not one drop of French blood. I am Irish, *irlandaise*!'

No one believed her.

'You are French,' they laughed, 'you are lying, Citoyenne.' They looked at her strangely and made her feel uncomfortable.

The gardeners abandoned Soisy in search of less controversial employment. The clipped hedges grew unchecked; the topiary peacocks and pigeons turned into ragged, unidentifiable monsters; the vegetable gardens ran to seed; the lawns grew waist-high. Nature set at liberty ran riot, like the Nation.

Army officers resigned and emigrated as a matter of honour, vowing to enlist in foreign armies and restore the monarchy of France when they could. The Comte d'Ayat refused to resign. He stayed with his regiment and was quick to advertise his revolutionary sympathies.

He received small packets of white feathers through the post.

Émigré officers sent him abusive letters reproving him for his recalcitrance, accusing him of cowardice and lack of loyalty to the royal family.

But d'Ayat felt no loyalty to the royal family, 'the tyrants,' as he called them, and his revolutionary fervour only increased. He discovered that a soldier with fifteen years' service was a man that the revolutionary army had some use for at last: a man who might be promoted. The Revolution was what d'Ayat had been waiting for. He was a revolutionary at heart.

He stopped using his title, and in 1790 he was appointed to a committee at the Ministry of War for the reform of the cavalry.

The authorities had realized that he knew something about horses.

In 1791 he was transferred to a cavalry regiment and made a lieutenant-colonel. His superiors consulted his opinion on the incidence of anthrax in horses and were impressed by his spectacular cure for equine dyspepsia.

Before the year was out he was promoted to full colonel of the Second Carabiniers, and covered himself with glory and other men's blood at the taking of Menin and Courtrai.

He dropped the '*de Beaufranchet*' from his name and became loud in his condemnation of the aristocracy.

Then he dropped his apostrophe and started calling himself *Dayat*.

He made a point of informing his fellow-officers that his mother was the daughter of a shoemaker. His colleagues laughed in disbelief.

'Your mother is a Comtesse!' they said. 'You are lying!'

Colonel Dayat worried about it.

Later, he abandoned his Christian name.

'I cannot be called *Louis* any more,' he told his mother.

'I shall call you Charles, then,' she said.

'No,' he said, 'you must call me *Citoyen*, Citoyen Dayat.'

He burned all his wigs and wore his own hair, growing it longer and wilder, like a haystack.

He poured away anything that could be classed as scent. He washed less and went about smelling of honest sweat, like a true *sans-culotte*.

He ground his gold-handled lorgnette beneath the heels of his riding-boots.

He snapped his silver-topped cane in two and threw it on the fire.

He stopped bowing to ladies in the street. He stopped kissing hands. He gave up all decadent activities that were unworthy of a revolutionary.

He worried about the ownership of property, and decided to pretend that Ayat did not exist, or belonged to some other, distant branch of the family.

'Property is all right,' he told his mother, 'as long as you don't have too much.'

It was his mother who owned the châteaux; he thought that if the authorities arrested anyone they would arrest his mother, not him.

He worried about surplus wealth, but that too he could pretend not to have. He moved out of his grand Paris apartment into drab lodgings and began to live like a poor man. He instructed his mother to smash the glass in the gatehouse windows at Soisy and to burn anything of any value. He might yet keep his head fixed to his body; he might survive, and so might she.

Dayat gave up betting, gambling and billiards. He threw his playing-cards into the fire and watched Kings, Queens, Hearts and Diamonds slowly curl up in the flames, turn black and burn away into nothing.

He drank more, one of the things a *sans-culotte* was allowed to do. But he still worried. He was careful to drink only the cheapest wines, or the roughest whiskey. He gave up drinking champagne.

Citoyen Dayat rose on the tide of Revolution. His colleagues and most of his relations fled France, or tried to, but Colonel Dayat was promoted again and again. He kept on rising in the world, as if to prove that his mother's action in carrying him upstairs the moment he was born did, after all, have some meaning.

Valdec de Lessart rose also. In 1790 he found himself appointed Minister of Finance, the position once held by the Abbé Terray. He began to wear his own hair and cultivated a certain wildness of manner. He sat up late over his candles trying to balance the nation's accounts, making interminable calculations on vast sheets of paper, talking to himself, scratching his head and rumpling his hair.

In 1791 he became Minister of the Interior and sat up into the small hours writing letters, chewing his quill, trying to make sense of the mess that his country had fallen into, and failing to make any sense of it.

In the same year he was appointed Minister for Foreign Affairs and worked till dawn dictating letters to foreign embassies, shuffling diplomatic papers, making sense of coded communiqués. He would stand brooding in front of the giant paintings representing Africa, Asia and America that hung in his office in the Rue de Surintendence, within a stone's throw of the château of Versailles, and worried about abroad.

In his spare moments he would address a brief message to 'Marie Murphy' at Soisy. He sent his love and his hopes, fearful of writing anything too personal lest his letters were intercepted; fearful of doing almost anything, thinking it was dangerous to write anything down.

Marie Murphy threw off her aristocratic habits, so laboriously acquired, so recently perfected. She stopped dabbing Eau de la Reine on her wrists and behind her ears. She no longer had her hair coiffured. She ordered Brestat, her *femme de chambre*, to cut it off at the neck, roughly, with the shears formerly used to clip the hedges. Brestat shed tears and did as she was told, and her mistress's golden hair crackled on the fire.

She wore her oldest, filthiest clothes. She hid away her gold knives and forks and ate with her fingers. In the mornings she worked in the vegetable gardens with Brigitte, seeking to give her hands the patina that would declare her to be a good *citoyenne*.

Brigitte wore cotton gloves and declared that she would rather die, rather go to the guillotine, than get her hands dirty.

Marie Murphy gave up smearing her face with lotions and creams to preserve her skin. She clipped and pruned in the sun all afternoon and began to acquire the red face and weatherbeaten look, the smoked-bacon colour that proved her to be a working woman.

'Not an aristocrat at all,' she said to Brigitte, but Brigitte stubbornly kept her face covered up lest the Revolution should come to a sudden end.

Brestat, the last remaining servant, was dismissed, and the two sisters moved into just one room with the roughest furniture they could find.

A week later Brestat returned to Soisy, tearful and dishevelled, with her dress ripped and filthy, saying, 'I cannot leave you, Madame.'

'I am not *Madame*,' said her mistress. 'I am *Murphy*, the gardener.'

But none of this altered the fact that Murphy was the owner of the château, of several châteaux, or that she was a Comtesse, or that she had links with the royal family and knew Versailles like the back of her hand.

None of her efforts to disguise herself altered the fact that all Soisy knew exactly who she was. It was impossible for her to pretend not to be herself.

To call herself the Comtesse de Flaghac seemed like an invitation for the authorities to arrest her. She began to wish she had never been married, never become a Comtesse, never been born.

'Call me *Murphy*,' she insisted, '*Citoyenne* Murphy.'

Revolutionaries burning châteaux came closer. Murphy went into her kitchen garden and burned all her finery: the Versailles dresses, the Court costumes embroidered with gold and silver lace. She burned the remains of her trousseau: the silk sheets with crowns in the corners, the red morocco trunks stamped with the insignia of the Bourbons, the hundreds of pairs of damask shoes with the toes embroidered with silver wire and heeled with solid gold. Everything went up in smoke by her own hand before it could be burned by anyone else, before it led to her own destruction.

She was finished with finery. She had had enough of society.

'Be yourself, Monsieur,' she told Colonel Dayat, 'don't pretend.'

'I am not *Monsieur*,' he said, raging, 'I am *Citoyen* Dayat.'

In the Château de Soisy Murphy, Brigitte and Citoyen Dayat ate nothing but potatoes baked in their jackets.

'*Pommes de terre dans leur robe de chambre*,' Murphy told her son. 'Food for peasants, food for revolutionaries.'

*

Murphy reclaimed her past, climbed back into it. She told her neighbours she was a clogmaker's daughter.

'No, Madame,' they said, 'you are one of the *seigneurs*.'

She still had her property in Paris, but Paris was too dangerous, not a place where she could hide. She was too well-known. She feared for her life, was afraid she would have to quit Soisy altogether.

Mobs of peasants rampaged closer. Murphy hid leather bags full of coins beneath the parquet. She said her prayers, making constant use of her rosary. She pulled white dust-sheets over the gilded furniture that she could not bring herself to burn. She closed the shutters and locked up the château.

As she glided down the carriage-drive she paused briefly to look back at Soisy: made of honey, made of pâtisserie, made of gingerbread, melting before her eyes. She thought of the mob by night with burning torches, setting it on fire. She did not want to be there to see the flames. She turned, with tears in her eyes, and walked on.

She left Brigitte Murphy installed as the *concierge* in one of the gatehouses: to keep an eye on the estate, to deter intruders, to lie about where her sister was. She clung to Brigitte. They hugged each other, promised to write letters, said it would surely last not much longer.

'You'll be all right,' said Brigitte, 'you were born lucky.'

'Hedges have eyes, walls have ears,' warned her sister.

Brigitte rattled her great bunch of keys, let her sister out of the giant wrought-iron gates, and locked them behind her.

Murphy walked the half-league to the spot beside the road where the public conveyance would pick her up.

It was high summer. She carried a few possessions in a scarlet cloth, a woman of the hedgerows. Her face was a tear-stained purple. Her dress was ragged. She wore the red bonnet of liberty on her head, a red kerchief round her neck. Her sabots clumped on the road. She felt pleased that they chafed her feet and gave her sores. Her money she had sewn into her dress, round her waist, into her breast, so that she took on the appearance of a much stouter woman and moved not quite with her usual ease and grace.

Inside she grinned, almost enjoying herself.

She thought, The Murphys were always good at acting . . .

The diligence stopped, picked her up, rumbled on, and kept stopping so the coachman could pour cold water on the burning metal rims of the wheels; then ground on again, leaving a trail of sparks.

Citoyenne Murphy disappeared.

Citoyen Dayat continued to distinguish himself. He spent much of his time in the Jacobin Club drinking Irish whiskey, toasting the Revolution. He raised his glass repeatedly to *Liberté*, *Fraternité* and *Egalité*. He loudly endorsed anything anti-Royalist, anti-noble and anti-Versailles.

He smeared his hair with Pomade à la Sanson, named in honour of the public executioner, in affirmation of his patriotic convictions.

He called his wife *Citoyenne*, even in bed.

'It's a question of survival,' he told her, and addressed her as *tu* instead of *vous*.

He cultivated a certain roughness, rubbed the polish off his Versailles manners, grabbed food at meals, banged his fists on the table, talked with his mouth full, and shouted throughout every meal.

Citoyenne Dayat was appalled, but dutifully followed all her husband's instructions. She wore a red neckerchief, had her mane of black hair shorn, and ruined her complexion to keep the Colonel happy.

In tears, she locked up her Paris apartment and fled Paris till the troubles were over.

Murphy made her way down the Seine on the barge, watching the river change colour from azure to ochre, to gold, to bronze, to ebony. She floated past the laundresses' boats and the rocks sticking out of the water like decayed teeth. It was an easy journey, with the current, through the mist, to Rouen, which she saw with surprise, almost having forgotten that her birthplace existed.

Eventually she came to Le Havre where, if necessary, she could take the packet to Rosslare, to Dublin, to Ireland, to a new life, to the old life. She rented lodgings and made herself known to her Irish cousins living in the town.

She kept her head down and became just the woman who walked alone on the shingle beach with a large black dog: a mysterious woman who talked to no one but looked straight ahead of her, who sometimes called her dog *'Paddy'*.

She watched the sea, thinking of Agathe-Louise, and could not stop looking at it, fascinated. She thought of Ireland, lying beyond the horizon. She found herself wishing that her grandfather had never come over the water to France, but had stayed at home.

She attended the section meeting regularly. She did what was required to appear a good daughter of the Revolution. But she sat apart from the other *citoyennes*, upright and aloof. The nuns had made too good a job of correcting her posture.

The *citoyennes* sniffed as Murphy entered the meeting, catching the unmistakable odour of Olympian Dew that still clung to her clothes. Murphy did not smell of perspiration as she should.

The *citoyennes* looked hard at Murphy's shoes. They were too grand, in spite of being scuffed, too expensive for the *citoyennes'* liking. Her skin was still too white, too perfect for her to be anything but an aristocrat.

She tried to stop smiling, knowing she was not supposed to be enjoying herself, but she could not stop smiling: her Versailles smile was permanent.

She roughed up her hair. She bashed her shoes about. She did everything she could think of to improve her standing as one of the *citoyennes* of Le Havre. The women eyed her suspiciously and watched her when she was not looking. They took note of the way she glided about Le Havre and stored up information against her for future use.

Murphy was restless. She came and went between Le Havre – or Havre-Marat as it had now become – and Paris, still trying to settle the business of de Flaghac's will, still seeing to her financial affairs, making sure the bank had not burned to the ground with all her jewellery inside.

In due course the Comtesse Marie-Anne d'Ayat, now plain Citoyenne Dayat, joined Murphy at Le Havre with her children – who wore miniature *sabots* and small red caps of liberty.

Sometimes it was convenient for Murphy to pretend not to understand French, to be a foreigner. Sometimes it was useful not to be able to answer anyone, but to speak English.

She devoted her days to the education of her grandchildren:

Anne-Pauline-Victoire, and Alexandre-Édouard-Marguerite, now abbreviated to Pauline and Alexandre Dayat.

Marguerite-Victoire also brought her children to Le Havre: François and Alfred, little more than babes in arms, who had dropped their particle and were just plain 'Chousy'.

Murphy began to teach them to read and write in English and French. 'There's no knowing,' she told them, 'when we might not have to travel over the water . . .'

She taught them about Saint Patrick and the snakes, the Giant's Causeway, the banshee, the little people, the leprechaun, and the lucky shamrock. Her stories were second-hand, third-hand, fourth-hand, inherited from her parents, embroidered during their progress over the Irish Sea and half the battlefields of Europe, and over the half-century of Murphy's life. She added embellishments of her own. She exaggerated, she made tall stories taller, and the grandchildren were none the wiser.

They wore blue threads round their necks. They killed black beetles when they could. They placed snails on dishes of flour and traced the initials of their true lovers' name.

On wet afternoons, or when the sun was too hot for them to go outside, Murphy would settle down with her grandchildren and make them recite the *Déclaration des Droits de l'Homme*. Their husky voices parroted the words after her:

Les droits naturels, inaliénables et sacrés de l'homme . . .
Les hommes naîssent et demeurent libres . . .
La liberté, la propriété, la sûreté et la résistance à l'oppression . . .

In the evenings they sang the *Marseillaise* as they shivered round a slow fire, trying to keep warm.

After the children had been put to bed the three Comtesses, Murphy, d'Ayat and de Chousy, would sit by the light of a single candle chanting the *Déclaration* over and over again themselves, with all the solemnity of Ave Marias, against the day when their past caught up with them.

They went to bed wearing their red bonnets. The family diamonds and the family fortune were locked safely in the bank. Under the bedclothes Murphy's fingers moved across the forbidden rosary beads and she would murmur her prayers under her breath before drifting into an uneasy sleep.

*

To Le Havre eventually came the news that Valdec de Lessart had been arrested and imprisoned in the former monastery of the Minims at Orléans. Murphy knew nothing except that there were some fifty-two prisoners, among them a duke, a bishop, a judge and some officers, and that they awaited their trial.

She feared the worst and prepared herself for Valdec de Lessart's head to be separated from his body. She told herself each morning, It will only be a matter of days before he is dead.

She wrote letters to her friends in high places, those who had not already left France, urging them to do what they could to save him. She succeeded only in drawing attention to herself.

She was prepared for Valec de Lessart to die: nothing prepared her for what actually happened.

With his wife and family at Le Havre, Colonel Dayat was enjoying all the glory of battle. Images of the cavalry charge at Famars kept recurring in his dreams: he heard a constant ringing noise in his ears, he had a permanent panorama inside his head of screaming horses, bared lips, flashing teeth, eyes rolling with terror.

His fellow-officers screamed themselves towards the enemy with a wordless roar, terrifying, out of control, intent only upon death. Hoofs pounded the soil. Dayat was surrounded by the thud and thump of falling horses, the clank of harness, the ripping of flesh. The earth exploded beneath his feet and his intestines gushed through his stomach wall.

The Colonel's hernia made it difficult to mount his horse without screaming with pain. He spent his time not in the saddle, not in the cause of Revolution but in going to and from the truss-maker, cursing the loss of mobility, cursing the loss of his freedom, cursing the loss of his youthful vigour.

The Colonel was just thirty-five and had to be driven everywhere. He felt like an old man.

'You will have to learn to live with it, Colonel,' said his doctor.

Dayat returned to his regiment, bore the agonizing pain, and drank more to compensate. His revolutionary zeal increased. His intestines would have to protrude through his stomach wall for ever. The sour-sweet smell of death lingered in his nostrils.

On 9 September 1792 a procession of farm carts made its way

from Orléans to Paris with the fifty-two prisoners of the Constituent Assembly, among them the former minister Valdec de Lessart.

The convoy was escorted by 200 Marseillais, some 1,800 revolutionaries, and several pieces of heavy artillery. They made their way through a dying landscape, with the leaves changing colour from green to gold, to orange, to rust, and with the dead leaves falling on them.

Two thousand men had not gone to Orléans to protect the prisoners but to lead them to Paris and hand them over to the popular rage; there would be little chance of them receiving regular justice in the lawcourts.

Valdec de Lessart watched, helpless, his hands tied. He watched the sky and the dripping leaves overhead.

The Assembly decreed that the column should not enter Paris and ordered it to make for Versailles instead, a Versailles full of agitators who lurked on street corners and slept rough in the Parc: men who lit bonfires and splashed in the fountains; men in filthy clothes with too much time on their hands.

The convoy moved slowly. Valdec de Lessart watched the buttons on his coat and thought of Marie Murphy.

The Mayor of Versailles, anxious to avoid disorder, made preparations for the column to be diverted before it came too close to the town, and for the prisoners to spend the night in the recently-vacated cages of the royal menagerie.

Chance brought Marie Murphy to Versailles on the afternoon that Valdec de Lessart would pass through the town. She lingered in the Rue de Surintendence hoping to catch sight of him, a last glimpse. She waited and watched, dressed in mud-coloured clothes, thinking Valdec de Lessart would hardly recognize her now if he did see her.

The cortège approached the château, determined to go right through the middle of Versailles, about which everything was so symbolic. They marched on amid confusion, shouting and disorder, accompanied by a large crowd of Versaillais.

In the Rue de Surintendence the column came to a complete halt, jammed in by the crowd, more menacing, sinister, waving their arms and shouting '*A bas les têtes!*'

The Mayor pleaded with the mob to let justice take its course. 'There might be innocent men among them,' he shouted.

But the crowd's mood grew uglier. 'You're too good to them – they deserve death!' they shouted.

Valdec de Lessart looked up at the windows of his old office, the Hôtel des Affaires Étrangères and the Hôtel du Contrôle Général des Finances, now shuttered and deserted, places where he had kissed Madame de Flaghac behind the curtains.

Citoyenne Murphy followed the procession on foot, wearing a red cap, part of the mob, keeping her distance, her eyes fixed on the figure in the blue coat.

The crowd began to scream, 'You don't know the wrongs these men have done us, they deserve death.' They chanted, '*La mort! La mort! La mort! La mort!*' and would not stop chanting.

Marie Murphy watched dark sweat-stains grow in the armpits of Valdec de Lessart's coat. Then she did not know what was happening. She could not believe what she saw, but huddled in a doorway with her hands to her mouth, stifling her screams, unable to take her eyes off what was happening to Jean-Marie-Antoine-Claude de Valdec de Lessart.

Thousands of voices roared for death and howled for blood, and blood made its appearance. Death arrived and severed limbs fell on the streets of Versailles.

It appeared to rain blood. Blood spurted and splashed. The autumn sun caught the metal of swords, glinting. Men wielded axes and sabres. Hands were raised and lowered rhythmically, frenziedly, unable to stop beating and thumping, rising and falling. Bayonets jabbed into warm flesh. Swords hacked off heads and scissored genitals, stuffed them into gaping mouths. Death upon death, death after death.

A horrible silence fell on Versailles. The Rue de l'Orangerie was suddenly deserted. The escort of 2,000 men vanished. There was no sound but the steady drip-drip-drip of blood off a cart into a puddle of blood in the road; the last faint gurgling groans of a man not quite dead; the hysterical screaming of a woman, faint behind a locked and barricaded door.

A priest moved among the dead, closing the eyes of severed heads.

The massacre had lasted more than an hour. The assailants had stripped the bodies and left them naked, stark and bloody, like raw meat. The flies of Versailles swarmed over sticky pools of blood. The dogs of Versailles sniffed at the débris, licking up the blood, lapping noisily, chewing tentatively, an arm, a leg, their tails wagging.

On the other side of Versailles, in the Place Dauphine, where the King's executioner had formerly hanged criminals, the mob danced and sang round a bonfire of the prisoners' clothes.

In the Rue de l'Orangerie the Mayor had the bodies taken up and removed for burial. A cart piled high with flesh like a butcher's wagon rumbled through the empty streets.

In the calm of the Maison Commune the Mayor delivered his account of the incident to the *conseil-général*, his hair dishevelled, his clothes bloody and torn, his face splashed with blood. As he spoke the door burst open and the murderers, raucous, rowdy, crazy with slaughter, covered in blood, poured into the room holding aloft their trophies: ripped-out hearts and bloody hands.

The official taking notes received the relics with due ceremony, laid them in state on his desk, and wiped his bloody fingers down the margins of the page.

When they picked up the pieces to count the dead, the jigsaw of the massacre of Versailles did not fit together. There were two hands left over and no body to go with them.

They were marble-smooth, pale hands, a man's hands: hands that had not been used to hard work, except perhaps the work of holding a quill, a man whose only work was writing. They were a gentleman's hands, with bitten nails and a gold ring on each of the little fingers: bloody hands, cleanly severed by an axe – Valdec de Lessart's hands.

Fortunately the massacre had taken place on the doorstep of Valdec de Lessart's former secretary, who had dragged the body into his house with the help of Marie Murphy and barricaded themselves inside, where she had screamed, hysterical, unable to move.

Valdec de Lessart's fashionable clothes were drenched with blood. Straw from the bottom of the cart adhered to his coat. His blood dripped on to the doorstep. There was blood on the vestibule floor. There was blood splattered on the walls, blood on the staircase, blood on the carpets, blood on the sheets, blood everywhere. Valdec de Lessart's life had fallen out of him, spraying blood, sprinkling the house with blood, reminding Murphy of the goose.

They had bandaged him to staunch the bleeding and he lay motionless, half-way between life and death. He could think only of his hat, left in the road, kicked and trampled. He thought of his hands, left in the dust like a pair of white gloves someone had dropped. He felt the hammer blows, saw the glittering eyes of his assailant, grinning, drunk with murder, slicing him up like butcher's meat.

When Valdec de Lessart opened his eyes Murphy held out her hands to him, the last thing she should have done. He raised his bandaged stumps to her, bloody, hideous. His face bore no expression, was a mask streaked with blood, filthy, unrecognizable.

'If you bite your nails,' he said slowly, 'your hands will fall off.'

Valdec de Lessart made progress, relapsed, languished. Murphy stayed with him, nursed him, dressed his wrists, did what she could. She came and went between Versailles and Le Havre and Paris, trying to keep together what was falling apart.

Valdec de Lessart lay still. He felt his fingers twitching, wanting to touch her, wanting to stretch out and stroke her perfect face. Time after time he would raise a hand to deal with some foreign body in his eye, to brush away tears, before he remembered that there was no hand, no fingers to do what he wanted them to do.

Gangrene set in. Medical assistance was difficult to come by. Valdec de Lessart faded. Eight months after the massacre he was dead.

Murphy returned to Le Havre. She laid the extra place at table in case the ghost found its way to her lodgings. Then it occurred to her that Valdec de Lessart could not have wielded a knife and fork anyway. Her heart felt empty, heavy like a rock. She thought of her sisters way back in her past telling her, 'If you fall in love your heart will break.'

At night the gnarled, barnacled feet of turkey after turkey disappeared slowly inside her mouth but she lay awake, thinking.

XVI

Shortly before the massacre at Versailles Colonel Dayat, now thirty-five, was made a Maréchal de Camp, and then Chief of Staff of the Army of the Interior.

He saw action at Valmy among muddy fields where bullets did not ricochet and cannonballs whizzed past his ears. With his hernia under control he distinguished himself, covered himself with other men's blood once again, was commended for bravery, and revelled in the glory.

At Le Havre his mother lay low, trying to keep warm, trying to do all that Revolution required of her.

Anne Dayat, overwrought by the troubles, worn out by giving birth to three children in quick succession, shocked by her husband's complete abandonment of his aristocratic principles, fell ill, died, and was buried at Le Havre without religious rites.

The Maréchal de Camp shrugged, frowned, and chewed turkey feet in the evenings.

'Have to find another wife,' he said to his mother gruffly. But he had more important things to occupy him: how to keep his head attached to his shoulders; how to stay alive himself.

Murphy, left in charge of four grandchildren, set them to learning the next section of the *Déclaration*, and read to them from *La Vie et les Aventures de Robinson Crusoé*.

They lived quiet lives of genteel destitution, dressed plainly, spent as little money as they could, and hoped and prayed about the future. In the absence of soap they went unwashed and developed red patches on their skin.

As they grew older the grandchildren perfected the art of swiping the tops off their boiled eggs with one blow of the fork, in imitation of their father.

Murphy screamed at them to stop: 'Don't do that, it's dangerous.'

The Maréchal de Camp stepped up his revolutionary activities. As Chief of Staff he remained in Paris and was seen regularly at the Jacobin Club, leading a comfortable life, frequenting the cafés of the Palais-Royal, strutting in his new uniform, hobnobbing with ministers, and feeling he was a personage.

His half-sister, Marguerite-Victoire, Comtesse de Chousy, tried hard to be a daughter of the Revolution. She cut her hair off, wore the red bonnet and the red kerchief, but her bearing gave her away. She was betrayed by her clean white hands; her face, never in all her life exposed to the sun, was whiter than white.

She came intermittently to Le Havre, and with her came her new lover, the Baron de Tournehem, heir to the estates and fortune of his great-uncle, Lenormand de Tournehem – the early benefactor and, in fact, father of Madame de Pompadour.

'We are cousins,' Marguerite-Victoire told her mother.

'Kissing cousins,' said the Baron de Tournehem, kissing her.

'A Lenormand de Tournehem might surely,' Marguerite-Victoire said, 'be friendly with a Lenormand de Flaghac.'

She liked the Baron de Tournehem. She left the Comte de Chousy in Paris, and lived with de Tournehem in Le Havre, trying to become pregnant, for pregnant women were spared the horror of the guillotine. She cultivated the friendship of her cousin Louis Desaix as well, with a view to remaining perpetually pregnant and saving her neck.

The family had its feet in both camps. Among themselves they did not talk about the troubles. They read the *Gazette*, paid lip-service to liberty, wore their red cockades, and kept their fingers crossed.

Murphy herself grew weary of living a quiet life. Le Havre was too quiet. Her whole life had been too quiet. She was restless. She wanted to be in the capital. She worried about her property and her fortune. In the New Year of 1793 she took an apartment in the Rue Saint-Jacques in Paris, thinking she was sufficiently forgotten to wait for better times at home, where she belonged.

On 21 January her son found himself in a position of command on the Place de la Révolution, in the midst of a vast crowd waiting beside the guillotine in the snow, waiting for the execution of the King. 130,000 armed men lined the streets. Dayat watched the tyrant brought to the scaffold with drums beating. He heard the steady tread of boots, the rumble of wheels, the ceaseless murmur of the crowd. He watched the ordinary-looking man, wigless, in an ordinary puce-coloured coat, not looking like a King of France in the slightest.

Dayat thought of the time when he had waited hour after hour just to remove the man's slipper. He felt no emotion. He felt numb, doing what he did because it was his duty. One half of him revolted at the thought of what was about to happen. The other half of him was thrilled that the tyrant's head would roll. He thought of the chickens running about at Flaghac, decapitated chickens. He thought of his mother's clocks blown to pieces, of time standing still.

The tyrant moved through a sea of spiked bayonets, blue soldiers' coats, black hats, white waistcoats. The crowd seemed to hold its breath, as if about to witness a miracle.

Louis XVI mounted the scaffold, his face red as a page's uniform, blotchy with emotion. Now he moved and breathed: in three minutes his time would be up.

He watched the multitude, which stretched as far as his eyes could see. He asked if the drumming would never stop. The sinister roll, the grim drumming ceased, and Louis walked a few steps. The boards creaked under his feet, as if he might be catapulted through them.

He spoke a few words in a loud voice, words that afterwards no one could exactly remember, but which were reported as:

'I die innocent of all the crimes laid to my charge; I pardon those who have occasioned my death; and I pray to God that the blood you are going to shed may never be visited on France.'

Dayat sat motionless on his horse, wondering if the man on the scaffold was, in fact, his *nephew*, whether he was not half-uncle to the King of France. He thought of Casanova's words; of the old King his father, of the new King his nephew, of all the mystery of his past, of all the questions that his mother would not answer.

Louis XVI would have carried on speaking, but they decided he had said enough, that he had lived too long already, that his life must end.

A man on horseback wearing the national uniform gave the order for the roll of drums to recommence, with a ferocious cry of '*TAMBOURS* . . .' like the guttural cawing of a bird of carrion.

The drums beat again. Louis XVI's time ticked on beyond what they had allowed him and he was still alive, on borrowed time, his face blank, as if the machinery of his brain had seized up already.

Afterwards Dayat claimed that it was he, Dayat, who ordered the roll of drums to drown the King's voice. Later he boasted of it, and took care to alert posterity that the order came out of his mouth.

Later still men argued about it, as if it mattered whether it was Dayat or Santerre who had yelled the command, or someone else.

The Comte d'Ayat thought of his own head up there on the scaffold, still fixed to his body. He thought of the creaking boards, the glittering blade, the indifferent crowd. He saw his own head roll into the basket, the blood spurt from his neck. He saw his own blue eyes glaze over and flicker. He thought of the chickens at Ayat, running about after their heads were cut off.

He wondered again whether the man on the scaffold was anything more than the grandson of his mother's lover. He wondered whether he was about to witness the death of *family*.

He thought, A man must survive. A man must keep his head.

Dayat opened his mouth and screamed the cry of the rooks at Ayat, the black, wordless, frantic cry of the builders of nests and feeders of fledglings.

The shining blade of the guillotine fell.

The head of Louis XVI flew, and his blood splashed in the snow.

It was twenty past ten in the morning.

Dayat's mind was blank. He felt sick. He did not feel sick. Inside, part of him exulted, part of him was afraid. His hands were numb with cold, numb with the horror of it, as if they were another man's hands, as if one half of him did not know what the other half was doing.

The youngest of the guards, a youth of perhaps eighteen years, seized the severed head and held it up, dripping, to the crowd.

In the silence Dayat heard again the creaking of the boards, the snort and stamp of horses. Then suddenly the crowd was yelling '*Vive la république*' and every man's hat was in the air: black hats flying upwards, like crows startled by the report of a gun. The crowd cawed and Dayat cawed with them.

The citizens dispersed, awkwardly, in silence, having witnessed the miracle of a King's head separated from a King's body, like the top of a boiled egg sliced off with one stroke of a golden fork. There was little difference, except between the colour of the golden yolk and the dark red blood congealing on the dead man's chin.

Among the crowd in the Place de la Révolution stood a small, upright woman of fifty-five, who had watched, frozen, horrified, the death of a man who had once kissed her hand. Now that it was over she moved fast, her feet taking short, quick steps, making her appear to glide over the bloody snow. Her heart beat like one of the drums. The tears glistened on her purple cheeks.

In March Dayat was sent away into the Vendée to help put down the resistance to the Republic. Before his departure he was promoted again, to Général de Brigade, and appeared overnight in a tight, bright uniform, ignoring the fact of his hernia, strapped in by a new truss of the latest revolutionary design.

He was to be a general for 130 days.

At about the same time his cousin, Louis Desaix, aged twenty-four, was also made a General. He wrote love-letters to Marguerite-Victoire de Chousy, assuring her of the sincerity of his feelings for her. He rose like a star, like a firework, sending out showers of sparks, propelling him ever higher on his journey to glory.

He remained a general for eight years.

At Fontenay-le-Comte, now Fontenay-le-Peuple, General Dayat had his finest moment. Decree Number 981 of the Convention Nationale spoke of the General's brave conduct as he covered the retreat of his troops.

Beneath his uniform the General's body survived unscathed. His head stayed in its usual position. His limbs remained attached to his trunk. He came through his latest excursion to Hell without a scratch on him.

After the battle the General made his way to Niort to reorganize his men, to prepare to take up the offensive again, and to remove the bloodstains from his uniform.

In his cups, among his fellow-generals, Dayat boasted loudly of how he had spent the night before the execution of the tyrant drinking whiskey in the Jacobin Club. He spoke with disdain of the Louis whose grandfather he had waited on, the Louis whose family had supported his mother for thirty years, the Louis who had provided his own privileged education, the Louis who had done his best to ignore him.

With every mention of '*Louis*' the General spat vehemently on the floor.

The generals made inquiries about Dayat's past. They found him too conceited, too self-satisfied, too vain. They thought General Dayat was too pleased with himself and much too keen.

In July the Minister for War wrote to General Dayat informing him that he had been suspended from the rank of Général de Brigade.

He was ordered to remove himself immediately to a distance of twenty leagues from the section of the army he was then commanding; to place himself twenty leagues from any other army, and twenty leagues from the frontiers of the Republic of France.

Dayat blustered, failing to understand what he had done to deserve such treatment. He reminded his colleagues how he had been transferred to a regiment of carabiniers to hunt out the aristocracy that infected it. He proclaimed his wholehearted admiration for the Terror.

He regretted not having been able to gather in his hernia so that he could devote more energy to the Revolution.

He praised his mother's revolutionary spirit in educating his children in the true republican tradition.

He fought for his career and his life, but his fellow-generals had no sympathy for him.

'You are an enemy of Revolution, Citoyen,' one said. 'You are a noble. If it was all over this afternoon, you would go back to being a noble tomorrow. You must stop pretending.'

'You cannot have it both ways, Citoyen,' said another. 'Either you are a noble or you are a revolutionary. You cannot be both.'

'You are trying to be half and half,' said a third general, 'and we cannot trust a man like that.'

'I am only half-French, Citoyens,' pleaded Dayat.

'You are only half-human,' laughed the generals, and they could not stop laughing.

Dayat's remarks and pretences deceived no one. He was kicked out of the army, stripped of his rank and uniform, and turned back into plain Louis-Charles-Antoine Pelet de Beaufranchet d'Ayat, Comte d'Ayat, Comte de Beaumont, Comte de Grandmont, and Comte of other places.

Unable to comply with the Minister's instructions and lodge with his family at Le Havre, d'Ayat headed for Soisy and disappeared from public life. He had made the mistake of drawing attention to his mother.

In due course the authorities paid a visit to the former General at Soisy and confiscated his goods. He protested that none of the furniture belonged to him; that it was his mother's property.

'It makes no difference, Citoyen,' hissed the official in charge of the removal. 'If she died tomorrow it would all be yours. She *will* die tomorrow. She is an aristocrat. We are taking away your golden chairs all the same.'

D'Ayat camped in one of the gatehouses, opposite his aunt Brigitte, in a room empty of everything but a grimy straw mattress. He was obliged to purchase worm-eaten chairs from the flea-market at Corbeil.

At the local section meeting d'Ayat found that the *sans-culottes* sniffed the air when he made his entrance.

He gave up using even Pomade à la Sanson.

The *sans-culottes* turned round repeatedly to look at his hair. In response D'Ayat grew his hair longer, wore it more rumpled, and stopped combing it.

The *sans-culottes* stared at his expensive-looking boots and made loud remarks about the price of boots like that.

D'Ayat went to the next meeting wearing *sabots*, and he kept an eye on the *citoyennes* in the gallery, with a view to finding himself a good revolutionary wife.

Finding the former general wasting his time and talents, the Commune de Soisy gave him the job of Commissioner for Saltpetre and told him to get on with it whether he liked it or not.

Deprived of his horse, d'Ayat enlisted as a sapper in the revolutionary battalion, back in the infantry. He drilled up and down a hayfield with the gardeners who had once clipped his mother's hedges. He was given bayonet practice and elementary firearms instruction, as if he had never enlisted in the armies of France and had never seen active service at all.

He bore the humiliation, thankful that they had not arrested him; relieved that his head could stay in its usual place.

Brigitte Murphy continued to deny that she was any relation of the châtelaine of Soisy. Brigitte was afraid. She wondered whatever had induced her to apply for noble status. She had long since torn up the documents and thrown them on the fire. She had long since ceased to be *de Boisfailly*.

'I am no relation of the Flaghac family,' she told her neighbours. 'I am not a noble at all.'

But her nerves were in tatters. Her heart did not stand up to the strain of Revolution.

On 24 August 1793, with her nephew Citoyen d'Ayat holding her beautiful hands and telling her to think of Ireland, Brigitte Murphy died, aged sixty-six.

D'Ayat followed her strict instructions and unlocked all the locks in the gatehouse so that her immortal soul could pass freely out of the door. He covered the tarnished mirror with a dirty piece of white cloth. He turned the only picture – frameless and filthy, a still life with vegetables – to face the wall. There were no Irishwomen in Soisy to keen for Brigitte.

D'Ayat sent word to his mother, now back in Le Havre. She did not budge. She wrote back, 'It is too dangerous to move.'

She could not, in any case, imagine that Brigitte had been taken away from her. She had Brigitte with her still. She saw her every day. She talked to her. She asked her questions and laid her place at meals and saw her sitting beside her at the table, her blue eyes like cornflowers.

She thought, Brigitte will never die. Her hands are immortal. Death does not exist, there is no such thing.

She clung to life at a time when nobody could be certain of living another twenty-four hours.

Whistling porters carried Brigitte's earthly remains to the grave on a squeaking wheelbarrow and tipped her without ceremony into the common pit. Louis d'Ayat thought it just as well that his mother had not attempted the journey.

In the autumn the Comte de Chousy was arrested for no other crime than being the Comte de Chousy. Marguerite-Victoire applied at once for a divorce, seeking to distance herself from the nobility. She went straight to Paris to arrange the legalities and was promptly arrested herself, for the crime of being the Comtesse de Chousy.

Hysterical, she told her gaolers she was the granddaughter of a *savetier*.

'You are far too grand for a *savetier*'s granddaughter,' the turnkey told her. 'You are aristocracy! All the tyrant's family attended your wedding!'

Marguerite-Victoire protested that it was not true.

'You deserve what is coming to you, Citoyenne,' the turnkey laughed, as he locked her into her cell. 'Your head will not sit on your shoulders for much longer.'

In December Madame du Barry, the woman of the streets, the woman of the people, went screaming with terror to the guillotine. She had been the mistress of the tyrant and yet they had cut her head off – in spite of her origins.

It made Murphy more afraid than she had ever been. The guillotine loomed closer. She heard stories of the executioner having trouble with the du Barry's fat neck, of the repeated blows.

Murphy thought, But my neck is not thick. It will be like beheading chickens.

She stopped worrying and told herself there was nothing a Murphy could not do, even if it meant mounting the scaffold. If she had to die, she would die like a Murphy; she could not let the Murphys down.

The Comte d'Ayat's return to Soisy in disgrace drew attention to his family. Murphy's bailiff denounced his mistress as a noble in retaliation for her refusal to sell him part of her estate.

In January 1794 she made her way to Soisy to find out what the bailiff thought he was up to, and to visit Brigitte's grave.

She attracted notice once more, and the Committee of Corbeil felt obliged to investigate her case.

The woman was a Comtesse, a noble. Not having set eyes on her since 1792, they decided she must have fled abroad, that she was a returned *émigrée*.

While they waited for better evidence and new information, they put Madame la Comtesse de Flaghac under surveillance.

Back in Le Havre she was denounced for not having displayed the highest revolutionary principles. She had been heard to say 'It is not safe to breathe.'

In her defence some testified that she had not left France, but had been at Le Havre all the time.

Others said on her behalf that she had made patriotic offerings.

The Committee refused to be deceived by the mother as well as the son. They decided that she must have been abroad. No one would stay in Le Havre and not have been to England or Ireland.

The Committee confined her to her château, with permission to go to Paris only under heavy guard.

Citoyenne Murphy protested against the injustice of the accusations, but in vain. She paced about the empty rooms, chewing her fingernails, not knowing what to do with herself.

In February, thinking that they had forgotten about her, she committed the indiscretion of going to Paris without applying for a guard.

The Committee of Public Safety promptly issued a warrant for her arrest and charged one of its members, Citoyen Briquet, with taking the matter in hand.

Briquet found Citoyenne Murphy well known at her new apartment in the Rue Grange-Batelière. He settled down in the house opposite, followed her everywhere and made notes recording her every movement.

On the night of 8 March 1794 all the good luck of the Murphys ran out.

XVII

She was woken by a relentless pounding on her door in the small hours of the morning, a hammering that did not stop.

She did not answer, but pulled the bedclothes over her head, shaking, hoping it was not her they had come for. The blows continued, and they had come for her. Knowing she was inside, they took an axe to the door and burst in, holding lanterns and flambeaux high: two men, four men, a dozen, scores of grim-faced, frowning men filled her apartment.

Foul-smelling torches singed her wallpaper. Muddy *sabots* stood on her Aubusson carpets. The smell of sweat and wet clothes permeated her salon. She remembered the *eau de l'homme* of Versailles.

'We have come, Citoyenne, to place you under arrest and to seal up your apartment,' Briquet told her, impeccably polite, a grin on his face, waving an order of the revolutionary committee.

She did not resist them, said nothing, but watched and waited to see what would happen.

She kept under her bolster, at d'Ayat's insistence, a small pistol. 'To make you feel safe,' he had said.

'I can look after myself,' she had told him. 'I have been brought up to defend myself.' But he had left the pistol all the same.

Now absurd thoughts raced through her mind: that she might shoot her way out and evade arrest. But the pistol remained in its place until the men searching her bedroom emerged triumphant, waving it, firing it into the ceiling, leering at her, as if they had discovered proof that she was an enemy of the Nation.

Her rooms stank of the men's garlic and wine and onions. They tore her pictures down from the walls, looking for hiding places. They ripped up the carpets as if they thought she was hiding all the royal family, half the nobility. They tipped drawers on to the floor, searching for her jewels. They lurched about, drunk, knocking things over. She heard the tinkle of breaking glass and a crash as a heavy chandelier shattered on the parquet.

She watched one of the men urinating against the wall of her *salle à manger.* She heard the sound of her china smashing, her Sèvres porcelain hitting the floor. She watched the men hurl her gilt mirrors down into the street. They pushed her golden furniture out of the windows, then flung sheafs of papers into the night, into the wind and rain, turning her life inside out.

She went with the men silently, carrying a few belongings in a red handkerchief. She wore her blue beads, a rabbit's foot on a string round her neck; she wore her thickest clothes, remembering a different journey by night nearly forty years before.

In the Couvent des Bénédictins Anglais they locked her up in a dark cell containing nothing but a bolster and a mattress full of flea-ridden straw. She stood at her barred window and watched the dawn break over a prospect of tree-stumps and gravestones.

It was, they told her, gentler than the men's prison. It was violent enough even so. She listened all day to the screams of the women. She heard them throwing themselves against the doors of their cells, rattling their bars, throwing their furniture against the walls.

Gaolers prowled in the corridors, staring through the grilles, talking always of death, delighting to frighten her and deprive her of all comforts.

The talk of death was not idle. A few women would disappear each day. None of them came back. To leave the prison was to begin the journey to the guillotine. To go away was to die.

When they took Murphy away again, in the middle of the night, she said her prayers, thinking that the end had come, preparing herself for the silver blade and the last judgement. But she was not taken for trial, or to her execution. Instead she found herself in the prison of Sainte-Pélagie, near the Jardin des Plantes, and in harsher, grimmer conditions.

She signed her name in a grubby book with dog-eared pages. An unshaven gaoler poked in her bundle, leered at her, peered down the front of her dress. A drunken warder with rough, cold hands subjected her to an indecent search, hunting for something he knew was not there. She caught a familiar glint in his eye. This was the Revolution, where everything was forbidden, everything was permitted. He could do as he liked with her. This was Liberty.

'Next time, Citoyenne,' he laughed, 'it will not be my fingers under your skirts, and you will enjoy it.'

Her new cell was minute, with damp walls and a barred window overlooking a butcher's yard where the dogs of Paris howled and coupled and opened their bowels among old bones and pools of blood. She listened to the howling and thought of death – death that did not exist – and of the banshee, and of the security of the Auvergne.

Sainte-Pélagie was remote, isolated, formerly a refuge for prostitutes under the old régime. The previous year hundreds of priests had been massacred here and the gaolers liked to point out the bloodstains, the signs of multiple death still on the cobblestones: a reminder and a warning of what might yet happen to Murphy. The guillotine. Violent death. She thought of Valdec de Lessart.

She breakfasted on bread and water. Every day the turnkey brought her a portion of beans and half a pound of black bread. She suffered from diarrhoea and grew weak, her stomach unable to bear the filthy food.

Later, convalescing, she enjoyed the cooking of the governor's wife, who offered to feed her. A cutlet appeared in her cell one evening, and a spoonful of watery cabbage. The stew, with its peculiar smell and distinctive taste, she was reluctant to eat.

'Human flesh, Citoyenne,' laughed the turnkey, 'hot from the guillotine!'

There were stories of buttons and pale hairs found in the watery gravy.

'Boiled Marquis, fried Vicomte,' roared the turnkey. 'The nobles have their uses.'

Murphy tried not to think about what the meat was. She pretended it was horse, or donkey. In the end she was so hungry that she ate it, human flesh or not.

She had one wine-bottle of water a day for drinking and washing. In summer it was barely sufficient.

For those with money there were ways round the privations. It was possible to bribe the guards, to obtain luxuries in return for doing whatever the turnkey wanted in the middle of the night. Rumours circulated:

No water without taking your clothes off.

No bread without lying down in the straw.

No wine without my tongue down your throat.

But Murphy was anxious not to attract attention. She tried not to seem wealthy. She felt she was too old for what the rumours hinted at, and was afraid of the consequences.

Day after day she listened to the shriek of iron bolts in the cell doors. She breathed the foul air. She peered out into the dim corridor, choked on the thick fumes from the single oil lamp at night. She lost track of time, lost count of the number of days of her incarceration.

She told herself there was nothing a Murphy could not put up with. She kept herself cheerful. Her spirit fought.

She remembered Victoire saying, 'You can get used to anything.'

No one came to interrogate her. She was taken before no tribunal. She was not charged with any crime. She felt as if the authorities had forgotten about her. Under her window the guards swore, the dogs barked and fought. No one visited her, until one morning her door was unlocked at a different hour and the cell was full of men with pinched faces, unwashed hair and unkempt clothes: men with dirt under their fingernails, who fired questions at her:

'*Bonjour*, Citoyenne . . .'

'Are you satisfied with these premises?'

'Have you any complaints to make regarding your treatment?'

'Have you any requests to make?'

'Is perhaps your health affected?'

'Are you perhaps bored, Citoyenne?'

They gave her no chance to reply, as if they did not want to know what she thought; as if they had come to look her over with a view to making her lie down in the straw with them. But they stared at her disdainfully, as if they thought she had seen better days.

She wondered if they knew who she was, what she had been. She wondered if anyone remembered as far back as that.

She thought, No, I am long since forgotten.

People's interest had surely passed her by. She was just one more woman with a château, one more noble, locked up because they locked them all up.

She had not used her tongue in three weeks. She shook her head, could think of nothing to say to her visitors. The heavy door scraped shut and the key grated in the lock.

'*Adieu*, Citoyenne,' she heard. She listened to the heavy *sabots* echo down the corridor, to the groans of the women, to the shouts of the guards, the barking of dogs. In the distance she could hear a persistent murmuring roar, rising and falling, the noise of the mob. Flies and wasps buzzed in her cell. Her sweat dripped on to the filthy stone floor. In the heat of summer she became dizzy and confused, with all the noises of Revolution reaching her from afar.

Things slipped away from her. She could not remember her father's face. She lay awake in the dark trying to conjure up his beak of a nose, his domed forehead, the way the bristles grew on his chin. She had the separate parts but could not piece them together. It was as if she was trying to imagine something she had never seen.

Daniel Murphy had never sat for Monsieur Boucher, not even for a miniature. All she had left was a few memories, and she lacked the means to join them up.

Death, she thought, had done that, had taken him away, left only a memory. She wondered how long it would be before she forgot even the vague picture of her Papa; how long before even the fragments vanished; how long before he became just one twinkling eye and faded completely.

She thought, Please God I won't forget at all.

She could see her father's waistcoat clear enough: a chocolate-coloured waistcoat, made when their luck had turned up. Chocolate, with gold foliage twining up round the buttons, like plants growing out of the pockets, with buds and tubers hanging from it all the way up, and a leaf pattern all over it: like a family tree with potatoes hanging from it – like the Murphy dynasty that had come to a full stop already, uprooted too soon.

Now the waistcoat was gone, the thumbs in the waistcoat pockets were dead thumbs, and her father was gone for ever.

Her memory faded. She wondered again how long it would be before she too was forgotten. Except that there was a picture of her for people to remember her by. Even a picture that did not look much like her was better than no picture at all.

She passed her days thinking about old times.

Something set Murphy apart from the other prisoners. She had not had a hard life. She was different. She had known luxury.

'You are one of the *seigneurs*,' the woman in the next cell told her.

'I am not,' Murphy insisted. 'My mother sold old clothes.'

No one believed it. She could not be anything but a noble. The women slapped her face and pulled her about.

'Tell the truth,' her neighbour demanded. 'Don't lie!'

Murphy slapped and scratched back, and her accusers left her alone.

The turnkey continued to abuse her throughout the long hot summer, and she continued to plead her humble origins in her defence.

'My father was a workman, Citoyen, I assure you,' she told him. 'I have not one drop of French blood . . .'

'*Non*, Citoyenne,' he said, spitting on the floor. 'You are Comtesse. You have borne children to the tyrants. We know all about you. You are enemy of France. Enemy of Liberty. Enemy of Revolution.'

She pleaded with the turnkey to help her, to make them stop treating her as a criminal.

'I have been a prisoner half my life,' she told him. 'I would like to have my liberty. I would like to be free.'

The turnkey scratched his filthy red cap and sneered.

'We would all like to be free, Citoyenne,' he said. He turned the key in her lock and walked down the corridor, whistling the *Marseillaise*.

A week later Murphy mentioned money, wondering if she could buy her way out of Sainte-Pélagie after all.

The turnkey hissed at her. '*Non*, Citoyenne, you are *bourgeoise*. You are nobility. We can tell you are aristocrat by the way you walk.'

He spat on the floor.

'You have learned the walk. You have learned the voice. You have learned the language.'

He spat.

'You lived like aristocrat, you will die like aristocrat. Where you come from has nothing to do with it.'

He stooped, picked up the ragged hem of her dress, turned it over, and examined it. She watched a fly creep across his forehead. She could smell the smell of his sweat.

The turnkey looked up and said, slowly, 'Rue du Faubourg Saint-Honoré! 10,000 *livres*!' He spat in her face and ripped the dress apart at the seams.

The glob of froth dribbled down her cheek and she heard the cell door bang.

She saw his blackened teeth through the grille in her door.

'Bad luck, Citoyenne,' he leered, '*à la lanterne.*'

She escaped into her past, thought herself back into her childhood. She imagined herself out of the dark cell into the sunlight. She ran barefoot through the streets of Paris, across cobbles shining after rain. She remembered green grass. In her mind's eye she made her way from one side of the city to the other, and kept her thoughts away from the guillotine. She walked beside the Seine and paused to laugh with the washerwomen; she stroked stray cats, she picked wild flowers growing in the cracks between the stones, she watched a dog leaping into the river to fetch thrown sticks.

She made the time pass. She made her captivity less of a burden. She woke in the heat, or lay awake, unable to sleep, dripping with perspiration, feeling as if she was suffocating, with no water in her bottle. She drank tears. She licked the moisture off her palms.

On Murphy's arrest the authorities had compiled a list of witnesses concerning her case: relations, neighbours, men of affairs. But the situation deteriorated dizzily until people were reluctant to testify for fear of finding themselves among the suspects, or involving themselves in denunciations and trials that were parodies, and submitting themselves to the bloody delight of the men who sent everyone to the guillotine.

Citoyen d'Ayat did what he could. He wrote letters to his friends, to men who had been his drinking companions, to ministers he had known at Versailles. His friends ignored his pleas.

He dared not visit his mother in Sainte-Pélagie lest the authorities kept him there. He stayed at Soisy and immersed himself in the accounts of the saltpetre manufactories of the district of Corbeil.

And his mother stayed in her prison.

In July she saw a familiar face looking through the grille in her door. She thought, *Himself.*

He was dressed in Court clothes, wearing the Order of the Holy Ghost across his chest. His blackcurrant eyes shone in the half light. He looked younger, she thought.

'Louis,' she said.

'*C'est moi*,' he said, '*c'est nous.*'

And then he was gone. She told herself that Louis was dead; that she was seeing things.

The next day she saw him again. The blackberry eyes peered at her, laughing eyes. He said nothing, just looked and grinned. He seemed to know who she was, looked as if he knew all about her. Some official, some busybody, she thought, come to ask whether she was in good health. Then, before she knew where she was the key had rasped in the lock, she was out of her cell and riding in an open carriage down the middle of the Rue du Faubourg Saint-Honoré towards the Palais-Royal, with the sun shining and the troubles over.

Her face was painted white with plaster from her walls.

Her cheeks were rouged with a paste made from tomatoes.

Her eyebrows were painted with soot.

It began to rain.

Her eyebrows ran in a black stream into her cheeks.

Her rouge ran in red rivulets, like tears of blood.

Her chin dripped into her bosom.

Her bosom, padded with straw, became water-logged and sagged into her stomach.

Her stomach sank. Rainwater flooded the floor. The wind took away her wig. She sat in the carriage with her greying bristles revealed, a balding woman with a lined face, sinking, with bubbles rising all around her.

She woke up. Outside, a summer tempest threw rain in sheets through the bars of her window.

Living in filth, sleeping on straw, she felt as if all the fairy-tale of her life had turned to ashes; as if her carriage had become a pumpkin; as if her horses had been changed into mice. She dreamed of her prince coming to rescue her, but she knew he was dead. She felt her story must be near the end.

The turnkey regaled her daily with fresh reports of the scaffold awash with blood, of a dancing mob that clapped and cheered as the blade of the guillotine swept downwards, flashing in the sun, into the fat neck of yet another decadent aristocrat; stories of severed heads carried on poles through streets running with blood.

She heard that the Roué du Barry had been executed in Toulouse and that Lolo du Barry had been killed in a duel.

She heard that the Comte de Chousy had been guillotined.

She expected to hear that Marguerite-Victoire too had lost her head, as if a daughter was something fate could not allow the Murphys to keep. She feared for Louis d'Ayat. She prepared for her own death or, if she was allowed to live, for the rest of her life alone, with all her family taken from her. She wondered how long it would be before they cut off her own head, Murphy's head, as well.

In the month of Thermidor Murphy still languished in Sainte-Pélagie. The armpits of her only dress were rotting. Her face ran with perspiration. Her overriding sensation was of stickiness, of being unable to breathe, of a raging thirst she could never satisfy. The flies buzzed. In the sweltering heat of the corridor she fainted.

At the end of July Citoyen d'Ayat sat in his gatehouse with a list of the inhabitants of Soisy-Marat on a table in front of him.

Towards midnight he would set off, cloaked and muffled, to visit his neighbours, carrying a leather bag full of cash. He emerged from each house with the leather bag lighter, and his list of signatures longer.

At the beginning of August the Committee of Public Safety received a petition demanding the liberation of Citoyenne Murphy, signed by the entire population of Soisy-Marat: some hundred signatures, right down to the mark of the village lunatic.

The petition stated that neither Citoyenne Murphy nor her late husband had ever belonged to the caste of the privileged.

On 8 August 1794 the Committee of Public Safety dispatched a document to the Governor of Sainte-Pélagie.

Two days later the leering turnkey unlocked the door of Citoyenne Murphy's cell and led her to the end of the corridor.

She feared the worst: that she would be forced to kiss him; that this was the beginning of her final journey.

The turnkey left her with the Governor, who escorted her across a courtyard to a gate in the wall.

'*Au revoir*, Citoyenne,' he said, '*à la prochaine.*'

The gate closed behind her and she was on the street in broad daylight, locked into the outside world where the sun shone.

She walked beside the Seine towards the centre of Paris, pinching herself to make sure she was not dreaming. The Tricolour flapped on every building. The sky was blue. She picked her feet up, making a conscious effort not to glide.

After 155 days she was free.

At Soisy she found the locks had been prised off all the doors of the château. Her looking-glasses were shattered. The shutters had been hammered from the windows. Someone had smeared revolutionary slogans on the walls: *Vive la Nation* – *A bas les têtes* – *A la lanterne* – together with ruder slogans and obscenities.

Her salon, her *salle à manger*, her bedroom, all her white and gold rooms, were full of cows – white cows, black cows, black-and-white cows – all of them defecating on her parquet, eating the remains of the damask hangings. Cows browsed on her gilded staircase, cows chewed the cud in her white and gold bedroom. There was cow-dung everywhere.

Outside her formal gardens were blackened and charred. Fire had reduced the topiary peacocks and *fleurs-de-lis* to skeletons. Her pleasure grounds were a charred wasteland, with leafless trees, and blackened, ruined shrubs. A powdery white ash blew about in the wind. The rooks, homeless, screamed.

A dishevelled Citoyen d'Ayat appeared, embraced his mother warmly and kissed her on both cheeks. They wept together and their tears gradually turned to laughter.

'I saved the château,' he said. 'I stopped them burning it down. No one has been inside . . .'

She looked at him, astonished. '*You* have done this?' she said.

D'Ayat grinned. He remembered the gold clocks, the blowing

up of the tree, his vow to destroy Flaghac. '*Je tue le temps . . .*' he said.

Murphy bit her lip. She looked at the devastation. She waved her arms at the cows, but they carried on chewing her curtains.

D'Ayat stopped grinning. 'Be yourself yourself,' he said. 'Stop pretending. You can't go back to being a *seigneur*. You are a shoemaker's daughter . . .'

Murphy retrieved her bags of coins from their hiding places and left Soisy for Paris and the Rue Grange-Batelière, where there was a sofa to sleep on, and no cows. Her dream was over. She would never live in a château again. She was finished with being aristocracy.

A few days later she saw a face, a young man's face, looking through the *boîte aux lettres* in her newly-repaired door.

She first saw just the lips, full, sensuous. He moved, and she saw just the dark eyes, the gleaming whites. He moved again, and she saw his hair, dark, luxuriant. She saw the parts first, the pieces. He moved again and the parts fell into place, like bits of a jigsaw: they locked together and made a face, and smiled.

'I've seen you before,' she said, her heart fluttering like a bird. She opened the door and let him in.

XVIII

Murphy emerged from the dark of Sainte-Pélagie as from a chrysalis. Her skin, not having seen the sun, was whiter. She looked younger and thinner, and smiled as never before. Her blue eyes sparkled. She glowed with health.

It was as if she had saved herself up for one last adventure, as if Time had given her stay of execution. She was aided by her own particular magic, by artifice, and by all the luck of the Murphys – now back in its rightful place.

She was miraculously preserved.

Somehow – by sitting in the kind light of candles, by having spent a lifetime smoothing her skin with lotions -- she managed to attract a man nearly thirty years her junior.

He was, she thought, the most handsome young man she had ever seen. His hair was dark, shining, curly. His skin was the colour of pale mahogany. His eyes were an electric blue. His looks stopped the carriages in the streets, turned people's heads, made them wonder if they had not seen an angel fall to earth, a god walk past. Her knees felt weak when she saw him, and not just the first time, but every time, all the time.

He wore white *pantalons*, boots of highly-polished leather, a white linen shirt. With his boyish looks, his mischievous smile, he was something that Louis XV had once been but which she had never seen. He was something Lenormand and Terray and Valdec de Lessart, worn down by worry, had never been. He was like the young men who had visited her when she was young: the men who had arrived after dark and left before dawn, so like fragments of dreams that she had wondered whether they were real.

The new young man was real. She found him irresistible.

He talked to her as if she was a human being, not some girl he had hired for an afternoon till someone more interesting came along.

'What is your name, Monsieur?' she asked him.

'Louis,' he said.

She smiled. She thought of the white snails oozing about in the flour fifty years before. She kept smiling. She thought, *Louis and Louise*. She thought, Surely this was meant to happen.

'Louis-Philippe Dumont,' he said. '*Citoyen* Dumont.'

She felt that had they not been in revolutionary times he would have bowed and kissed her hand. His voice was husky, like that of another Louis. It made the hair on the back of her neck prickle.

'What age are you?' she asked him, casually.

'Thirty,' he said, grinning, as if he thought thirty was old.

She wondered, Will my age put him off? Will I lie about how old I am? She thought, No, age does not matter. She thought, Old meat makes good soup. She would tell the truth. If he asked.

Louis-Philippe Dumont wondered how old she was, and decided not to ask. He thought, Age has nothing to do with it.

Murphy the rogue turned up her charms to their fullest extent. She felt herself smiling as she had smiled at no one in half a century. She willed him to love her, if only for a day, if only for a night. She prayed all the prayers she ever knew, to all the gods she had ever heard of, and kept her fingers crossed.

She drew reckless sums of money from her bank. She bathed in raspberries and strawberries. She made the freest use of musk and civet and ambergris. She had the faithful Brestat – now restored to her – massage her with sponges soaked in milk and perfume.

Murphy the rogue, Murphy the Queen of the Parc-aux-Cerfs, would keep her clothes on until the candles were guttering. She would make sure that Louis' glass of wine was always full. Only by the light of the dying fire, she thought, would she allow his fingers to run across her satin skin.

She willed herself to be young, young enough. She was no longer fifty-six. With her face painted, in the full light of day, she was ageless. In certain lights she was thirty. At dawn she could be twenty-five. With the shutters closed, by night, she regained her youth. By the light of candles she was in her prime. Her voice would convince him he was with a girl of his own age. In the darkness she willed herself to be fifteen. In the dark she could be any age she liked. She thought, In the dark one's age does not matter at all.

She thought, By candlelight all girls are beautiful.

She looked into her mirror and remembered her mother saying 'At night all cats are grey ...'

In the apartment in the Rue Grange-Batelière, empty of all furniture except a yellow-green sofa too big to hurl through the window, she entertained the young Deputy of the Convention Nationale who had been elected to represent the people of Calvados.

She fed him celery soup.

She laced the soup with ambergris.

She stirred in triple vanilla.

Louis-Philippe Dumont was charmed. He thought Murphy looked ravishing, and said so.

She fed him truffles from Périgord.

She filled him up with chocolate.

He listened to her story, and her silver tongue charmed his silky feet out of the knee-length boots and on to the yellow-green sofa that he thought he had seen somewhere before.

She kept talking, as if she had kissed the Blarney Stone after all.

She fed him more truffles, and her golden tongue charmed him out of his dark-blue coat, a coat without gold braid, without gold or silver lace: a plain blue coat with plain buttons.

She poured him more chocolate, and her velvet tongue charmed him out of his tight white *pantalons* and into her silky arms.

She talked her smooth pink tongue inside his mouth, and fell silent. They shut their eyes, wrestling among the pink and white drapery. Her tongue made its way behind his ivory teeth – white and straight as the keys of her daughter's fortepiano – and the fifty-six-year-old widow proved that she still had it in her to go like the proverbial pair of lobster claws.

She thought of the lizard, of Himself, of de Lessart, of Terray, of de Flaghac, of Daniel Murphy, of Jacques de Beaufranchet and his black eyebrows. She thought of her past.

She thought, The heart breaks, the heart mends.

In a whirlwind, the next morning, they stood before the civil authorities and signed documents with scratchy quills, and the Comtesse de Flaghac became plain Madame Dumont, Citoyenne Dumont, and told none of her family what she had done.

She daydreamed. She saw the carriage stop in the Rue Grange-Batelière. She saw Dumont carry her over the threshold of the apartment. She saw him put her down. She dreamed the long moment, the whole of her married life, as he kissed her and her wig slipped and she changed into a woman old enough to be his mother. She saw the door wrenched open and watched Dumont run for his life, down the stairs, his shirt-tails flying, running away from her.

She imagined him removing his clothes and climbing into the bed to find her in a haze of scent, with her golden hair spread about her. She saw her pristine, perfect face crumple like a paper bag before his eyes. She saw her taut skin sag and fall in rolls under his smooth fingers. Her bright hair faded and fell away in his hands. She saw the distracted Dumont, frantic to pull on his clothes and flee from the room, running away from her for ever.

She allowed her mind to drift into the future: Murphy in her false colours, false hair, false breasts, false bottom, false face, false virginity, revealed on her wedding night as a bride with no breasts, no bottom, no hair, her skin shrivelled like last year's potatoes.

She heard the roar of the mob in the street: the traditional charivari under the window on finding a young man married to an old woman. They shrieked and howled with laughter, banged on pots and pans, and would not go away. She saw Dumont, husband of half a day, half a night, half an hour, running along the Rue Grange-Batelière, his bare feet slapping on the cobbles, running, running.

She dreamed the first kiss and herself, an old woman, turned into the girl of fifteen, the girl on the sofa, lying on her stomach with her feet in the air, musing on her life spread out before her and what she might do with it, and where it might lead her. The frog prince and the frog princess.

And she knew that dreams never come true, and that it would all go wrong, as everything else had gone wrong.

Afterwards, when the marriage was over, Louis-Charles d'Ayat asked his mother how she had managed it all.

Murphy laughed her old laugh, the roar, the guffaw. She could not stop laughing.

'Miracle!' she said. *'Un miracle!'*

It was said that Louis-Philippe Dumont would do anything for money, and that when he found his wife had no intention of giving him any, he abandoned her.

It was thought that Dumont was worried by talk of a tax on bachelors and that he wanted to do the correct revolutionary thing.

It was noised about that Dumont could put up with a year or two of marriage to an old wife in return for the rest of his life living on the widow's fortune.

It was rumoured that Dumont simply liked older women; some men did.

Some swore that Murphy simply did not look her age. She had all her hair, golden-yellow just as it had been when she was fifteen. She had hardly a wrinkle on her face. It was a miracle and she had no intention of telling Dumont how old she was.

The Legislative Assembly had authorized divorce by a decree of 1792. Divorce could be pronounced by mutual consent, for simple incompatibility of temperament, in cases of dementia or brutality, serious injury or abandonment of the marital home.

The divorce between Louis-Philippe Dumont and Marie-Louise Murphy or Dumont was pronounced on 16 December 1798.

Madame Dumont went back to calling herself Madame de Flaghac, or Madame d'Ayat. Sometimes she signed herself Comtesse Murphy, Madame Murphy, Mademoiselle Murphy, Citoyenne Murphy, or just plain Murphy. She shifted her shape and was free.

Marguerite-Victoire shed few tears for the dead Comte de Chousy and married the Baron de Tournehem as soon as she could.

She continued to write intimate letters to her cousin, General Desaix, assuring him of her undying love.

'Louis Desaix is family, Monsieur,' she told her new husband. 'You must not be jealous. No one else will ever love him.' And the Baron de Tourneham had to put up with it.

He made some remark about it not being particularly fashionable to sleep with your own husband. He asked Marguerite-Victoire, 'And what did your mother say when she heard you had married the first cousin of Madame de Pompadour?'

'She just laughed,' said Marguerite-Victoire. 'She laughed. She would do anything for the money herself.'

In the New Year of 1795 the Committee of Public Safety was pleased to lift the suspension of the former General Dayat and authorized him to take his retirement.

He was thirty-seven and an invalid, but not too much of an invalid to remarry. He stopped looking for a revolutionary wife with the termination of the troubles and married Charlotte-Josephine Kempfer de Plobsheim, the Comtesse de Sayn-Wittgenstein, whose husband had been sliced up like bacon in the September Massacres.

The former Comtesse de Sayn-Wittgenstein would wake regularly, screaming, towards five in the morning, dreaming of the severed head and limbs of her late husband. In her quieter moments she would forget that she had lost him, and murmur 'Georges-Ernest' instead of 'Louis-Charles' in her new husband's ear, and Louis-Charles would wake her up to remind her who he was.

D'Ayat was red-faced and prematurely grey-haired. He would grow his moustache or shave it off, depending on which was the correct post-revolutionary thing to do. He quietly returned the apostrophe to his name when signing letters. He experimented with calling himself 'General', and found that his friends had forgotten that he was not a general at all. He experimented with using his title and monitored his acquaintances' reactions. He appeared again in respectable clothes. He squeezed into fashionable tight *pantalons* that made him gasp. The Revolution had made him fat.

The General's children put away their *sabots* and red caps until the next revolution and flopped about their new house in Paris wearing cocked hats and blunt swords and velvet tunics embroidered with gold braid, like miniature generals. They resumed their triple-barrelled Christian names, and Alexandre-Edouard-Marguerite d'Ayat enlisted in the Imperial Army.

The General furnished his residence in white and gold, with

gilt *fauteuils*, gilt lion's-foot centre tables, and gilded clocks by Leroy à Paris.

A marble bust of the Emperor Napoleon watched over the *salle à manger*. Like the Emperor, he had a phial of the finest Eau de Cologne poured over his head and shoulders each morning. Like the Empress Josephine, he dined on potatoes.

The Revolution had not managed to deprive the General of his wealth.

He held his head up among the returned émigrés as one who had weathered the storm most successfully and obtained the best of both worlds. He would sit in his gilded library full of books with gilt spines, flipping through the plates of *The Anatomy of the Horse*, and browsing through the diagrams in *Les Grandes Opérations Militaires*. He drummed his fat fingers on his desk. All the General needed was something to do.

General Desaix continued to nurse his deep affection for Marguerite-Victoire. He was twenty-nine, amorous, and ugly – with thick lips, the big black eyes of an Auvergnat, and a melancholy pallor.

Marguerite-Victoire was not deterred by his appearance.

'There are more important things than how you look,' she told him. She liked the little man with dark, flowing hair, the romantic hero, the great general, who did not try to order her about as other men did.

'Louis is the only man I shall ever love,' she told her mother. But Desaix was rarely with her. He had followed Bonaparte to Egypt, where the burning sun had turned him into a black man. He pursued the seduction of his cousin Marguerite-Victoire through the post. He told her he loved her and could not live without her. He promised that when he returned to France they would meet in the Jardin des Plantes, or walk in the alleys of mulberries at Soisy. He did not know that the alleys of mulberries had been reduced to cinders and no longer existed.

It was General Desaix who pulled strings for General d'Ayat's military pension to be put in hand, and it was thanks to Desaix that d'Ayat was re-employed, as a member of the council of administration of military hospitals.

While General Desaix sweated in Egypt and loaded himself

with honours and medals, d'Ayat supervised the rolling of bandages and dealt with the supply of crutches and wooden legs.

Later d'Ayat was appointed a director of the military hospital at Mézières and spent his days arranging the transport of maimed soldiers and discussing the design of hospital beds. He felt as if the authorities were trying to lose him.

On 14 June 1800 Marguerite-Victoire noticed that all her gilded clocks had stopped. The Irish part of her knew why. The French part refused to let her give in to the irrational.

When the news of General Desaix's death at the Battle of Marengo reached Paris, strangers shed tears for him on the streets.

Marguerite-Victoire took the blow with all the sang-froid that her upbringing demanded. She locked the lid of her fortepiano, wore black dresses for a year, and devoted her time to nursing the soldiers in Les Invalides, some of whom, in certain lights, bore a passing resemblance to her beloved General and made her heavy heart seem lighter.

When the colossal Egyptian-style monument to General Desaix was erected in the Place des Victoires, Marguerite-Victoire would go and stand by it every afternoon, in all weathers, and dream of his tomb in far Milan that she would never see.

D'Ayat followed the progress of war after war from afar, in the pages of the *Gazette de France*. His eyes flickered down endless columns detailing France's fate at Hohenlinden and Trafalgar and Austerlitz and Jena. In 1808 he found the name of Alexandre-Édouard-Marguerite d'Ayat among the lists of the dead fighting in Spain.

The General raged and wept for his son and heir.

Having proved himself useful, and battling successfully with the twin demons of hernia and sarcocele, the General was in 1809 appointed Inspector-General of Studs – the studs set up by Napoleon to supply cavalry horses for the armies of France.

The General threw himself into being General d'Ayat again, and tried to forget about death. He could still make the most intractable horse dance. In his heyday he could make any horse write VIVE LE ROI in the sand of the riding-school with its hoofs, describing large circles, loops, convolutions. He began to practise his tricks.

The General discovered his lost *joie de vivre*. He gave his considered opinion on glass eye, azoturia, cataract and diabetes in horses.

He personally experimented with the steaming of horses' nostrils with eucalyptus oil in cases of laryngitis.

He travelled from stud to stud: from Pompadour to Deux-Ponts, from La Mandria to Pau-le-Pin, shaking his head and saying, 'Women and horses, none of them without their faults.'

Reluctant to let the Inspector-General out of their sight, his wife and mother travelled with him whenever they could. The two Comtesses talked endlessly of war and wars, of their late husbands' battles. They argued ceaselessly about strategy and ballistics. They spent all day sipping chocolate and fanning themselves with copies of *Le Journal de l'Empire*.

When the horses were restive in their stalls the General would say, 'The fairies are riding on their backs' and spit three times at each one.

'The most ancient cure, Messieurs,' he told the grooms, 'is the cure by saliva.'

He would demonstrate his expertise in equine obstetrics, assisting at the covering of mares, wielding a giant brass syringe himself, and hauling damp foals steaming from their mothers' flanks.

Then he would dance round the stable yard on the best horse, showing off to his staff. Or he would grow impatient with the slowness of his carriage, irritated by the presence of the two Comtesses, and gallop ahead of his entourage alone, in his quest for the perfect horse, the fastest horse, the finest cavalry horses in the world. Until the hernia popped out again, and left him writhing, screaming and swearing on the ground. Until, in the end, his doctors ordered him to give up riding and he had to content himself with being a spectator.

He grew more red-faced, more portly, and more cantankerous.

The General's health deteriorated steadily and he began to tour the spas as well as the studs, in search of a miracle cure. He sweated heavily whatever the temperature. He sought relief in alcohol and spent whole days sitting motionless in a gilded chair, thinking that death was in the room with him.

In June 1812 he found himself *en route* for Vichy, with the two Comtesses left firmly behind in Paris. The General was ill. He felt heavy, as if his legs were made of lead. There was something wrong beyond the hernia, though he did not know what it was.

At Vichy he shambled from café to café and drank deeply at the fizzy Source des Célestins, recommended for stomachic and intestinal complaints. His health did not improve.

Each morning he limped on to the bridge across the Allier, paused halfway to look down into the water, thought about throwing himself in, and limped back towards the bank, leaning heavily on his stick, unable to walk in a straight line.

He could smell the smell of something rotting on the breeze.

One morning he turned round to see a black dog trotting across the bridge behind him. The General sighed. He was tired of the malfunctioning of his bowels. He was tired of scraping the whiskers off his face. He was tired of being fat. He was tired of being tired. He wanted to die.

The smell of decay hung in his nostrils.

He listened to the sound of soldiers drilling on some waste ground in the distance. He felt as if he was a ghost looking on, as if he might have died without realizing it.

He turned and saw three black dogs loping after him across the bridge.

Weeks passed. The General kept taking the waters but felt no better. He was fifty-four, an Inspector-General of Studs who could no longer mount a horse. His legs ached from walking too far. His hand ached from gripping his stick too tightly. His soul ached and he did not know why.

By July a pack of dogs pursued the General wherever he went, as if they sensed a meal.

The General decided that the smell of corpses was the smell of himself.

Three weeks after the General arrived at Vichy the weather was intolerably hot and the Vichy flies settled in clouds on the butcher's meat. Mosquitoes kept the Vichyssois awake with their ceaseless whining, and the insupportable smell at the thermal baths induced the authorities to order the sprinkling of chloride of lime as a precaution against disease.

At Les Bains the attendants poked about in the drains looking for a missing General.

Eventually a stout, bloodstained body was found floating in the river and was laid on a marble slab in the morgue.

No one could remember exactly what the General looked like. Without his clothes no one knew General le Comte d'Ayat and no one wanted to know him. Someone sold the General's sodden uniform to an old-clothes woman, who dried it out and sold it to the Vichy theatre. The General would make his reappearance in due course.

The Vichyssois shrugged their shoulders and carried on living much as they had done before the General arrived. Invalids often died at Vichy. Death was unmentionable in such places; it was bad for business.

The General's mother sat in her Paris apartment, dressed in black again, surrounded by pink roses, listening to the steady tick of golden clocks. She thought about Louis Himself, Louis-Charles, Louis-Philippe, all the Louis, about the snails, about the passage of time.

She was seventy-four. She found it difficult to remember what her son had looked like without taking his miniature portrait as a royal page out of the drawer of her gilded escritoire.

She sat alone, thinking she would outlive all her contemporaries. All her sisters were dead. She had only Marguerite-Victoire and the grandchildren left.

At Vichy the noise was that the dogs had consumed the General's genitals and the fleshy parts of his face.

XIX

Marie-Louise Murphy lived increasingly in her past. She remembered things. She did not remember things. Or she half-remembered. She sat brooding, dreaming of what had been and of what might have been.

She wandered about Paris at all hours of the day and night, answerable to no one. She had her liberty.

Her eyes wandered down the columns of the *Gazette*, through reports of battles, abdication, restoration, retreat, banishment, and none of it seemed real, until the Comte de Provence was returned in triumph to the throne as Louis XVIII and all that had been swept away seemed to have been swept back again.

She slept easier in her bed, stopped feeling that it was dangerous to breathe, and began to enjoy herself.

She found herself one night looking at an old woman standing in front of her. She realized she was looking into the mirror, looking at herself. She saw an ancient woman with beautifully-kept hair and a network of fine lines all over her face.

She laughed, and her laugh came out as a cackle.

She had turned into the banshee.

Her mood varied. There were days when she talked of nothing but her affair with the King.

'The *old* King,' she would say, lest there should be any doubt, to the embarrassment of the Baron de Tournehem and his dinner guests.

'I do not care who knows about it!' Murphy cried, guffawing. 'Why should I be ashamed?'

The Baron grimaced and talked about finance.

'And most of the things in this room were paid for with His money . . .' she went on, tapping the gilded table with a forefinger.

The Baron preferred to forget. He frowned and talked about racing.

But Murphy could not forget. There were days when she said nothing of her affair with the king, and was silent.

Marguerite-Victoire would ask what she was thinking about, trying to snap her out of her sombre mood.

'I was thinking of Agathe-Louise,' she said. 'I was thinking of a wasted life.'

In her dreams she returned to Versailles and got lost. She found herself in the Galerie des Glaces behind doors she knew were locked. Then she would lose the doors because they were mirror doors. A thunderstorm would rage in the Parc and she smashed the mirrors because she could not turn them to face the walls.

She saw herself reflected and distorted, shimmering, mis-shapen in a cracked mirror, fish-faced in a convex mirror, unlucky in a mirror by candlelight, or with a devil laughing over her shoulder: and the devil had the face of Louis XV or the Abbé Terray.

She was reflected in mirrors directly opposite each other so that her image repeated itself, disappearing into infinity, as if she would go on for ever.

She watched herself walking down the middle of the Avenue de Paris, aged thirteen, away from Versailles, with the golden château behind her, and all her life before her, free. Then she would wake up.

With Versailles on her mind she made one last visit, to exorcize the past for good.

The château was desolate and deserted. The painted ceilings had peeled. The crimson tapestries were faded and ripped. She walked through doors, and cobwebs wrapped themselves around her face. She stood in silent rooms where the sun streamed in on dusty furniture, and flies buzzed against window panes, caught in spiders' webs. Her shoes left footprints in the dust.

She found lilies left in a vase, rotting, unrecognizable.

She came across baths still half-full of grey water, with a scum of insects that had flown too near the surface and drowned.

She lingered in chambers still filled with powerful, trapped scents that might last for ever.

She disturbed dresses mouldering in armoires full of clouds of moths. 'Ghosts,' she said to herself.

She opened a chiffonier full of wrinkled potatoes and laughed, remembering.

Back in Paris she told Marguerite-Victoire, 'Forget the past. Yesterday is no use to you.'

But Marguerite-Victoire thought constantly of General Desaix. The past was all Marguerite-Victoire had left.

When Marguerite-Victoire called on her mother in the Rue Grange-Batelière she would ask, fifty years after it was all finished, 'What was he like?'

Sometimes Murphy could hardly remember. She thought of the various portraits, none of them like the Louis she had known. They flattered him. He would be called away in the middle of a sitting. The artist never had a chance. Portraits were full of lies.

'What was he really like?' persisted Marguerite-Victoire.

Every day he was less distinct, nothing of him left but his portrait on a coin, a fading profile. Sometimes he was just a wig, with no face under it. Sometimes he was just two blackcurrant eyes that had lost their sparkle.

Some days she saw him wherever she looked: among the gangs of shaven-headed convicts making their way to the galleys at Nantes. She saw him among the bands of criminals working on the roads, his eyes glistening with the suggestion of a tear, a man deprived of his freedom. He was the howl of a chained dog. He was the pacing of a caged wolf. She said nothing. Her thoughts wandered away.

'Did you like him?' asked Marguerite-Victoire.

'I did,' she said at last. 'He was a lovely man, to be sure.'

Sometimes he was a lovely man.

'But did you *really* like him, though?' asked the Baronne, who had heard the stories.

'I did,' she said vaguely. 'I liked him well enough.'

Sometimes she liked him.

'What sort of a man was he, though?' demanded the Baronne.

'Well, he didn't say much,' she said. 'I never did really get to know the man at all.'

Sometimes she would simply reply, 'He took away my *baby*. A mother never forgets that.'

From time to time the de Tournehems were disturbed to hear that Murphy had been seen ripping up a banker's draft, not caring any more what happened to her money. She would stand near the Palais-Royal throwing money into the air, wanting to be free of it, doing as she liked for the first time in her life.

The de Tournehems made known their displeasure.

Murphy laughed. 'It's not my money,' she said, 'it belongs to France.'

On fine days she would sit in the Jardin du Luxembourg beneath a plane-tree, surrounded by hundreds of pigeons, with the birds perching on her head and hands, feeding them: an old woman nobody noticed, laughing, thinking her life had begun, that it was never too late.

Her cheeks were caked with rouge and white lead, livid, jowly. She was a pantomime old woman, with her hair awry, wearing a necklace with large pearl drops and large pearl earrings.

'I shall wear the pearls,' she said to herself, thinking of Brigitte, 'and to Hell with the bad luck. I have had all the bad luck in the world already.'

Her dress hung off her. Her breasts sagged, shrunk away into almost nothing. She shuffled along in a half-run, wearing an old pair of shoes with the toes cut out at the sides to ease the pain of her bunions. Her chin was whiskered with white hairs. She was an old woman with a beard, her back bent, but with her eyes still sparkling, alive, full of laughter: an old woman who never stopped smiling.

When she had a fall the de Tournehems took her into their own house. They could not, after all, allow her to throw their money away. She drifted quietly from room to room, sliding her gnarled fingers across yellow silk damask chairs with gilt frames, and yellow silk curtains embroidered with a *fleur-de-lis* motif. She tapped at the gold clocks that filled the house and her mind lost itself in her past.

She handed all her diamonds to Marguerite-Victoire, saying

she had no need and no wish to own diamonds any more. She divided her entire fortune among her surviving family.

'I do not need money,' she said. She settled down to wait for the end. She was just seventy-seven.

In the second week of December 1814 Murphy heard a noise like cats howling, and knew at once what it was.

She put her affairs in order, sent for the priest, and composed herself on her pillows under a cloth-of-gold counterpane.

The priest sat on a gilded *fauteuil* beside the bed, listened all evening and left her only when she began to snore. He returned the next morning and listened all day. At dusk he left her with the rosary in her hands, calm and peaceful. His ears burned.

Murphy was, as usual, reported dead, but was still alive.

On 16 January 1815 she heard the howling of cats again and retired to bed early, saying she felt tired. The noise went on and on, at times low and soft, a strange, mournful lamentation: no word, only a bitter cry of deepest sorrow and agony.

Towards eleven o'clock she called Marguerite-Victoire to her. 'I can hear the *banshee*,' she said.

Marguerite-Victoire smiled. 'Don't be daft,' she said, 'do you think the banshee would cross the Irish Sea in all this awful weather just to haunt you?'

'Well,' said her mother, 'I do. I do.'

The Baronne held her hands, talked, listened, reassured her, kissed her goodnight and returned to her fortepiano.

Murphy heard the distant applause of the Tournehems' dinner guests and the tinkle of the gold clocks chiming midnight. Music by Rameau floated up the staircase to her, as if she was back in the attics at Versailles with the music of the King's band drifting out of the open windows of the Hall of Mirrors on a hot summer night sixty years before.

She fell asleep, dreamed, floated away, slept more soundly than she had ever slept before.

XX

The Baron de Tournehem would have none of his mother-in-law's superstitions.

'I will have no Irish women keening in my house,' he said.

Marguerite-Victoire dabbed her eyes with a black lace handkerchief.

'This is modern times, Madame,' he said. 'The nineteenth century.'

He put on his tall black hat.

'And we shall not be eating the plate of peas,' he said.

The Baronne sniffed into her black silk taffeta sleeve.

'I told them to nail down the coffin lid,' he said. 'We've seen quite enough of the old woman's face.'

The Baronne frowned and pulled on her black silk gloves.

'We are civilized people,' said the Baron, 'and there will be no Irish nonsense.'

The Baronne stopped the gilded clocks all the same. There was a profound silence in the house, without the usual heavy thump of pendulums, without the tinkling, sonorous chimes.

She covered the gilt looking-glasses with fine white linen cloths.

She turned the pictures in gilt frames to face the walls.

She unlocked all the locks in the house so that her mother's soul could pass to its eternal rest.

Later the Baronne opened the street door to a dozen ancient nuns of the Couvent de la Présentation, contemporaries of Marie-Louise Murphy, who stamped the snow off their black boots and ascended the gilded staircase like a flight of crows.

They sat up all night with the coffin, telling the dead woman's story by the light of four giant beeswax candles, one at each corner of the coffin of finest mahogany with gold handles.

They told her story as best they could, having been locked up in their convent for more than three-quarters of a century. They were full of good intentions but told it as they had received it

233

from others, at second-hand, third-hand, fourth-hand, full of
rumours. Some of it they told all wrong, full of mistakes and
exaggerations, but it was a better story for all that.

The nuns preferred the marvellous to the true.

White lilies filled the room, vying with the faint odour of cam-
phor. Marie Murphy lay with her hands clasped over her breasts,
her face a pearly white, made up by the Baronne de Tournehem
with a cream that filled in the wrinkles of her skin and made
her seem hardly more than fifteen years of age.

The sisters set up a subdued ul-lu-lu so as not to discommode
unduly the Baron de Tournehem, writing in his study on the
floor below.

They set the legend going, kept the legend alive, seated on
gilded chairs, dressed in black, with their white headdresses like
giant butterflies, casting shadows on the walls all around them,
quivering.

Towards midnight the Baronne served *thé à l'anglaise* in Sèvres
cups, and they ate the traditional plate of *petits pois* after the
custom of the Auvergne. Gold forks and spoons clinked in
the silent house.

Between episodes of the story the sisters clacked their rosary
beads and chanted cycle after cycle of 150 Hail Marys, and
prayed the prayers for the old woman's eternal repose, and gazed
at her white face.

Towards two in the morning Soeur Concordia yawned, put her
hand over her mouth to keep out the Devil, and nudged the
Baronne, whispering, 'Did you ever see the lovely lovely picture
of your mother how she was when young at all?'

'I did not,' said the Baronne, surprised, 'I never did.'

Soeur Concordia elbowed Soeur Felicitas, who fumbled
beneath her skirts and fished out a crumpled sheet of paper: an
engraving of Boucher's painting.

Soeur Felicitas unfolded the treasure she was not supposed to
have laid up, but had preserved intact for more than half a
century.

'There she is now,' she sighed, passing the engraving round
the circle of women, 'the immortal Murphy.'

Marguerite-Victoire began to understand.

Murphy lay back to front on her sofa, the engraving a mirror image of the painting, as she might have recognized herself.

'There now,' said Soeur Perpetua Flaherty, 'little Marie Murphy in just her skin, for all the world just like a great potato.'

'God have mercy upon her soul,' sighed Soeur Concordia O'Brien, 'she was a lovely lovely girl.'

'The most famous Murphy of us all,' sighed Soeur Immaculata Murphy. 'She had a beautiful death, God be praised . . .'

Soeur Felicitas O'Reilly folded the engraving, hid it away, and cleared her throat loudly.

The murmuring of the sisters started up again:

Ave Maria, gratia plena,
Dominus tecum:
Benedicta tu in mulieribus,
Alleluia . . .

The click of wooden beads and the murmured chanting went on into the night, like pearls rattling in a snuffbox. The nuns expected miracles but their perfectly white headdresses rose and fell like giant lilies in a gentle breeze: they could not keep awake. One by one their heads nodded on their breasts, the chanting and the rattling died away, and they were all asleep.